I0646352

TED TAYLER

INTO THE SUNLIGHT

BOOKS

By Ted Tayler

The Freeman Files

Red Herring Season
Gathering Clouds
Still Standing

Vinci Books

vinci-books.com

Published by Vinci Books Ltd in 2025

1

Copyright © Ted Tayler 2021

The author has asserted their moral right to be identified as the author of
this work in accordance with the Copyright, Designs and Patents Act 1988.
This work is a work of fiction. Names, characters, places and incidents are
the product of the author's imagination or are used fictitiously. Any
resemblance to actual persons, living or dead, places and incidents is
entirely coincidental.
All rights reserved. No part of this publication may be copied, reproduced,
distributed, stored in any retrieval system, or transmitted in any form or by
any means, including photocopying, recording, or other electronic or
mechanical methods, nor used as a source for any form of machine
learning including AI datasets, without the prior written permission of the
publisher.
The publisher and the author have made every effort to obtain permissions
for any third party material used in this book and to comply with copyright
law. Any queries in this respect should be brought to the attention of the
publisher and any omissions will be corrected in future editions.
A CIP catalogue record for this book is available from the British Library.
Paperback ISBN: 9781036705022

Chapter One

GUS AND SUZIE went through their regular routine in the morning. Gus flashed his lights as Suzie turned into the London Road HQ and continued towards the office. Neil, Blessing, and Luke had arrived before him. As Gus locked his car door, Alex and Lydia entered the car park.

"Another glorious morning, guv," said Lydia when she got out of her Mini.

"It's certainly bright, Lydia," said Gus.

"My suit's still at the dry cleaner's, guv," she grinned.

"What are we expecting this morning, guv?" asked Alex.

"We can't hope for too much from Divya and the Hub," said Gus as they entered the lift. "They will need time to carry out search routines over an extended period. An international search will take even longer to arrange, let alone produce results."

"We're not out of Europe yet, guv," said Alex. "I hope

their co-operation in finding a serial killer wouldn't get mired in petty squabbles. If that's what we're facing."

The others were chatting when they exited the lift.

Blessing Umeh notified Gus she was about to call Eve Chaloner. They needed to follow up on Richard Chaloner's bicycle. Neil wondered whether Stan Jones Junior could monitor what was going on at the garage via a camera in what had been his bedroom.

Gus knew tying up these inconsequential loose ends wasn't vital, but it might add icing to the cake. So he suggested Luke and Neil drive to Swindon on Monday to check Neil's theory without antagonising Stan's father.

Blessing reminded Neil to look for the gold chain the killer had stolen; Lydia pointed out there could be other items young Stan might have kept as trophies. Souvenirs of what he saw as good times in his life. Gus felt it more likely they would be with him in the cab of his truck.

"When was the last time you investigated a case like this, guv?" asked Alex.

"A possible serial killer, Alex?" said Gus. "This is my first. Murder is rare in Wiltshire. Moreover, a serial killer is as common as snow in July."

"It hurts not to get the chance to see the case through to the end, guv," said Lydia.

"That goes for me too, guv," said Alex.

"If either of you wants the opportunity, you need to spread your wings and fly from this nest," said Gus.

Blessing soon received confirmation that Richard's bicycle had been returned after the original forensics crew finished their work. Eve Chaloner told her she hadn't been able to throw the bicycle out.

"It can stay where it is, for now, Blessing," said Gus.

"Whichever Murder Investigation Team gets assigned to the case can decide what happens next."

"I believed Eve when she told us they were trying for a baby, guv," said Blessing. "When I asked whether the safe's contents helped her decide to stay home rather than look for a job after Richard died, Eve admitted the truth. However, it was a shock to open the safe and find over twenty thousand pounds inside she knew nothing about."

"Leave it to me, DC Umeh," said Gus. "I'll mull it over and decide what would be for the best."

"Got it, guv," said Blessing.

"Let's update the Freeman Files," said Gus, "and wait for news."

Lydia fetched coffee at ten. Alex's phone rang five minutes past.

He listened to the voice at the other end, took notes, and ended the call.

"Emma Fox, twenty-three, guv," he said. "They found her body on November the sixteenth, 2007, on an embankment beside the motorway. Police believed she died after leaving a truck stop on the M6 where she may have attempted to hitchhike south. Emma left home at eighteen, and the police could not identify her or contact her family for ten months. They eventually identified Emma through fingerprints. Death by strangulation. No forensic evidence was recovered at the scene."

"Anything else, Alex?" asked Gus.

"The cashier from the nearest service station thought she remembered Emma wearing a distinctive silver necklace and pendant, with the head of a fox and its brush studded with red stones. I haven't received a photo of the victim yet, guv, but Divya said the resemblance to Tara Laing was uncanny."

"Thank you, Alex," said Gus.

It promised to be a long day.

Monday, 10 September 2018

"THE START of another new week, guv," said Neil Davis.

It surprised Gus to find anyone in the office. He'd left the bungalow thirty minutes earlier than usual. Suzie had only just been making her way to the shower.

"I thought when we left here on Friday afternoon, I'd put everything to bed, Neil," said Gus. "While I worked on the allotment yesterday afternoon, I thought it best to run through our files one last time in case we missed something. What brought you here so early?"

"Melody didn't have the best of nights, guv," said Neil.

"Everything okay with the baby?" asked Gus.

"I hope so, guv," said Neil. "The high temperatures earlier in the month didn't do Melody any favours. I was wide awake at six o'clock, so I thought, blow it, I won't get back to sleep before the alarm. I could start clearing the decks for our next case if I drove here while the roads were quiet."

"Good idea," said Gus.

"By the way, I bumped into Rick Chalmers on Friday night, guv," said Neil.

"Did you take Melody out for a meal?" asked Gus.

"No, guv. I met up with a couple of mates for a few cold beers. We were in the Silk Mercer in Devizes when Rick wandered in alone."

Gus wondered whether Rick and Vera ever saw one another these days.

"How was he?"

"Rick had plenty to say, as usual, guv, but Friday night wasn't the right time or place for work. He'd spent the past six weeks undercover."

"It seems to be the role that suits him best," said Gus. "Unsocial hours, with plenty of scope for fast food and casual relationships."

"Harsh, guv," said Neil. "Rick wouldn't go into detail in front of my mates, but he spoke to DS Mercer after he returned to London Road from this office in mid-July. The boss sent him to join a task force from Avon & Somerset Police. Rick's involvement in the undercover assignment ended Thursday evening, and he delivered his report in person on Friday afternoon."

"I'm intrigued, Neil," said Gus. "Any idea where Geoff Mercer might send Rick next?"

"Rick's on holiday for a week, guv," said Neil. "The boss told him to recharge his batteries and prepare to return to the seaside."

"Chasing illegal immigrants again," said Gus. "I don't envy him that job. But at least the weather's fine. Did he give a hint to where Avon & Somerset had him working undercover?"

"Rick said he thought it might interest you, guv," said Neil.

Gus heard the lift return to the ground floor. The rest of the team was on the way.

"Any idea where Rick's spending his week of relaxation?" he asked.

"He's got a flat somewhere in Devizes, guv," said Neil.

Alex Hardy and Lydia Logan Barre exited the lift and crossed the room to their desks.

"Morning, guv," said Lydia.

"Did we miss something?" asked Alex.

"No, Alex," said Gus. "Nothing further yet. Neil and I couldn't sleep. We were chatting about Rick Chalmers."

"I saw him on Friday night," said Neil. "Alex, you know where his flat is, don't you?"

"I picked him up on the way to the Hub when we worked on the Grant Burnside case," said Alex. "A tad ambitious to call it a flat; it was more of a tip."

Luke Sherman and Blessing Umeh were next to arrive. They were deep in conversation, and Lydia could tell Blessing had plenty to tell Luke. Jamie Barnes-Trewick was the chief topic, no doubt. Luke seemed more animated than usual, too.

"Now everyone's here," said Gus. "Neil has offered to prepare the office for the next case. Can the rest of you double-check everything we added to our files last week, please?"

"Sure, guv," said Lydia. "No problem."

"I would prefer to spend two hours ensuring we haven't dropped the ball rather than having our reputation shredded by the Chief Constable," added Gus. "When he hands the case onto MCIT, he can be confident we did everything by the book."

"Got it, guv," said Alex.

Gus checked his mobile phone. Yes, he had Rick's number. Something told him Rick would enjoy a chat.

Luke and Neil set off for Swindon to check for the hidden camera. After a quick phone call to Rick, Gus drove to Devizes twenty minutes later.

Their meeting took place over an extended brunch in a town centre café. After Gus dropped Rick back home, he headed for London Road. At last, there was a light on the horizon. Rick's undercover work might have allowed them to put a tick against the only case the Crime Review Team hadn't solved. Gus thanked Rick and looked forward to hearing officially from Geoff Mercer that Avon & Somerset Police at Portishead had removed any obstacles preventing them from getting Rusty Scott to court.

Minutes after leaving Rick, Gus turned into the London Road car park. He skipped up the steps to the front door and made his way to reception. When he reached the mezzanine, Vera Butler nodded towards a pile of folders on her desk.

"Alex Hardy dropped these off ten minutes ago. Gus. Geoff is free if you want to pop in. Kenneth is with the PCC and won't be available until after lunch."

"Many thanks, Vera," said Gus, gathering the files without stopping for a chat. He tapped on Geoff Mercer's door.

"Come in," said Geoff. "Gus, it's usually good to see you, but Vera suggested I looked at a couple of these files before you got here."

Geoff handed Gus a folder with two sheets of paper inside.

Gus studied the first sheet. On November the ninth, 2010, a woman's body was found in a storage cupboard on an abandoned industrial site near Smethwick. She had been suffocated. Molly Phelps, twenty-two years old, had been dead for several days. Originally from Paisley in Scotland, Molly's parents said their daughter was trying to get a lift home for the weekend and never arrived. The photograph they gave the police showed Molly wearing a gold choker chain with a cross. Police found no jewellery with the body.

Gus stared at the photo of the young girl. There was no mistake. The hair colouring was different, but Stan Jones would have been reminded of Tara Laing the second he set eyes on the poor girl. Gus turned over the second sheet.

On November the twentieth, 2013, a dog walker found Sammy Yendall, twenty-two, near Wentwood Forest in Monmouthshire. The similarities were there again. Gus sighed. What did he take as a trophy this time? The cause of death differed from the others, and the violence was more significant. Sammy had been struck several times with a hammer or similar object on the skull and about her face. The killer wanted to obliterate her facial features. Her family, from Newport, said she always wore a charm bracelet by Pandora that, at last count, had eleven charms.

"Alex received more information just before he left the office, Gus," said Geoff. "There's another note here he left with Vera."

Luke and Neil had visited young Stan's bedroom on Ponting Street. The camera itself had gone, but the window sill held evidence someone had fixed something there for a lengthy period. Stan's father hadn't been inside his son's room since he was thirteen.

Luke had checked the bedside table drawer under the bed, inside and on top of the wardrobe. He found no sign of any trophies. Neil had taken Stan Jones downstairs to look at the mail awaiting his son's return. His subscription to the Swindon Advertiser would be due for renewal in mid-November.

"Grim reading, Gus," said Geoff.

"We need to find Jones before he strikes again," said Gus.

"We owe it to any girl who reminds him of Tara Laing. They deserve to be allowed to look forward to a normal November."

"Everything's ready on the Chaloner case in these files

when Kenneth's free," said Gus. "Who do you think will get the pleasure of making the headlines?"

"They've got plenty to choose from these days, Gus," said Geoff. "You know the Metropolitan Police have twenty-four teams for the capital. We wouldn't warrant many teams on our patch, so our Major Crime Investigation Team is a collaborative unit comprising officers and staff from Wiltshire, Gloucestershire, Avon, and Somerset Police areas. The unit's remit includes the investigation of Category A-C homicides throughout the tri-force areas."

"I wish I hadn't asked," said Gus.

"I guess it will be sent out of the county to one of our neighbours. Does that bother you?"

"Not at all," said Gus. "Our remit was to put a name to Richard Chaloner's killer. I'm confident we identified the guilty party. There was no sign in the original murder file to suggest we were hunting a serial killer. The trick cyclists will agonise over why Jones waited so long before taking revenge on the lad who threw the firework that scarred him. Would he have attacked the others in time? When Stan Jones is in custody, someone can pose the question."

"I see your point," said Geoff. "He went after girls who reminded him of Tara Laing. But am I being too optimistic? There's a three-year gap between the murders you've identified."

"Stan was due to marry Tara in November 2004," said Gus. "Jeanie, his mother, hung on for a year. He'd already left home by then but returned for her funeral. Maybe you're right, and the ghost wedding, followed by his mother's death, were two events he kept churning over in his head as he drove for hour after hour. Emma Fox could have been his first victim. But after that, why should he stop? If Jones's anger gets the better of him every three years, then this November, he'll target another Tara look-alike. My worry is he gets angry several days before Halloween, regardless of the year."

"God help us if there are half a dozen more bodies out there," said Geoff.

Gus looked at his watch.

"How long before the Chief Constable can escape the clutches of the Police and Crime Commissioner?"

"These meetings tend to run on," sighed Geoff. "Ah, I see where this is heading. As Kenneth's with the PCC in an unscheduled meeting, Vera won't have cancelled the regular lunch order. I'll give her a shout, and she can bring the grub into my office."

"Do you know what he's lined up for us to tackle next?" Gus asked.

"Not the specifics," said Geoff. "You know what he's like. Kenneth wears his heart on his sleeve. Look at how he rescued Kassie Trotter from the perils of life on the streets."

"His faith in whatever denomination church he attends is commendable," said Gus. "Does that suggest we're heading for the seamier side of society on this occasion? Kenneth and his wife are more interested than most in the young women who fall through the safety net."

"It appears so," said Geoff. "On Friday afternoon, we chatted before we went our separate ways to drive home. He'd been reading another of those reports on his desk you ribbed him about last week."

"Never a good idea on an empty stomach," said Gus.

"Sorry," said Geoff. "I'll call Vera now."

Geoff made the call.

"That was lucky," he said. "Vera had just left to take her thirty-minute break. Thank goodness Kassie picks up her calls. We're okay. She'll be right in."

Gus could hear Kassie singing as she pushed her trolley along the dark corridor towards Geoff's office. He wanted to learn what Kenneth had been reading, but Kassie did enjoy a chat. Whatever it was could wait a few minutes.

The door swung open, and Kassie entered.

"I've taken a liberty, Mr Mercer," she said, giving Gus a cheeky grin. "You would have only made a pig of yourself trying to eat the Chief Constable's share as well as your own. So, I let the young lad in reception have Kenneth's baguette."

"As long as I have my usual order, that's fine," said Geoff.

"You can manage two wraps, can't you, Mr Freeman?"

"If I must, Kassie," said Gus. "What's on the secret menu this week? Will there be something scrummy to collect on my way back to the office?"

"I had another bash at making cream horns," said Kassie. "They look good, even if I say so myself."

"I'll take one back with me," said Gus.

"Might I have two?" asked Geoff.

"Sorry, Mr Mercer," said Kassie. "I only have one spare now that Mr Freeman's agreed to give them another try."

"What happened to Kenneth's cake?" asked Gus.

"The lad on reception's got it, I bet," moaned Geoff.

"Are we talking about the comedian I met a few weeks ago?" asked Gus. "I didn't think you fancied him."

"I don't," said Kassie. "But if I feed him up, he might do, at a pinch."

"Young men around here must feel like turkeys at Christmas," said Geoff.

"Enjoy your lunch, you two," said Kassie. "I'll see you later, Mr Freeman."

With that, Kassie, together with her heart and lovebird tattoos, had gone.

"I'll run through the content of Kenneth's reading material after we demolish this food," said Geoff. "Did you have a good weekend, Gus? Anything exciting planned this week, depending on where your next case takes you, of course?"

"Suzie and I spent a quiet weekend at the bungalow or the allotment," Gus said. "As for this week. I need time off on Wednesday afternoon."

"Interesting," said Geoff. "DI Ferris made the same request this morning, A couple of hours late on Wednesday afternoon, she said."

"Suzie didn't give any further details?" asked Gus.

Geoff Mercer shook his head.

"Then I'll await further instructions," said Gus.

"Fair enough," said Geoff. "No problem. I presume DS Hardy will take control while you're absent?"

"That's standard procedure," said Gus. "Have you heard any more from DS Sherman?"

"Not a whisper, Gus. Has he spoken to you?"

"We've not had much chance, but he did seem in a better mood this morning. So perhaps Luke and his partner got through the weekend without a blazing row for a change."

"It might pay you to take Luke on the early interviews in your next job. Then, he might open up away from the office. Someone has to go with you. You might as well use it to your advantage."

"I'll bear it in mind," said Gus. "Right. What was it that piqued Kenneth's paternal instinct?"

"Human trafficking," said Geoff. "Especially where these unfortunate souls end up. In the past decade, the number of people trafficked into the UK for sexual exploitation has risen. Ten years ago, a modest five hundred, three-quarters of whom were adults, but that number had doubled within four years."

"Still a relatively small number compared to other countries worldwide," said Gus.

"The numbers continued to rise," said Geoff, "and those were just the known victims."

"Where do the majority come from?" asked Gus.

"Many make the short trip from the Baltic States," said Geoff. "Some are from Russia and Eastern European countries, Ukraine, Romania, and Albania. Then, of course, others originate from Africa and South East Asia."

"No doubt there's a financial cost to this misery?" said Gus. "Criminal gangs have always been involved in this business. Any commodity that has value to them is fair game. So what are the gangs paying for these women?"

"Perhaps an average of five thousand pounds," said Geoff. "The girls work sixteen-hour days and are expected to service a client every thirty minutes."

"Why do these women come to this country?" asked Gus.

"They get lured here under false pretences, expecting to have a restaurant job or as a nanny," said Geoff. "Instead, they get moved around the country as money passes hands between the gangmasters. You might assume they only gravitate to the major cities. But the problem has grown so large they can turn up anywhere from Cornwall to Cumbria."

"After Terry Davis's murder, I visited Donna, one of his informants," said Gus. "A note Terry passed her helped put Culverhouse and Plunkett in the frame for the hit-and-run they tried to hide. Donna likes to tell people she runs a business in Devizes in the care sector. Several of her staff arrived in the county from those European countries you mentioned, but they're not exploited in the same way as those that fall into the hands of criminal gangs."

"It's a fine line, Gus," said Geoff. "As soon as more than one person uses the same premises to sell sex, we should act. I'll have to accept that Donna runs a care home until I can prove otherwise. I don't suppose you remember where it was?"

"It slipped my mind completely as soon as I left with the clue that Terry gave us," said Gus. "Was there a particular story in that report that got Kenneth agitated?"

"He spoke of a girl called Olga from Krakow," said Geoff. "She was seventeen and leaving school when she saw an advert online for a nanny. The couple claimed to have an eighteen-month-old daughter and wanted an au pair to live in. The story was that the wife wanted to return to work full-time. Olga replied to the advert, and weeks later, she flew into Exeter airport. The couple had paid for her passport, sent her a one-way plane ticket, and agreed to help her learn English. Olga thought everything was legit and looked forward to the experience. The wife collected her from the Arrivals area and led her to a people carrier outside the airport. They drove to a detached house in a leafy suburb where Olga was introduced to the husband."

"And the eighteen-month-old daughter?" asked Gus.

"She never existed. The couple took everything from Olga except the clothes she was wearing and locked her in an upstairs bedroom. Her nightmare had begun; no passport, money, or mobile phone. The husband told her she needed to work to repay the money. Olga asked about the baby, and the wife told her there were other ways she could earn enough money to pay them back. They forced Olga to call her parents to tell them she'd arrived safely and everything was fine. The wife held the phone while the husband held a knife to the poor girl's throat. Fifteen months later, Olga was spotted soliciting in the nightclub area near Little Castle and Bailey Street. The officers took her to a nearby café, and Olga revealed she was being put to work by an organised crime gang. The police soon learned that the couple who lured her to the UK had sold Olga to a local gang. Olga showed the police the house where she had originally lived and worked. The couple kept her in that bedroom twenty-four-seven for eight months."

"Nobody noticed numerous visitors?" asked Gus.

"They had chosen the property well," said Geoff. "It was the last house before an electricity sub-station, and there was plenty of passing traffic, but the driveway couldn't be seen from other houses on the road because of a bend and a row of leylandii."

"Were the couple still there?"

"No, but after months trawling through financial records and liaising with neighbouring forces, the couple were discovered in Wareham, Dorset. Further examination of mobile phones and computers seized at their new address showed they ran a highly organised operation for more than five years, trafficking vulnerable women, usually from mainland Europe. They targeted women who couldn't speak English and had no way of securing legal work in the UK. The wife uploaded profiles of the girls onto adult websites and after a while moved them around the country to carry out sex work."

"When they sold Olga to this other Devon-based gang, she went from the frying pan to the fire, I presume," said Gus.

"Olga said the couple used drugs to control her. Every day was a blur; then, one night, she tried to escape. Olga told the police she was heading for the railway line. They had passed it on the drive to the house from the airport. She just wanted to end the nightmare. When the husband caught her, he punched Olga half a dozen times in the stomach. The next night, Olga was driven from the house and dropped near the car wash at the back of a garage forecourt a few miles out of Exeter. Olga said she was ordered to wear a white blouse, a short black skirt, and knee-high white socks. She stood shivering in the dark, awaiting her fate. A van with tinted windows pulled into the parking bay beside her. The driver got out and went inside the garage shop. The passenger jumped out, bundled Olga through the van's side door, and told her to keep quiet. Minutes later, the van drove away from the forecourt. Olga had been moved on to another gang with girls in flats in Exeter city centre. She was expected to be available from six at night until six in the morning and earn a thousand pounds a night. If she didn't make enough money, the driver beat her."

"So, Olga suffered for a further seven months working for this gang?"

"Her torture ended when she left the café that night with the police. Olga is back with her family in Krakow, trying to rebuild her life. She was key to the investigation that led to the couple getting convicted under the Modern Slavery Act. They are now in prison. Work is ongoing to bring the other gang to the courts. They profit from the misery of others and show no regard for the welfare and wellbeing of the women they exploit."

"We have to celebrate every small success, I suppose," said Gus. "The gangs have accumulated so much clean cash they can afford the best legal representation. So it's hard to make charges stick."

Geoff and Gus sat quietly, drinking their coffees.

"Grace would have something to say if she found us spinning our wheels," said Gus.

"I blame the PCC," said Geoff. "He wants a lean, mean fighting machine, and then he whips our leader away at a minute's notice. So you're stuck here until Kenneth becomes available. It makes no sense to drive back to the office. As for me, perhaps I should throw you out and get on with that pile of paperwork in my in-tray. If I did, you could guarantee Kenneth would call me into his office before you reached the top of the stairs."

Gus heard singing in the corridor.

"Kassie's on her way," he said.

"Someone's made her life brighter," said Geoff. "A brave man, but not before time."

Kassie knocked but was through the door before an echo had a chance to escape.

"Vera will be back in five minutes," she said, "then I'll get a chance to enjoy thirty minutes of late summer sun myself. I brought your cream horns in person."

"Brilliant," said Geoff, licking his lips.

"You won't get this service every week," said Kassie. "It's just that the boss is back in his office. He asked whether I'd seen you two. I've taken his coffee in, so give it five minutes, and he'll expect you."

"Thanks, Kassie," said Geoff.

Gus inspected the white paper napkin contents as Kassie breezed out of the room. It looked tempting, but it could get messy. Discretion being the better part of valour, he decided to wait until he was in the Focus. Geoff Mercer had no such qualms; he was already wiping the excess puff pastry crumbs and sweet vanilla cream from his lips.

"I know," he said. "Don't give me that look. Christine

tuts if I have two chocolate digestive biscuits with a coffee on Sunday morning as a treat."

Gus wrapped his treat in the napkin and placed it on Geoff's desk.

"I'll pick it up when we've finished our meeting with Kenneth," he said. "Don't get any ideas."

Geoff was still grinning when his phone rang.

"That was Vera," said Geoff. "She's back from lunch, and Kenneth is ready and waiting."

Chapter Two

GUS AND GEOFF took the short walk across the mezzanine to the Chief Constable's office. His door was open, and they could see Kenneth Truelove seated at his desk.

"Sorry for the delay, chaps. Come in," said Kenneth. "The PCC had a bee in his bonnet."

"Anything to concern us, sir?" asked Gus.

"I stopped listening after the first thirty minutes," said Kenneth, puffing out his cheeks. "It was the same old, same old. More, better, with less every day."

"We do what we can," said Gus.

"The PCC can hardly have a go at the Crime Review Team on that score, sir," said Geoff. "I've seen Gus's latest report. Did you have time to catch up with the Chaloner case yet?"

"Vera left a copy on my desk," said Kenneth. "That's as far as it got. I believe one of your team delivered it, Freeman. Where were you?"

"I was following up on the Burnside case with Rick Chalmers, sir. We had an early morning meeting in town."

It was early for Rick Chalmers, but Kenneth didn't need to hear the details.

"Any progress? Didn't you update me on that last week, Mercer?"

"I told you Chalmers had returned from his undercover spell with Avon & Somerset Police, sir. We agreed to let Rick have a week's leave, and then he will return to the South coast helping stem the flow of dodgy Channel crossings."

"He's your odd-job man, Mercer, isn't he? Chalmers always strikes me as another Terry Davis in the making. A detective with his finger on the pulse wherever he's put to work but with little drive or ambition to progress further. Sometimes it's better not to ask where they get the key pieces of information that crack a case."

"When I started as a DC at Bourne Hill," said Gus, "my first Sergeant told me every police station needed someone who did the dirty work. Someone prepared to rummage around in the muck looking for diamonds."

"I imagine you view those as the good old days, Freeman," said Kenneth. "I could not possibly comment."

"The days when dinosaurs ruled the earth, sir," said Gus. "We've come a long way since then, although not always in the right direction. Rick updated me on his recent team's progress on charging the man we believed responsible for the hit on Grant Burnside."

"Yes, Mercer did mention that. We must rely on Portishead to prepare a solid case. As for this folder in front of me. What do I need to know before I give it my full attention?"

"Richard Chaloner was killed by Stanley Jones, the thirty-seven-year-old son of a gentleman with the same name, who lives opposite Chaloner's garage on Ponting Street. The bare bones of the case were that when Jones was a young boy, Chaloner and his mates threw fireworks for a laugh on Bonfire Night, regardless of where they landed. Young Stanley suffered scarring of the face and hands in an incident in 1989."

"Twenty-odd years is a long time to wait," said Kenneth. "And murder seems an extreme way to get his own back. I sense there's more to it."

"Jones was engaged to be married when he was twenty-four, but the young lady, a Tara Laing, got cold feet," said Geoff Mercer. "By this time, Jones had taken a job as a truck driver. He travels throughout the UK and Europe. His visits to Ponting Street are rare, certainly since his mother died in 2005."

"Something had to give," said Kenneth. "A series of negative life events and this chap flipped; he identified Chaloner as the root cause of his misfortunes and shot him."

Geoff Mercer looked at Gus. If only it were that simple.

"We believe your first action should be to pass this case on, sir," said Geoff.

"Tara Laing might have triggered the first murder, sir," said Gus.

"The first? How many are there, for heaven's sake?"

"We can't answer that yet, sir," said Gus. "Jones suffered from being jilted, and then he lost his mother to cancer eighteen months later. Then, in November 2007, the body of a young woman, Emma Fox, was discovered on an embankment on the M6. We've compared photographs of Tara Laing and the twenty-three-year-old victim. They could be twins. The murder took place in November."

"DS Hardy also provided you with two additional murders that appear related, sir," said Geoff. "Vera would have dropped a folder onto the pile on your desk."

Kenneth flicked through the items at the top of the enormous pile.

"Got it," he said grimly. "Two more young women in the UK, two more murders which occurred in November. The photos on the sheets of paper in this folder suggest we're dealing with a serial killer. The similarities are undeniable. Unfortunately, as much as I would love for the Crime Review Team to trace Jones and bring him to justice, they don't have the resources. It's above the pay grade of the detectives under your wing, Freeman. I'm sorry."

"We understand, sir," said Gus. "DS Mercer and I are concerned we haven't identified every victim in this expanded case yet. So we involved the Hub last Friday. Divya Yadav is searching for matches between November 2005 and 2017."

"She's hunting for young women with the physical appearance of this Laing woman," said the Chief Constable. "I have no problem with the Hub's resources getting used on that task; it's why they're there. You say this Jones character travels in Europe too?"

"He does. We thought if the contact with the Major Crime Investigation Team came from you, sir, they would be more likely to get a wiggle on," said Gus. "November isn't far away, and I want Jones arrested before he can add another Tara Laing look-alike to his list."

"Fair enough. I'll handle that," said Kenneth. "I'll have a word with Mrs Yadav too and inform MCIT we should be able to identify the scope of the UK murders in a matter of hours. What about the attack on Chaloner, though? That was two years ago now. You mentioned he was with other teenage tearaways back in 1989. Have any of those men been attacked since 2005?"

"No, sir," said Geoff Mercer. "I've contacted Gablecross

and asked for the necessary surveillance during November to keep them out of harm's way."

"I would hope Jones was in custody before we get that far, Mercer," said Kenneth.

"He's clever, sir," said Gus. "At least three young women plus Richard Chaloner died without either investigation into their deaths having any success. He's never left discernible DNA at the scene. Until we worked on the Chaloner murder file last week, nobody had established a link between Jones and these random killings in three separate parts of the country."

"Did Tara Laing come from Swindon?" asked Kenneth. "Have you asked Gablecross to provide her with protection, Mercer?"

"Tara Laing had an interesting career after she ditched Stan Jones," said Gus. "Ms Laing recently retired to an island off the Scottish coast searching for anonymity. However, the local police have been advised to look out for Stan Jones as a foot passenger or in a hire car on the ferry."

"You appear to have thought of most things, Freeman," said the Chief Constable. "But. I'm concerned we haven't started searching for this killer's vehicle. Have you issued an APB, Mercer?"

"We considered an alert broadcast to police officers within our area, sir, instructing the arrest of the suspect," said Geoff. "That approach has drawbacks. First, we don't know whether Jones is working in the UK, meaning we would need co-operation from various forces across the UK and mainland Europe. Second, because of his childhood experience, Stan Junior wasn't keen on having his photograph taken."

"He has a driving licence and a passport," said

Kenneth. "He must have provided legitimate photos for those."

"True," said Gus, "but what Geoff meant was Stan Jones has done everything possible to mask his scars. He wears gloves, whatever the weather. He has grown a beard. Although we can get a copy of the images he used for those official documents, we've got nothing current to distribute. So, do we stop every truck driven by a bearded man wearing a baseball cap and sunglasses in the hope the driver has significant scarring?"

"Registration number?" said Kenneth, opening his arms wide. "Surely, we know the registration of his tractor unit?"

"We know what it was when he bought it, sir," said Geoff. "However, he's avoided the nationwide CCTV coverage here in the UK, which might have tipped off detectives investigating the murders of those three girls."

"Which suggests he has a selection of vehicle registration plates, sir," said Gus. "The firms he works for wouldn't find it odd. Jones would automatically need to match the front and rear plates."

"He is clever," said Kenneth. "I'll give him that. I don't know how many firms he works for, but he needs to use the same false plates every time. That takes a good deal of planning and forethought."

"He will have several sets of foreign plates, too, sir," said Geoff. "It provides an extra layer of confusion for any traffic police watching for him."

"That's why we thought it best for you to hand everything over to Major Crimes," said Gus. "They have the necessary expertise to handle complex operations with multiple partners and international implications."

"What does that even mean?" asked Kenneth.

"No idea, sir," said Gus. "I only speak dinosaur. But that

sentence reminded me of what I hear from the bright young things who have reached the top of the tree in today's police service. In short, it's going to be a devil of a job. We're talking needle in a haystack territory, with thousands of vehicles that need pulling over to check whether the driver is our Stan Jones. But the alternative is just as risky. Neil Davis and Luke Sherman visited our suspect's father this morning. I haven't talked with them about everything they learned, but we know the Ponting Street address is young Stan's base of operations. He collects his mail on the rare visit he makes. One method he used to keep in touch with what was happening in Swindon was to pay for a subscription to the digital version of the Swindon Advertiser. That needs to be renewed in November. Gablecross can monitor the house and arrest Jones when he comes home."

"A huge risk if he doesn't turn up until the end of the month," said Kenneth, "and he's already murdered another girl. Why visit Ponting Street, anyway? He'll sort it online, won't he?"

"Too easily traced, sir," said Gus. "Stan Jones chose the lonely life of an independent trucker for a reason. Divya Yadav could probably tease out every phone call and bank transaction Jones made since he moved out of his family home if he ran his business and personal life online. But for a start, his father doesn't have a mobile number for him. We thought we would check the Ponting Street landline for an incoming call, telling his father he's staying overnight to get hold of his number. But Stan told Neil his son often arrives out of the blue. He parks his truck on the outskirts of Swindon, gets a taxi into the centre, and has a few beers. The first Stan knows his son is arriving is when he stumbles through the front door late at night."

Kenneth leant back in his chair and stared at the ceiling.

"He must have a bank account somewhere," he said.

"If I were him, I'd use cash wherever possible," said Gus. "If we traced a business account, the statement would be populated by payments from the firms he's worked for and direct debits and standing orders he's set up to keep his business afloat. Any transaction revealing his location, such as a till receipt for fuel or food while he's hunting his next victim, has to be avoided."

"If the address in Ponting Street is his base of operations," said Kenneth. "Then, surely, any business-related mail gets delivered there."

"I can't recall the exact section of the Postal Services Act 2000," said Gus, "but it is an offence to intercept any communication in the course of its transmission by post."

"What about the Investigatory Powers Act 2016?" asked Geoff Mercer. "That gives us routes to lawfully intercept postal communications after they get posted and before they get delivered."

"We could get a targeted interception warrant," said Gus. "Royal Mail will always co-operate with the police and other law enforcement agencies and assist them as far as the law permits."

"Is the father co-operating, Freeman? Has he impeded your investigation in any way?"

"We haven't told him of our suspicions, sir," said Gus. "He was an eyewitness mentioned in the original murder file. Stan Jones Senior saw someone peering through the garage windows on the afternoon of Richard Chaloner's death. He's been co-operative throughout."

"You might struggle to get that targeted warrant," said Kenneth. "The letters his father keeps for his son contain nothing dangerous or illegal. We can't expect to get permission to go on a fishing expedition."

"I understand, sir," said Gus. "We rely on that mail holding the missing pieces of the jigsaw. It could help locate our man and get him into custody before he strikes again. We have to place him in Swindon and Ponting Street on the day of Chaloner's murder. Young Stan didn't visit his father on that occasion. It was a flying visit. Access to his vehicle and his accounts could reveal where he was at the time of each of the murders we've traced so far."

"There's another reason we need access to his truck, sir," said Geoff.

"I'm ahead of you, Mercer," said Kenneth. "I'm multi-tasking and skimming through the report to get up to speed. You believe there will be trophies, Freeman?"

"We do, sir. Each girl wore a unique item which their family confirmed as missing."

"Let's park this case for now," said Kenneth. "I'll hand everything we have to the Major Crimes Investigation Team. After you've left, I'll speak with the Hub to check on progress. Whatever they dig up must get handed to the MCIT as soon as possible. Some steps they need to take will be challenging. But, as you pointed out, they are best equipped to negotiate their path through the minefield."

Kenneth Truelove opened his desk drawer and removed a thick folder.

"On July the twenty-first, 2014, Danute Zukas was found beaten to death and burned in a field on farmland near Claverton Down, three miles from Bath. The twenty-three-year-old was a Lithuanian national who hailed from Kaunas, a city of around three hundred and fifty thousand inhabitants. She was last seen alive on the nineteenth in Trowbridge town centre at ten-forty-five. Danute had been hit over the head repeatedly with a heavy object. An accelerant had been used in an attempt to burn the body, but this was only partially successful. The body was spotted by a man walking his dogs just before seven o'clock in the morning."

"Where would we be without the dog walkers?" said Gus.

"Uniformed officers arrived from Bath, and by lunchtime, the body was removed. A forensic post-mortem examination followed, which judged time-of-death occurred between midnight and four that morning. It was several weeks before they could make an identification. The police carried out a finger-tip search of the field and the immediate locality, looking for a handbag, purse, or mobile phone, but they found nothing. Dental records finally enabled the detectives to name the victim. Danute's mother, Karolina, said she hadn't known where her daughter was since moving to England three years earlier. Within twenty-four hours of landing at Bristol International airport, Danute had called home to say she'd arrived safely, and that was it. As far as her mother was concerned, Danute had moved to England for a better life."

"Were there problems at home?" asked Gus. "Was this a case of a twenty-year-old young woman kicking over the traces and wanting to escape from an unhappy situation?"

"Her mother had been widowed six years earlier," said Kenneth. "She looked after her other daughter, Natasha, two years younger than Danute. Life wasn't easy, but there was nothing to suggest any friction between the family members. Certainly not enough to cause Danute to sever all ties."

"What did the sister have to say?" asked Gus.

"Police interviewed Natasha, and she told them her sister called her every week at first, telling her she seemed happy and enjoying her job."

"Were they able to locate where the calls were made?" asked Geoff Mercer.

"In the Bath and Trowbridge area," said Kenneth.

"When did the calls stop?" asked Gus.

"Around nine months after Danute left home. Natasha and her sister had been very close. Even closer after their father died. In Kaunas, they went around together, dressed alike, and had the same hairstyle. Natasha showed the police the tattoo they got the same day without their mother's knowledge. Because of the fire, that fact couldn't be verified. However, the dental records removed any doubt. The girl in the field was her sister."

"What triggered the sudden break in the regular phone calls?" asked Gus. "How did Natasha explain why Danute hadn't called her mother?"

"Natasha told the police her mother wouldn't have approved of the work Danute was doing. She worked in a late-night bar in Bath."

"What did the police learn when they spoke to the management and staff there?" asked Gus.

"The manager, David Hodges, said Danute was a beautiful young woman, popular with her colleagues and customers," said Kenneth. "Her English was limited at first, but by the time she left, it had improved. Hodges said they were sorry to see her go."

"Did the halt in phone calls to her sister and a change of job overlap?" asked Gus.

"Danute started working at Nyx in the summer of 2011," said Kenneth, referring to the murder file for confirmation of the dates. "Hodges told the police she left at the end of April the following year."

"Natasha said the calls ended nine months after her sister left home. So, that was a month before she quit a job she enjoyed; at a place where she was welcomed. So, that's worth a look."

"Were there any recorded incidents at Nyx?" asked Geoff. "Did David Hodges know of any trouble Danute experienced with an over-attentive customer or another staff member getting out of line?"

"Nothing at all," said Kenneth.

"Where in Bath was Danute living?" asked Gus.

"She was living in Trowbridge," said Kenneth. "I don't suppose that should come as a surprise. Bath is an expensive place to live, especially for a girl barely out of her teens arriving from Lithuania."

Kenneth Truelove dug deep into the reports he had accumulated since accepting the role of Chief Constable. It never seemed to stop growing; he missed the days when he was at the sharp end. These weekly meetings with Mercer and Freeman were invaluable. They reminded him he had been a proper copper many years ago.

"Levels of poverty in Lithuania rose after the financial crisis a decade ago," he said. "Many areas maintain a low standard of living, with poor access to education and social services. Rural communities are the worst affected. The Zukas family lived in the second-largest city in the country. Vilnius, the capital, is the largest. So, comparatively, they were better off. However, the lack of opportunities and government assistance drove many like Danute from the country seeking better employment after 2008."

"The cost of renting a flat in Trowbridge would still be high compared to those at home," said Geoff. "But less eye-watering than anything available in the Roman city. Bath is the second least-affordable city in England for rental properties."

"Trowbridge might be a cheaper place to live, that's

true," said Gus. "But the job Danute secured presented her with another problem. I've heard nothing yet to suggest she owned a car. So, Danute could only get to work by using public transport. Good luck getting home after finishing work at three in the morning. You might still get a train at midnight, but buses would have stopped running as soon as her night shift started."

"Someone could have given her a lift," said Geoff.

"We'll dig into the thick folder to answer that question," said Gus. "Taxi costs would blow a large hole in her wages, so that would have been out of the question."

"Most young men baulk at the idea of thumbing a lift these days," said Geoff, "let alone young women. We thought nothing of it when I was a teenager."

"Perhaps another staff member took her home," said Kenneth. "Or maybe there was someone from Trowbridge working at Nyx when Danute arrived. If there was, it should be in the file somewhere."

"That could explain the job change," said Gus. "If her regular lift was moving on to new pastures, she could no longer make the journey. On the other hand, if Danute enjoyed what she was doing, she'd be upset, and that could have triggered a temporary break in the calls to Natasha."

"Did Natasha ever confide in her mother about the regular contact she had with Danute?" asked Geoff Mercer.

"Karolina always believed Danute had left to search for a better life," said Kenneth. "That was her choice. It was tough for Karolina, with no husband bringing in a wage. She and Natasha worked in Kaunas, and for the first few weeks, she prayed her daughter would save enough money to send something home for luxuries. Unfortunately, the money didn't materialise, and Karolina's concerns for her daughter grew. There are charities and foundations in places like Poland and the Baltic States trying to raise awareness of the dangers lurking for young immigrants. Karolina knew many young Europeans were living rough on the streets of London."

"They soon learned the streets weren't paved with gold," said Gus.

"Who handled the case, sir?" asked Geoff. "Did Bath run with it after they were first on the scene?"

"We got lumbered with it out of the blue," said Kenneth Truelove. "I'm surprised you don't remember, Mercer. As soon as Bath confirmed the body had been dumped and learned that the victim lived in Trowbridge, they suggested the detectives at Polebarn Road searched for the crime scene."

"They couldn't get rid of the case fast enough," said Geoff. "I remember now. Thousands of tourists arrived in Bath the following weekend for a festival. The city was swarming with visitors. The last thing they needed was a full-scale murder investigation disturbing the ambience."

"Who got the short straw?" asked Gus.

"Detective Inspector John Cook, together with Detective Sergeant Susannah Fry," said Kenneth, taking a quick peek at the murder file.

"Cook and Fry, sir?" asked Gus. "They sound like the dream partnership to me."

"Nothing to joke about, Freeman," said Kenneth. "They were dealing with a brutal murder on a quiet summer Sunday night. You can imagine the local press having a field day, but the commotion soon died, and reporters found other stories to print. Bath detectives wondered why nobody came forward to claim the victim as a relative in the first forty-eight hours. The file shows that a detective asked the pathologist and forensic experts to analyse the bones to determine the victim's race. The fire hadn't obliterated everything, but they needed to use facial mapping techniques to create an image of what Danute might have looked like. When they tried it in the local weekly paper, it didn't produce an identification."

"It couldn't have been a close match for the beautiful young woman David Hodges employed at Nyx, sir," said Gus.

"These mapping techniques aren't perfect," said Kenneth. "Cook's first breakthrough came when a young woman matching the victim's description was caught on a CCTV camera in the town centre late on Saturday night. The girl looked drunk or drugged."

"Where was Danute working between May 2012 and July 2014, sir?" asked Gus.

"Was Danute still living at the same address as when she worked at Nyx, sir?" asked Geoff.

"Good questions," said Kenneth Truelove. "Cook and Fry are still working out of Polebarn Road. Unfortunately, they couldn't answer those questions four years ago and never found the crime scene, which is why the investigation ground to a halt."

"I showed Gus the human trafficking report we discussed, sir," said Geoff.

"A minor success," said Kenneth, "although Olga suffered for far too long before being rescued."

"I can see why you took an interest in the case, sir," said Gus. "I guessed our new case might be linked."

"That remains to be seen," said Kenneth. "When Danute's identity became public, anti-trafficking charities suspected she had been trafficked. I don't accept someone paying her flight fare to get here as they did with Olga. I believe she fell under a predator's spell while working in

Bath. Her mother said Danute dreamt of going to Britain to make her fortune from an early age. Although she was twenty when she landed in England, she wasn't streetwise."

"Victims of trafficking often resemble victims of domestic abuse," said Gus. "They return to the abuser. If Danute had emotional ties to someone who befriended her in Nyx, or where she lived in Trowbridge, she didn't recognise she was being exploited."

"The CCTV picture supports that argument, Gus," said Geoff. "While she worked in that bar in Bath, everything was sweetness and light. Hodges said she was attractive, friendly, and a good worker he didn't want to lose. But, after two years in limbo, the girl had changed."

"Why didn't Cook and Fry locate the girl's whereabouts?" asked Gus. "Trowbridge isn't a vast metropolis. It shouldn't have been that difficult to check with the handful of letting agents in the area."

"You'll need to follow up on questions you have about how they handled the case," said Kenneth.

"Cook is a competent detective unlikely to have missed the obvious," added Geoff. "I've not met DS Fry, but no matter what steps they took, or didn't take, four years ago, this is your chance to follow different lines of enquiry."

"Until I read that file from start to finish, I'm not sure we've got a good place to start," said Gus. "This has the feel of a missing person case. My team will need to find a trace of Danute Zukas before we can start the search for her killer."

Chapter Three

"THAT SOUNDED LIKE THE LIFT," said Blessing Umeh.

"I was wondering whether the boss was going to make it back today," said Neil.

"The Chief Constable's meeting with the Police and Crime Commissioner must have dragged on," said Alex.

Gus strolled through the lift doors with a thick folder under his arm. He'd enjoyed Kassie's cream horn in the car before leaving the car park at London Road, and now he was thirsty.

"I know you want to learn about our next case," he said, "but first, can someone please fetch me a coffee?"

"On it, guv," said Luke.

"A tough day, guv?" asked Neil.

"I've had worse," said Gus. "Look, it would help if you and Luke told me about your visit to Ponting Street this morning. The Chief Constable is sending the Stan Jones case to the Major Crime Investigation Team. So if there's anything we can add to the file we've already handed him, it can only help them in their search."

"What's happening with the tasks we set Divya and the Hub, guv?" asked Luke, who was bringing Gus's black coffee to his desk.

"Kenneth Truelove will make sure she gets the support she needs. He wants to show the true scope of the investigation by the close of play tomorrow."

"Divya hasn't got back to us with any more bodies, guv," said Neil.

"Early days yet. Neil," said Gus. "Alex, can you dig into this folder and select the items we need on the walls and whiteboards, please? Blessing and Lydia will help you, I'm sure."

Luke and Neil joined Gus at his desk.

"Take me through what you found at the Jones's address in Ponting Street and everything Stan Jones told you."

Luke explained what had happened when they arrived. First, they asked Stan if they could check the front bedroom. He wondered why they needed to go in there. Luke had told him the first-floor bedroom on this side of the street might offer a better view of the garage and the surrounding area.

Stan had shrugged his shoulders but hadn't objected. Instead, he led them upstairs, opened the door and stood aside. Luke had entered the room, while Neil had encouraged Stan to return downstairs.

"I asked him if he ever went in the bedroom, guv," said Neil. "Stan said he hadn't been inside the room for over twenty years."

"I described what I found on the window sill to Alex, guv," said Luke. "I'd swear there was a camera there for a while."

"Don't doubt it, Luke," said Gus. "Yes, Alex passed that

information onto me. What did you two discuss while Luke was checking the bedroom, Neil?"

"Stan is proud of his son, guv. He hasn't got a clue yet that he's in the frame for Chaloner's murder. Heaven knows what he'll think when he learns of the other deaths. I hoped to get a chance to look at the mail that had arrived for young Stan, but I looked around and saw nothing. When I asked if much correspondence had come for his boy since his last visit, Stan said it was under lock and key. He stores it in that bureau standing against the wall by the window."

"Did that spook him?" asked Gus.

"What, because we appeared to be interested in the unopened mail, guv?" said Neil. "I don't think so. I changed the subject, anyway, to give him something else to consider."

"I had come downstairs by then, guv," said Luke. "While Neil gave Stan a chance to talk, I went into the kitchen to get three coffees. Stan sat in his chair by the window and told us how young Stan had gone from an awkward teenager to a young man with his own business. He wasn't happy when Stan started staying away so much after Jeanie died, but he understood it was necessary if his boy wanted his business to be successful."

"Stan told me young Stan worked for a big haulage firm for the first couple of years," said Neil. "Then, when work dried up in that sector, he took whatever he could get from a variety of smaller operators. In the end, young Stan decided he wanted to control his own success, pick his own work, and ultimately be the person benefiting from his hard work and effort. Deciding to become an owner-driver was difficult, and there were many things to consider before he took the plunge. Stan told us he knew nothing about running a business; he couldn't offer his son any advice, which made the success young Stan made of it even more satisfying."

"I checked a few of the facts Stan gave us, guv," said Luke. "Before he could apply for an Operator's Licence, young Stan needed a substantial sum in clear funds at the bank to operate one vehicle. He also had to find somewhere secure where his truck would be parked when he wasn't driving it."

"That explains his regular trips to the lorry park on the outskirts of town," said Gus. "As far as we can tell, there was only one occasion when the truck was parked outside the house on Ponting Street. So when did Stan stop driving for someone else and buy his tractor unit?"

"Early in 2006, guv," said Neil. "Stan told me his son was adamant he needed to buy from a reputable dealer and check the truck had a full-service history. That truck was to be his money-making tool, so reliability was imperative. In addition, the nearly new unit he bought had a warranty left, which gave him peace of mind when he was just starting."

"He was making good money if he could entertain buying his own truck," said Gus. "Where did he get most of his work? Do we know? It might narrow the field for MCIT when they start hunting for him."

"Stan told us on the odd occasion they spoke after a sleep-over young Stan grew his network of contacts in the first year with a haulage exchange firm," said Luke. "That way, he had daily access to thousands of load types from various companies. As a result, he quickly found haulage work and established himself as a reliable, independent trucker."

"He learned other ways to run the business," added Neil. "Stan could work as a sub-contractor for one leading haulage company, float between different hauliers utilising a freight exchange, or find work directly with customers, cutting out the middlemen and earning more money."

"His parents were simple folk who lived and worked in Swindon their whole lives," said Lydia. "I doubt they ever even travelled overseas for their holidays. Yet young Stan has proved to be an astute operator at home and abroad."

"It's a shame his experiences as a child, and a young man, had such a terrible impact," said Blessing. "The enterprise he's shown in his business has helped him murder at least four people."

"We have to hope the crew the MCIT select to carry on our good work will catch Jones before he can add to that number, Blessing," said Gus.

Alex Hardy's phone rang. Gus looked across from his desk as Alex listened to the caller. He realised at once it was bad news.

"That was Divya," said Alex, replacing the phone. "The Hub has flagged two unsolved murders in Germany and Belgium that carry uncomfortable similarities to the others. On November the seventh, 2012, Petra Fischer, a twenty-seven-year-old factory employee living in Frankfurt, disappeared. They found her strangled body in a vacant lot on the twentieth. Then, on the fifteenth of November 2015, the body of twenty-two-year-old Zoe Dubois was discovered in woodland four miles from the port city of Ghent. She had been suffocated."

"Has Divya got photographs of the victims?" asked Luke.

"Yes," said Alex. "There's a definite likeness to Tara Laing."

"Is it common for serial killers to vary their method, guv?" asked Blessing. "Emma Fox and Petra Fischer died from strangulation. Molly Phelps and Zoe Dubois were suffocated, while Sammy Yendall died from blunt-force trauma. The killer tried to obliterate her facial features with repeated blows from a hammer. Meanwhile, when he came back for Richard Chaloner, Jones used a gun."

"I suspect Jones used the gun to confuse the police," said Luke. "That way, the murder could never connect to those he'd committed elsewhere. Physically, Richard Chaloner would have been a tougher proposition to strangle. Jones needed to get into the garage, take his revenge, and get out. Why he did it when he did is another matter. It could have been something simple, like Chaloner getting his picture in the Swindon Advertiser for another charity sponsorship. Chaloner's friends told us he did it to appease his guilt over what they did all those years ago. We can't know what Stan Jones thought about it."

"I hadn't thought of that," said Blessing. "It's difficult to get my head around the concept of a serial murderer."

"Serial murder is not a recent phenomenon, Blessing," said Gus. "It's a relatively rare event, comprising less than one percent of murders in any given year. However, there has been a macabre interest in the topic since the late 1880s."

"Jack the Ripper," said Neil.

"Those unsolved murders in Whitechapel led to many newspaper articles and books," said Alex. "They created a lot of public interest, which over future decades was exploited by the burgeoning movie industry and television."

"The facts got lost in the sensationalised versions that followed," said Luke. "The public could no longer separate fact from fiction. No wonder so many myths surround serial killers."

"The media fuels the idea that serial killers are white males," said Lydia. "Sex-crazed predators who are misogynists and loners."

"Not all serial murders are sexually based," said Gus.

"Stan Jones doesn't molest his victims. What sets him apart is that he has killed women in different areas of the UK and Europe. Most serial killers have very defined geographic areas of operation. They conduct their killings within comfort zones. Those zones can be defined by where they live or work."

"Surely there are examples of killers moving their activities outside their comfort zone, guv?" asked Luke. "Stan Jones isn't unique in that regard."

"Their confidence grows if they commit several murders without getting caught," said Neil. "That could see them moving to another area to start another killing spree."

"True," said Alex. "But I guess some make the switch to avoid detection. Fishing in the same small pool increases the risk of detection, doesn't it?"

"We're entering territory the MCIT team will find the most challenging," said Gus. "Few serial murderers travel overseas to kill. Those that do tend to be individuals whose employment lends itself to travel, such as truck drivers. The difference between Stan Jones and other serial murderers is the nature of his travelling lifestyle, which provides many zones of comfort in which to operate. Each of his female victims came into contact with Jones on or near a motorway or trunk road. Service stations, garages, truck stops, and highways are his hunting ground. Whether it's in the Midlands or the outskirts of Munich or Marseilles is irrelevant to him. Jones feels at home. His truck *is* his home for extended periods. Jones plans his attacks more thoroughly than other criminals, and his learning curve is steepest once he had killed Emma Fox. After that, he's learned to select, target, approach, control, and dispose of his victims with no one suspecting his involvement."

"How does Jones function during the other eleven

months of the year, guv?" asked Blessing. "What if he sees a girl resembling Tara Laing in March while driving on the M4, heading for Bristol? Why doesn't he kill her, there and then?"

"His trigger centres around November and Bonfire Night," said Neil. "She would be one of the lucky ones."

"Maybe not," said Luke. "Jones might spot a potential target and organise his schedule to re-visit this part of the country in November. Then, as an independent trucker, he decides where and when he collects and delivers a load."

"Until Jones is in custody, we won't know whether he chose his victims well in advance," said Gus. "What is clear is the logistics involved in committing a murder and disposing of the body can become complex, especially when multiple sites are involved. Another myth that has grown around serial killers is that they are criminal masterminds. I believe Jones to be of average intelligence, yet he's developed an effective strategy to commit these murders at a time of his choosing, without leaving forensic evidence leading to his capture."

"Jones drives thousands of miles, alone in his cab, with nothing else to think about except how to kill Tara Laing repeatedly," said Blessing. "Why hasn't someone realised that was what he was doing? Or at least anticipate his childhood traumas might send him down this path? Surely, doctors must have treated him for more than his physical wounds. If only he'd been put on a watch list or a register. Or am I being fanciful?"

"There is no generic profile of a serial killer, Blessing," said Gus. "They differ in many ways, including their motivations for killing and behaviour at the crime scene. Identifying motivations when investigating a crime is a standard procedure for the police. Typically, motivation allows us to narrow the potential suspect pool. We follow the same logical steps when investigating homicide cases. As someone known to the victim commits most homicides, we focus on the relationships closest to the victim. That approach works for most murder investigations, as we have discovered. However, most serial murderers are not acquainted with or involved in a consensual relationship with their victims. Since there are no obvious connections between offender and victim, detectives instead try to figure out the motivations behind the murders to narrow their focus. In our case, Jones is motivated by hostility towards women who remind him of the hurt caused by Tara Laing. The methods of strangulation and suffocation offer him the time to savour the experience. With Sammy Yendell, perhaps she said something that Tara Laing had said to him. Maybe a stinging reference to his scarring. Whatever it was, it sent Jones into a violent rage that led him to vary his method. Those spells of extreme rage may escalate if he's not caught."

"You said any Major Crimes Investigation Team faced a challenge, guv," said Neil. "Was that because the murders took place at different sites?"

"To date, the nearest team of detectives has handled each of the murders," said Gus. "Ditto, the forensic teams, laboratories, coroners or police surgeons. Documentation should be similar within the UK, but you can bet there are minor differences. What any documentation available resembles in any European country, heaven knows. So, the MCIT will find varying levels of detail gathered at each crime scene, photographs, and test results. Each force will have its particular methodology. Can you imagine how difficult it could be, in other instances, to convince a German police officer the crimes were linked?"

"Photographs of Tara Laing and the victims should be enough to get them to listen," said Lydia.

"We might have had a lucky escape, guv," said Alex. "I wouldn't fancy MCIT's job."

"Oh, how fickle the youth of today can be," said Gus, shaking his head. "It wasn't long ago you were itching to leave the CRT office and gallivant across Europe hunting for Stan Jones and his truck. You wanted to see the case through to the bitter end. You weren't content with having identified Richard Chaloner's killer."

"It's tougher to let some cases go than others," said Neil. "We couldn't have dreamt we'd uncover what we did when we re-opened the Chaloner murder file. The Chief Constable and DS Mercer hinted the crime tied in with the theft of those catalytic converters."

"Just coincidence," said Gus. "Same postal district, but a fresh set of criminals. Has Jake Latimer ever mentioned nicking those guys, Neil?"

"Not a whisper, guv," said Neil. "Was Tom Spencer involved in that caper, Luke?"

"Tom was chasing combine harvesters around country lanes last week, Neil," said Luke. "Although he worked with DI Sengupta on the Chaloner case first time around, I haven't spoken to him to learn whether vehicle thefts are a speciality of his."

Lydia was sure she spotted Luke blushing. Had she missed something?

"Can we move on now, guv?" asked Neil. "We're keen to see what you've got in that thick folder."

Gus glanced at the clock. Perhaps he could give the team a flavour of the case. He wanted to leave on time tonight, taking the file with him to study it closely before they ripped it apart and began the inevitable round of interviews.

"We're looking at the murder of a twenty-three-year-old Lithuanian girl in July 2014," said Gus. "A man walking his dog in a field at around seven in the morning found the body. Danute Zukas had been beaten to death, and her killer, or killers, had attempted to burn the body to destroy forensic evidence."

"Where was this, guv?" asked Neil.

"Near Claverton Down, Neil. Three miles from Bath."

"Avon and Somerset should have picked up that case, guv," said Neil.

"Uniformed officers from Bath attended the scene, Neil," said Gus. "But it was soon clear the murder site was elsewhere. Danute was last seen alive in Trowbridge town centre two nights earlier. She was caught on a CCTV camera outside a bar at ten forty-five."

"How long had she been in the country, guv?" asked Alex.

"Three years, Alex," said Gus. "Danute flew into Bristol International airport from Kaunas."

"Never heard of it, guv," said Neil.

"It's the second-largest city in the country," said Gus. "With a population of three hundred and fifty thousand, which makes it around half the size of Bristol. Ryanair has direct flights daily from Bristol International."

"Typical," said Neil. "They're just like EasyJet. They fly to places in the middle of nowhere for next to nothing. Not that it's somewhere anyone wants to go. Is it near a beach?"

"No, Neil, the Baltic Sea is two hundred and fifty miles away," said Luke. "Kaunas is in the middle of the country, and the airport is a twenty-minute drive from the city centre."

"Have you been there?" asked Blessing.

"I haven't," said Luke, "but Nicky flew there on business once."

"What were the nuts and bolts of the post-mortem, guv?" asked Neil.

"Death occurred between midnight and four," said Gus. "Danute died from blunt force trauma; her injuries indicated she suffered multiple blows to the head and body. One small mercy, she was dead before someone poured the accelerant on her body and set it alight."

"When someone sets out to destroy their victim, it points to it being personal, doesn't it, guv?" asked Lydia.

"That's a potential line of enquiry to follow, Lydia," said Gus. "How the body was dumped certainly shows a complete disregard for human life. However, if someone planned the murder and what was to follow, I would expect them to have been better prepared."

"Do you sense burning the body was an afterthought, guv?" asked Luke.

"Danute could have died as late as four in the morning," said Alex. "Maybe the killer had to get out of the field in a rush. On the other hand, if the murder occurred in Trowbridge, and the killer drove towards Bath, it was fast approaching dawn."

"The dog walker found the body at seven," said Gus. "It would have been light for two hours by then. He told police there were no cars parked near the field, and he didn't see anyone else on the pavement as he walked his dog from home. However, he saw the occasional vehicle travelling in either direction, as you would expect on that road on a Monday morning."

"We haven't confirmed the murder took place in Trowbridge yet, guv," said Luke.

"True, but the forensic crew found nothing to suggest the attack took place in that field. So, the body was transported from somewhere within a few miles. Unfortunately, there was no identification on the body, bag, phone, or purse. That led to a lengthy delay before the police traced Danute's dental records to the city where she lived with her mother and sister."

"What a terrible shock for her family," said Lydia. "Was her mother divorced from Danute's father?"

"Danute's father died in 2008," said Gus. "Karolina Zukas lived with Danute's younger sister, Natasha. They were both hard-working individuals doing what they could to survive."

"Danute came to this country, as many others have from the EU, hoping for a better life," said Lydia.

"When had they last spoken to Danute, guv?" asked Alex. "Did she regularly write or phone? Was she sending money home to help her mother cope with the loss of her father's income?"

"We only have what's in that murder file, Alex," said Gus. "I reckon we need to dig deeper because Karolina told detectives from Trowbridge police she hadn't known where her daughter was living since moving to England. Danute rang to say she'd arrived safely at Bristol International, and then nothing."

"Had they fallen out over something, guv?" asked Lydia.

"Not according to Karolina. Natasha gave a different account of events following the first phone call. She told police Danute rang her weekly, telling her she was happy and working at a job she enjoyed."

"But she didn't speak to her mother, guv? Why not?" asked Blessing.

"Natasha said their mother wouldn't have approved of

the work Danute was doing. Karolina is a devout Roman Catholic who wanted her daughters to stay on the straight and narrow."

"Hang on, guv," said Neil. "Are you telling us Danute was on the game?"

"DI Cook from the Polebarn Road station didn't find evidence to support that theory while Danute worked in Bath," said Gus. "Perhaps, Danute and Natasha might have convinced their mother working in hospitality was legitimate employment, and normal lines of communication could have resumed. As it was, Danute worked at a late-night bar called Nyx. When DI Cook asked, Bath police gave the place a reasonably clean bill of health. They weren't looking to oppose licence renewals because it was a regular trouble-spot. Like many licensed premises, Nyx had the occasional fight break out in the early hours, but nothing pointed to the bar being a drug or vice den."

"Were the detectives able to show Danute's calls home came from Bath, guv?" asked Luke.

"The analysis of Natasha's phone records showed the calls originated in the Bath and Trowbridge area," said Gus. "Unfortunately, the calls petered out around nine months after Danute arrived here. The break appears to be linked to a change of job. Danute couldn't afford to rent a place in Bath, so she found a flat in Trowbridge soon after she arrived."

"Do we have an address, guv?" asked Neil.

"Not at this stage, Neil," said Gus. "But I'm ever hopeful."

"How do we know it was Trowbridge, guv?" asked Lydia.

"David Hodges, the bar manager, told police Danute told him that was where she lived. She travelled into the city six nights a week. Her shifts covered eight in the evening until two in the morning, Monday to Thursday. Then, the bar stayed open on Friday and Saturday until two o'clock instead of one."

"The extra hour was to get rid of the punters and tidy the place ready for a noon start the following day," said Alex. "That's common practice, guv. When we were investigating Trudi Villiers's murder, that extra hour was a bone of contention for the cleaning staff the landlord brought in on Sunday mornings."

"Trudi and Krystal weren't keen on staying behind to tidy up," said Lydia. "They rushed away with their latest conquests, leaving the Sunday crew with twice the work to do."

"A thirty-eight hour week," said Neil, "working unsocial hours. It would be nice to think this bloke paid good wages."

"Natasha reckoned her sister was happy working at Nyx, guv," said Lydia. "Why did she change her job? Or did she get the sack?"

"David Hodges told DI Cook that Danute was a beautiful young woman, popular with her colleagues and customers," said Gus. "He was sorry to see her go. There don't appear to have been any issues over pay or conditions. Danute certainly didn't get the sack, but she left Nyx at the end of April 2012."

"That was when Danute stopped calling her sister," said Blessing.

"No," said Gus, "Natasha said the last call she received was around a week before."

"Do we know what that last conversation was about, guv?" asked Luke.

"Natasha said her sister was still happy and enjoying her

job," said Gus. "There was no hint of an imminent career change, no mention of a boyfriend, and no complaints of harassment from a customer. So Natasha was surprised when her sister didn't call the following week but not concerned."

"How did Danute travel to and from Nyx, guv?" asked Alex.

"She didn't drive, Alex," said Gus. "My first thought was public transport, but although she could get there alright, there was no way she could make the return journey by bus or train."

"Did she stay in Bath with a friend?" asked Blessing. "Another person from the bar, perhaps."

"We need to check the file, but David Hodges mentioned nothing."

"Another staff member could have driven into Bath, guv," said Lydia. "Or someone Danute knew in Trow-bridge who also worked unsocial hours somewhere in the city."

"Why didn't the detectives learn these details during the initial investigation, guv?" asked Neil.

"DI Cook and DS Fry are still at Polebarn Road," said Gus. "We can ask. Hospitality work in a cosmopolitan city such as Bath will attract people from many countries. They are young and liable to move around frequently. So, with the murder occurring two years after Danute left Nyx, there may have been a raft of staff changes, both at Nyx and other similar businesses catering to the night-time economy."

"So, it might not have been simple to locate the person who gave Danute a lift, guv," said Blessing.

"Exactly," said Gus. "We don't yet know what prompted the change of job. If her regular lift was leaving the area,

Danute couldn't get back from Bath without paying over the odds for a taxi."

"I'd find a way to get home every night, guv," said Lydia. "I know it's cheaper to rent in Trowbridge, but I couldn't spend only one night a week in my bed and crash on someone's sofa for the rest of the week."

"Didn't Natasha tell her mother about the lack of phone calls, guv?" asked Blessing. "After the first week without contact, she must have worried."

"I saw a reference in the folder," said Gus. "Karolina was disappointed with Natasha for hiding that she was in touch with her sister. For the first nine months, Karolina had believed Danute left home to forge her way in the world, and she respected that decision. Karolina had enough trouble affording to feed her and Natasha and keeping a roof over their heads."

"There was quite a time from that initial break in communication and what we know happened to Danute two years later," said Blessing. "How did Karolina deal with that?"

"They heard nothing to make them think differently, so they stayed positive," said Gus. "It might seem odd to us, but we do not know what conditions they lived under. The family was in no position to jump on a plane to come and search for Danute. Although Natasha knew about Nyx and that Danute had stayed in Trowbridge, they had no address for her and no clue where Danute went after she left her job."

"Did Karolina go to the authorities, guv?" asked Lydia. "To get help in discovering her daughter's whereabouts?"

"Karolina approached a Lithuanian charity set up to raise awareness for anyone emigrating to the UK and other EU states. She asked for their help tracing Danute a year after Natasha's confession. The charity warned her that many young Europeans were living rough in London, and her daughter could have suffered the same fate in the West Country. The reality of working abroad was much tougher than the dreams they had when they first left home."

"Why didn't Natasha simply phone Danute after that first missed call, guv?" asked Blessing.

"Danute was earning better money in Bath than in Kaunas," said Gus. "She told Natasha it was better if she called her. Danute knew money was tight for the two of them. Karolina had started the ball rolling with the charity to get news of her daughter and kept hoping that, in time, a call would come. The number Natasha had for her sister was no longer in service by the time they approached the charity, anyway."

"Although the murder occurred two years later in mid-July," said Neil, "they still didn't hear the news for several weeks. That must have been a nightmare."

"The police did not know Danute's nationality at first," said Gus. "When Trowbridge police took over the case from Manvers Street in Bath, they thought someone local would have contacted the police to report a missing person. For instance, a landlord missing a tenant or someone Danute shared a flat with. Given the circumstances, nobody had gotten in touch, and it wasn't easy to post a photograph in the local press. John Cook realised he was in for the long haul. The dental match was confirmed by Bath police days before the handover, and Cook soon had a photograph of Danute, aged nineteen, to use. They caught a break when a fellow officer, reviewing a separate case, spotted a young woman matching Danute's description caught on a CCTV camera in Trowbridge town centre late on the Saturday night before her murder."

"Could DI Cook and his team identify the people Danute was with that night, guv?" asked Lydia.

"Danute was standing alone on the street corner leading to a popular drinking hole. Another late-night establishment."

"Perhaps my earlier comment wasn't so wide of the mark, guv," said Neil.

"If so, I want to know what caused Danute to stray from the straight and narrow," said Gus.

Chapter Four

GUS WRAPPED things up for the day. He'd given everyone a taste of what lay ahead. It promised to differ from every other case they'd handled. He told his team to get off home, get a good night's sleep, and they'd start afresh in the morning.

As Gus drove past Crook's Way en route for Devizes, he made a mental note to tell Luke he wasn't working on Wednesday afternoon. One of the first tasks Luke would tackle was the interview schedules, and if the others picked up the slack, they might not ask why he was taking time off at the start of a cold case review.

So far, Suzie's parents and the two people in the village who knew about the pregnancy had kept things secret. In forty-eight hours, anyone who was interested would know everything. First thing Thursday morning was soon enough for Alex and the others.

Gus passed the London Road buildings and looked for Suzie's Golf but saw no sign. He resisted the temptation to drop by the allotments on the way through Urchfont village and swung the Focus through the gates of the bungalow a few minutes after half-past five.

He found Suzie in the kitchen, preparing their evening meal.

"Will a salmon traybake with new potatoes tickle your taste buds?" she asked.

"After today," said Gus, "anything will do the trick. As long as a large glass of single malt can follow it."

"Oh dear, did you have a tough day?"

Suzie knew Gus had driven into town to meet Rick Chalmers before visiting the Chief Constable at London Road.

"We got off to a decent start, but the PCC derailed my lunchtime meeting with Kenneth. So I had to hang around with Geoff Mercer while we waited for him to return to his office."

"That's no hardship, surely?" asked Suzie. "You two get on like a house on fire these days."

"Sometimes, I suspect they're working in tandem," said Gus.

"Our meal will be on the table in forty minutes," said Suzie. "Have a shower, slip into something comfortable, and you can tell me what you think is going on."

As always, the meal was excellent, and they moved into the lounge, ready for another quiet evening at home. Gus felt guilty enjoying a glass of Chardonnay while Suzie stuck to water, but it had helped him get his ducks in a row. So he brought two coffees from the kitchen and joined Suzie on the settee.

"Tell me more," said Suzie.

"It was something Neil said that started me thinking," said Gus. "He said we could never have expected Chaloner's murder in his garage to turn into a nationwide hunt for a serial killer. When he handed me the murder file, Kenneth's first move was to spin a yarn about catalytic converter thefts. That could have set us on the wrong track altogether."

"You questioned the details of the attack," said Suzie. "I remember you giving me the lowdown this time last week. It never felt gang-related to you, and I trusted your judgement that it was personal. You were right."

"Geoff used our spare time to tell me a story about a young Polish girl. Her name was Olga, and she lived with her family in Krakow. At seventeen, she secured a job as a nanny, flew into Exeter Airport, and you can guess the rest."

"They had conned her," said Suzie.

"The couple running the show put her to work in a house on the outskirts of the city. Twelve months later, they sold her to another gang in Plymouth. This gang had her working on the streets rather than behind closed doors, and luckily, the police rescued her. Olga told them everything she could, and the couple has since been arrested and jailed. Olga is back in Krakow with her family. A harsh lesson, but at least she's alive. Unlike the girl Kenneth told me about when he handed me our next case."

"Your new case concerns yet another victim of a sex-trafficking scandal," said Suzie.

"Or does it?" asked Gus. "Ever since Neil put the idea in my head, I've been going over the cases Kenneth's given us, searching for hints our leader knew just which buttons to press."

"Are you sure you're not overthinking things, darling?"

"I brought the file home this evening to look for clues that Kenneth had seen another possibility," said Gus. "How the two young women reached this country differed. The events that followed differed, yet everything points to the same result. Olga disappeared within hours of reaching Exeter. Her captors never allowed her to see the light of day and used drugs to control her. Only once did she find a chance to escape. During that moment of freedom, her only thought was to head for the nearest train tracks and commit suicide. Instead, Olga was caught, beaten, and watched more closely until the man and woman running the premises cashed in on their asset. In Plymouth, the control pattern through drugs and punishment for failing to reach targets continued. Olga was one of the lucky ones. Two uniformed officers patrolling the darker corners of the city's late-night entertainment district spotted her. Thank goodness they didn't treat her as a bog-standard streetwalker and move her on with a warning."

"Did Olga give them information about the gang that had bought her?" asked Suzie.

"Devon and Cornwall Police handled that aspect of the case.," said Gus. "Olga's story was more recent than the one Kenneth tasked us to review. Information Olga gave the detectives in Plymouth regarding her time in the Exeter property was circulated to other forces in the south of England. It took eighteen months, but Wiltshire's forensic accountants traced the couple from Exeter to Wareham. That wasn't the only house move they'd made during their criminal career. When Dorset Police raided a property in Wareham, they discovered three young women being held against their will. A man and woman, both Romanian nationals, were arrested, and evidence gathered from mobile phones and laptops at the property sealed their fate. Police found passports and other personal items belonging to the girls in a safe and twenty thousand pounds in cash."

"Where did these three girls come from?" asked Suzie.

"Europe, Africa, and Asia," said Gus. "The approach

they used for dozens of girls over the years was similar on every occasion. They advertised online for a girl between seventeen and nineteen to work as a nanny, au pair, or housekeeper. After a year, eighteen months at most, they sold the girls to another group of traffickers. Then they started covering their tracks—a change of venue and new girls. Every connection to the girls they'd sold on was destroyed, or so they thought. The lines were faint, but those forensic guys were bloodhounds. Unless you physically destroy every phone, tablet, and laptop, you can't be sure you've erased every trace."

"Is there any possibility your latest case is connected?" asked Suzie.

"If you had asked me that when Kenneth briefed me on the case, I'd have said never in a million years."

Gus gave Suzie the salient details of Danute Zukas's background, her time working at Nyx, and her murder.

"What did Danute do after she left her job at the bar?" asked Suzie.

"For some reason, DI Cook and his colleague never learned where Danute was working between May 2012 and July 2014," asked Gus. "They never identified where she lived in Trowbridge either."

"That's odd," said Suzie. "Someone must know."

"Danute lived in rented accommodation," said Gus. "That offers more opportunity for anonymity than if she were a householder. Unfortunately, the 2011 Census took place on the twenty-seventh of March 2011. Danute didn't arrive in the country until several weeks later. So, that opportunity to fix her location was missed. I don't know the exact figure for the number of licenced HMOs in Trowbridge, but something between twenty and thirty feels reasonable in a town of thirty thousand people. There's even a licenced HMO in this village, Suzie. Can you tell me who lives there?"

"Not exactly, no," she replied. "I could hazard a guess at five single people, based on the cars in the driveway and parked on the road. One guy is a stylist at the hair salon I use. Jamie is his first name, but that's as much as I know about him."

"Urchfont has a population approaching one thousand," said Gus, "and we've got at least four people we can't identify. Who owns the property? Do they keep detailed records of the people renting rooms? Licences last for five years, but there's more to renting a property than finding a tenant and handing over the keys. We need to check the Trowbridge rental market to separate unlicensed properties from those following the rules. Danute should have paid a deposit to a landlord when she first rented a place back in the summer of 2011. We need to find that first piece of the jigsaw, then follow the trail to her final property in July 2014."

"The police never found the crime scene," said Suzie. "They had a body but nowhere to gather forensic evidence, which might have led them to Danute's killer."

"Eight weeks after that dog walker found her body," said Gus, "the investigation ground to a halt, and the Bath detectives were moved onto different cases. Kenneth believes a predator groomed Danute while working at Nyx."

"So, did this man, if it was a man, live and work in Bath?" asked Suzie. "Was he a regular customer? If so, the manager should have been able to identify him. Or did the grooming, or stalking, take place in Trowbridge?"

"Kenneth preferred the simplest option," said Gus. "A customer visited the bar, realised Danute was naïve and impressionable and made his move. Perhaps, if we trace the person who gave Danute lifts to and from work, we will discover someone else took over. Think what Natasha, the sister, told the police. The phone calls were regular until just before she left Nyx. Throughout the first nine months, Danute was happy and talkative. So, whoever we're talking about didn't arrive on the scene until after the New Year. Maybe in February or early March. That's a narrower window when we talk to the manager and staff at Nyx. Kenneth thinks Danute became emotionally involved with this man but was blind to the fact his only aim was to exploit her. She probably thought he loved her. When Danute's mother sent Bath police a photo taken the summer before she left home, they showed it to the manager and staff at Nyx. They confirmed it was the girl they knew. Bath police handed the file over to Polebarn Road within a week. The murder happened on their patch. It was the only logical conclusion. Soon after, the CCTV image from Trowbridge town centre materialised, and the new guy in charge, DI Cook, studied it for a time before agreeing it was the same girl. While she worked in Bath, everyone said she was attractive and friendly. Then, two years later, Danute had changed."

"Did the autopsy show evidence of regular drug use?" asked Suzie.

"I need to study the file's contents in greater detail," said Gus.

"I'm keeping you from doing what you planned to do, aren't I?" said Suzie.

"We often make more progress by chewing a case over in the first forty-eight hours after I pick up the murder file. I value your input."

"You say the nicest things, darling," said Suzie. "I'll pour that glass of single malt now while you dig in the folder for the autopsy summary."

Gus soon found the sheet he wanted and scanned it while Suzie almost emptied his bottle of eighteen-year-old Macallan's whiskey. Gus made a mental note to replenish stocks after payday.

"Cause of death was the prime concern," said Gus, "plus an estimated time at which it occurred. The fire-damaged parts of the body are detailed in the report. Drugs didn't feature in the cause of death. Therefore, it appears they did not carry out tests."

"I don't think you can make much headway with this case until you've had several preliminary interviews," said Suzie. "You need to trace where Danute lived, who she associated with in Trowbridge and more details about her movements in Bath from staff and customers at that bar. Those interviews should give you a better handle on what type of life Danute led and what persuaded her to change her job."

"You're probably right," said Gus. "I'll brief Luke in the morning. Then, he can get the ball rolling. I won't be able to attend the early interviews, anyway, as I've booked time off for your appointment."

"I had to tell Geoff Mercer I needed time off this week," said Suzie. "Did he query why you booked time off at the same time?"

"Geoff knows me well enough not to ask," said Gus. "A raised eyebrow was his response, as I recall. Nevertheless, having the news out in the open will be good."

"I'm glad you're coming with me," said Suzie.

"The procedure isn't something to worry over, is it?" asked Gus.

"Not in itself. It's just an ultrasound scan showing how

the high-frequency sound waves from the probe pass over my tummy reflect off our baby in my womb."

"It's all new to me," said Gus. "I can't imagine what the experience would have been like for Tess if she'd wanted children. No doubt things have changed over the decades. My mother said my father was never allowed anywhere near whenever she saw the doctor. It was as if it had nothing to do with him. As for antenatal classes or being present at the birth, you could forget it."

"That's progress for you," laughed Suzie. "I wouldn't twist your arm to accompany me on every occasion, but this scan could be important because I've asked them to check for certain conditions and provide the due date."

"I think I understand the reasoning behind that," said Gus. "You're saying the scan could highlight any potential disabilities our baby might have."

"Fingers crossed, it's something we won't have to worry about, darling," said Suzie. "I'm looking forward to learning the size of our baby, an indication of its sex, and how many babies I'm having."

"Twins aren't the same as London buses, are they?" asked Gus. "You wait for ages, and then several arrive at once."

"If it were twins, it would be because of my genes, not yours. I was at school with a girl from Worton who had two sets of twins. Don't look like that. Emma had left school and got married before she had her first two. It's amazing how the odds against giving birth to twins change if twins run in the family. There was a one in eighty chance she would have twins, which didn't put her off in the slightest. Normally, the odds would be over three times as high if it were a natural pregnancy."

"Why didn't Emma call it quits after the first two?" asked Gus. "What did she have?"

"Two boys," said Suzie, "so they tried again because she wanted a daughter. Eighteen months later, Emma had another set of twins."

"Two girls?" asked Gus. "Or one of each?"

Suzie shook her head.

"Two boys," said Suzie. "When the doctor saw her after the birth, he said he should have warned her that after having twins, given her history, the odds halved to forty to one."

"Blimey, time to call it a day, I reckon," said Gus.

"They adopted a little girl, Jamila," said Suzie. "A three-year-old who arrived in the UK in 2010 with a group of Iraqi refugees. Her parents died, and the grandmother was too frail to care for her."

"I'm not sure I'm in favour of big families these days," said Gus, "given the state of the world."

"We didn't plan this one," said Suzie, patting her stomach. "Emma and her husband are happy enough with their brood. He's had the snip, so there's no prospect of adding to their number. As a young girl growing up on the farm, our animals regularly churned out calves and foals. I imagined it happening to me one day, but I thought I had the means to decide how often it happened and when. Although I must admit, after I started taking the pill at sixteen, I never thought about the matter until I realised I was pregnant three months ago."

"One step at a time," said Gus. "That seems the sensible approach. We're a team, and we'll adapt to having a third person in our relationship. We don't need to decide what comes next, not yet."

"At least we have a future to look forward to," said

Suzie. "Unlike that poor girl whose death you're investigating."

"Which one?" asked Gus.

"The Lithuanian girl," said Suzie.

"Sorry," said Gus. "It's getting late. It's been a long day. Alex heard from Divya Yadav that two young girls had been murdered in the past five years in Europe. Unfortunately, they could be more of Stan Jones's victims, and in time that number could grow."

"What a dreadful thought to go to bed on," said Suzie. "No wonder you're concerned with the state the world's in. I keep clinging to the belief that far more decent people are around than monsters. We must teach them how to tell them apart when our little one arrives."

Tuesday, 11 September 2018

GUS WAS first out of bed in the morning. He wandered through to the kitchen and prepared his breakfast. Suzie joined him five minutes later.

"Was it a struggle to get going this morning?" asked Gus as he buttered a second slice of toast.

"You kept me awake with your snoring," said Suzie.

"That large glass of whisky you poured me helped," said Gus. "At least I didn't have nightmares."

"Be thankful for small mercies," said Suzie.

"Always," said Gus. "Can I get you something?"

"Today feels like a cereal and yoghurt day."

"I'll pour your coffee, and then I'll get your breakfast. Will you be home at half-past five this evening?"

Suzie nodded.

"Do you have any plans for this evening?"

"Nothing concrete," said Gus. "A brief visit to the allotment to check on my winter cabbage, that's all."

"I told you when I visited Vicky Bennison last week; she was on the mend. I got a text from one of her colleagues. There's an outside chance they could let Vicky come home today. If so, I'd like to pop round to help her get settled. Of course, someone else might think to call in, but there's nothing worse than coming home to an empty house."

"So, you might be out for a couple of hours early in the evening?"

"If you stop at the allotment on the way home, we can have a meal here later," said Suzie.

"That's fine with me," said Gus. "All things being equal, we could visit the Crown tomorrow evening."

"Either to celebrate or to drown our sorrows," said Suzie, nursing her cup of coffee and staring out the kitchen window.

Gus stacked his breakfast things in the dishwasher and headed for the shower. Least said, soonest mended. Suzie kept insisting this procedure was nothing to worry about, but it was clear she wouldn't relax until they'd heard the results of the scan tomorrow evening.

By twenty-past-eight, they were both dressed, ready for work, and making their way outside to their cars.

"I'll see you tonight," said Gus. "I hope you hear good news on Vicky."

"Me too," said Suzie. "Either way, will you cook tonight?"

"Not a problem," said Gus. He waited for Suzie to ease her Golf through the gateway and followed her through the village. They negotiated the traffic on the outskirts of Devizes and slowed on London Road, waiting for a gap in traffic for Suzie to turn into the Police HQ's car park.

Gus parked the Focus in the last remaining space at the rear of the Old Police Station at five minutes to nine. As he rode in the lift to the first floor, he wondered what the next forty-eight hours would bring.

"Morning, guv," said Neil as Gus exited the lift.

"Someone's been busy," said Gus.

"We thought we could benefit from keeping relevant items from the Danute Zukas murder file on one wall, guv," said Alex Hardy.

"Luke and I are using the back wall to post the most up-to-date situation on the Stan Jones case," said Lydia. "We may have handed the file over to the Chief Constable, but we're still receiving add-ons that might get missed if we're not on top of things."

"Not just the bare-bones of the fresh cases unearthed by the Hub, but our interpretation of how they relate to what we already had, guv," said Luke. "We believe we're best-placed to make those observations. It will save the team that eventually picks it up a lot of time."

"I can't argue with any of that," said Gus. "What have you been doing with the restroom wall, Blessing?"

"I found a map of the area near my parent's home in Englishcombe, guv," said Blessing. "The manor house you visited and the grounds are outlined in red. I've also posted a summary of the original Burnside murder, plus the subsequent events that directly or indirectly impacted this team. We want permission to ask DS Mercer for a copy of the file he received from DS Chalmers relating to the Portishead team he worked with undercover."

"You can ask, but he might want to know why you need

to see it," said Gus. "What do you hope to gain? When did you start this, anyway?"

"Luke suggested we met up for a drink and a chat over the weekend, guv," said Neil.

"But everyone wasn't available," said Alex, "so when we left last night, we agreed to drive out to that new pub on the outskirts of town."

"We didn't stay long," said Neil, "But we decided to get here earlier this morning to get the office ready for when you arrived. As for Rick's report, we were in at the beginning of this team unravelling the Grant Burnside murder. If Portishead carries out a raid in the coming days, it would be fun tracking events via Rick's bodycam."

"I suppose you've spoken to Rick, have you?" asked Gus. He'd given up walking from one wall display to the other. Instead, he sat at his desk and waited to hear what else they'd been scheming.

"Rick couldn't make the meeting last night, guv," said Lydia. "He's somewhere on the Dorset coast, between Seaton and Weymouth, keeping watch for small boats. Rick thought our idea was great. DS Mercer told him yesterday afternoon Portishead had enquired whether he would be available next Sunday evening for a particular operation. They thought Rick deserved to be in at the death, considering the hours he'd put in on the assignment. So DS Mercer gave Rick the green light.

"Rick's sent me the necessary details for us to follow the raid," said Luke. "We must be in the office at dusk on Sunday evening."

"I'll have to check my diary to see if I can join you," said Gus. "I hope you don't expect to claim overtime."

"We wouldn't dream of it, guv," said Blessing.

"So, now we've got three cases to progress instead of

one," said Gus. "Do we have any interviews scheduled for today?"

"DI John Cook will see us at Polebarn Road this afternoon, guv," said Luke.

"What time?" asked Gus.

"One o'clock, guv,"

"Right, Alex and I will attend that one. I shall only be here until lunchtime tomorrow, Luke. I'm taking a half-day holiday. That doesn't mean you can't arrange interviews for the afternoon, though. Split the tasks between the teams as you see fit. Alex will be in charge while I'm away and can take the lead at meetings with leading witnesses in the Zukas case. I can't guarantee whether I'll be in the office on Thursday, so Alex will need to step up if the need arises. I know you'll give him your full support."

Lydia Logan Barre was itching to ask Gus if everything was alright, but the look he gave her when she opened her mouth convinced her to keep quiet.

Chapter Five

"DO you mind if I drive, guv," asked Alex, as he and Gus travelled in the lift at twelve-fifteen.

"Not at all, Alex," said Gus. "Do you know where we're going?"

"I checked the directions with Luke. We've driven through Trowbridge on other cases but never needed to stop."

"Some say that's the best option," said Gus. "but I couldn't possibly comment."

"I gather the new station building attracted opposition when they built it back in 2004, guv," said Alex.

"From what I remember, the Trowbridge police station was always on Polebarn Road," said Gus. "The address was the same all the time I was stationed in Salisbury."

"Yes, that was the original station they built in the 1920s. I think both of us can visualise that. Lots of red brick and wooden windows. Fifteen years ago, the Home Office issued a directive that stations should include safe zones and at least try to look more welcoming to the local citizens."

The A361 eventually disappeared into Roundstone Street, and Alex turned left onto Polebarn Road. A futuristic building loomed large on their left-hand side.

"The only people likely to be welcomed by this would be lovers of 50s sci-fi films," said Gus. "Did you ever watch the Day of the Triffids?"

"That was the post-apocalyptic black and white film, wasn't it, guv?" said Alex. "I think I caught it once, late at night, after I'd fallen asleep in the chair. When they replaced the old building, they got little change out of two million pounds."

"Imagine how many police officers would pay for," Gus said. "It doesn't fit in with its surroundings, does it? So why here, in a conservation area? At least our steel and glass command centre and custody suite is hidden away on an industrial estate on the outskirts of town.

"The authorities cited a lack of suitable alternatives to demolishing and replacing the existing building, guv. Local councillors suggested half a dozen appropriate sites, but after London Road threatened that they might have to move out of the town if they did not approve the plan, the die was cast.

"Trowbridge should have a police station in the town centre area, and the existing Polebarn Road site was the only sensible option," said Gus.

"That's the size of it, guv," said Alex. "While disagreeing on the design and location of the building, councillors agreed the police could not carry on working from the cramped 1920s building."

Alex parked the car under the lofty canopy, and they approached the glass-fronted building. Once inside, regular service resumed, and Gus and Alex had to suffer the rigours of a twenty-first-century reception.

"I bet you're glad we left ten minutes early, guv," said Alex, while they waited for a fresh-faced officer to verify Freeman and Hardy were bona fide visitors.

DI John Cook arrived at the front desk at a minute to one o'clock. Tall, with his dark hair carrying a few flecks of grey at the temples, the detective appeared to Gus in his early forties. The hangdog expression was all too familiar. John Cook was another world-weary officer drowning in a sea of paperwork and new initiatives handed on tablets of stone from above.

After a brief nod to the youth behind the counter, the senior detective led Gus and Alex into the bright interior. DI John Cook had an office that matched his rank, and when they were sitting comfortably, Gus broke the silence.

"Thank you for agreeing to meet with DS Hardy and me today, John. I'm Gus Freeman, employed for the past six months as a consultant by the Chief Constable. After forty years in the force, I retired as a DI four years ago. Our colleague, DS Sherman, will have told you why we're here."

"The Zukas mystery from four years ago. Yes, he said you needed to revisit the original investigation. I'm hoping to learn why you're bothering me. We spent weeks on the case getting nowhere," said DI Cook. "It was a nightmare from the start."

"Let's be clear, John," said Gus. "We're not asking for your cooperation in a box-ticking exercise. The Chief Constable tasked us with taking a fresh look at several unsolved murder cases. The Crime Review Team I work with will refer to the murder file you and your colleagues compiled, but we won't stick to the methods you adopted. Four years on, there could be something we can do differently. DS Hardy and the others have already succeeded in solving cases that went into cold storage up to twenty years ago. So, let's not waste any more time."

"That wasn't my intention," said John Cook. "We're under the cosh here, working around the clock to ensure the local community feels safe and supported. Polebarn Road acts as a hub for the police force to represent the public and let everyone know of their presence. I have been here since 2010 and have been an active police officer since 1996. Our responsibility is to deliver local policing to Trowbridge and six surrounding towns."

"Highly commendable," said Gus.

"What happened to your DS on the Zukas case, Susannah Fry, sir?" asked Alex. "We understood from DS Mercer at London Road both of you were still stationed here."

"Susannah got married several weeks ago," said John Cook. "She's returned to work, but not here. You'll find DS Lamb at the Warminster station."

"A subtle change of name," said Gus, "but neither of you have moved up the ladder since 2014."

"Susannah had risen as high as she wished," said John Cook. "I believe her stay in Warminster alongside her husband, Bradley, will be brief. Once they start the family she's always craved, we'll see the back of her."

"Another able officer lost to the force," said Gus. "I sense you aren't happy in your work, John, or am I mistaken?"

"I can't swear it was the Zukas case that marked my card, but it appears I'm going nowhere. We have plenty of uniformed officers here, plus almost twenty PCSOs, but we don't warrant any ambitious crime investigation officers, given the nature of crimes in the locality. We get far more anti-social behaviour incidents than serious crimes. There's only room for one crime investigation coordinator. So the likes of me, the wrong side of forty, will tread water until they show me the door."

"You referred to the Zukas case as a mystery rather than a murder, sir," said Alex. "Why was that?"

"And why was it a nightmare from the outset, too?" asked Gus.

"I can't recall the exact date," said John Cook. "But in July 2014, someone spotted a smouldering corpse at the edge of a field in Claverton. They called the police, and uniformed officers drove the three or four miles from the centre of Bath. The caller had asked for all three emergency services to attend. The fire crew didn't have a role to play by the time they arrived, but their chief's incident reports explained in detail how the accelerant had been hastily distributed over the body. It led to severe damage in certain parts, but they failed if the killer hoped to obliterate the woman's remains. The paramedic's only role was to declare life extinct, and the uniformed officers cordoned off the field. At the same time, they waited for the detective team, a pathologist, and a forensics crew to arrive from Bath."

"When did you get the call, sir?" asked Alex.

"At the end of September."

"You're not serious," said Alex.

"There was a long delay in identifying the body, Alex," said Gus.

"If I remember the sequence of events correctly," said John Crook. "A paramedic was the first person to reach the scene. The 999 caller had left the field already and was standing by the gateway with his dog. I appreciate why he wasn't keen on keeping guard of the poor girl's body. Have you seen the crime scene images, Mr Freeman?"

Gus nodded.

"Call me Gus, John. Do we know what happened next?"

"The caller said the paramedic opened the gate and drove across the field to see if he could do anything. Maybe two minutes later, the dog walker saw the paramedic making a phone call. Two uniformed officers from Manvers Street arrived next and started putting traffic cones at the side of the road and stringing crime scene tape across every opening into the field. As the paramedic drove back across the field, the dog walker could hear the siren of the approaching fire engine. When they arrived, the paramedic had parked on the grass verge at the side of the road. A police officer held the gate open for the fire appliance to get close to the body. The four firefighters got out and studied the remains. But, of course, there was nothing they could do, and as they were about to return to base, the pathologist drew up by the gateway. He wasn't happy."

"Not used to an early start, I suppose," said Alex. "People die at such inconvenient times, don't they? No consideration for others."

"That may have played a part in his demeanour, DS Hardy," said Gus. "My guess is he was more concerned the two uniformed officers had done little more than the basics. Although they decided the entire field was pertinent to the murder scene, they did nothing to protect its integrity by the sound of it. For example, the paramedic's car and the fire engine could have obliterated tyre tracks left by a vehicle bringing Danute Zukas's body to the field. In addition, there should have been clearly defined entrance and exit points to the spot where the body lay."

"The pathologist said he then walked to the top of the field to approach the body," said John Cook, "keeping as near the hedge and ditch as possible. He estimated the body had been in the ditch for four hours. As you know, he later confirmed the time of death as between twelve midnight and four a.m. The fire in no way contributed to the death. The victim was repeatedly struck with a metal object about the skull, face, and upper body. Apart from the clothes she was wearing, nothing else was discovered next to the body."

"How long after the pathologist arrived did the other emergency services stay on the scene?" asked Gus.

"I believe the paramedic waited until the ambulance he'd requested came, and then he was re-assigned to a home address in Newton St. Loe to see an elderly man with a suspected broken hip following a fall. The ambulance and its crew parked outside the field, waiting for the call to ferry the victim's body to the morgue at Flax Bourton. You would need to verify this sequence of events with DS Lamb. When we eventually got handed this case, we liaised with the lead detective at Manvers Street. He will have retired by now. I don't know whether you knew him, Gus. Terry West was the fellow we dealt with."

The name meant nothing to Gus. Since West worked for Avon & Somerset, Portishead, rather than London Road Devizes, that was no surprise.

"So, much of what happened and the order in which it happened was provided second-hand," said Gus. "You didn't interview these people yourselves?"

"Susannah and I got handed a sparse murder file ten weeks later and were told the victim's identity. Our priority was clearly defined. But, first, we needed to find where she'd lived and worked in the past two years and where she died."

"Flax Bourton seems a distance away," said Alex. "That's out by the airport, isn't it?"

"Just past Bristol International, yes," said John Crook.

"Danute landed there in April 2011, and her body went

into cold storage a mile up the road three years later," said Gus. "She deserved better."

"We know the dog walker made the emergency call around seven o'clock, sir," said Alex. "Can you give us rough times for the various arrivals after that?"

DI Cook sighed, stood up, and hunted for a folder in a filing cabinet. Gus and Alex waited while he found the relevant report.

"The paramedic arrived eight minutes after he received the call from dispatch. I reckon that meant he got to Claverton at around ten past seven. The dog walker told police the paramedic spent around ninety seconds to two minutes on the other side of the field before making a phone call and driving back. The uniforms were next to appear and started work. So, the fire engine must have arrived between seven-fifteen and seven-twenty."

"Which means the pathologist also drove up at around seven-twenty," said Alex. "He took a circuitous route around the field, carried out his investigations, made notes, and walked back to the gateway. Yet, he still didn't report his initial findings to the Bath detectives. So where the heck was this DI West and his colleague?"

"You need to ask him," said John Cook.

"Sorry, sir," said Alex. "I thought you might have done that when you first learned of their response time. The pathologist had already seen the mess the uniformed officers had made of keeping a tight grip on things. Claverton isn't a remote village. If you find one dog walker in a field at seven in the morning, you can guarantee several others will wander through those fields eventually. What was on the other side of the hedge from where Danute's body had been dumped?"

"Another small field, with a herd of cows on the far side. An electric fence kept them away from the public footpath. Look, fields and woodlands surround that stretch of road. Susannah and I drove out a week after receiving the files to familiarise ourselves with the layout. You don't get the full picture by looking at a map and photographs taken at the crime scene. By the time we inherited the case, any hope of seeing what that paramedic had when he had set foot on the murder scene was long gone."

"Did the public footpath only bisect the adjoining field?" asked Gus.

"Yes," said John Cook. "I suppose you're wondering why the gentleman who called the emergency services was in the field with the body in the first place?"

"Well," said Gus, "if a farmer has gone to the trouble of separating his cows from the footpath, it suggests local people and ramblers regularly used the route."

"There is a well-publicised circular route for those interested in using Claverton Down for sightseeing and exercise. Not that there would have been many people about that early in the morning. When they asked the dog walker why he hadn't kept to the path, he said he'd worked for the farmer who owned that field before retiring. So it was somewhere he could let his dog off the lead without consequences."

"What happened when DI West and his crew finally arrived?" asked Gus.

"West paid a brief visit to the crime scene and spoke with the pathologist," said John Cook. "His sergeant reprimanded the uniformed officers and installed the protocols that should have been in place from the outset. The forensic team's van logged in at nineteen minutes past eight. Crime

Scene Investigators remained on-site, gathering evidence for the rest of the day. The ambulance crew removed the victim's body at eleven twenty-eight and drove to the morgue at Flax Bourton. The pathologist carried out the post-mortem there the following morning. DI West and DS Barge were in attendance."

"Is DS Barge still working in Bath?" asked Alex.

"No idea," said John. "We have little contact with them. She was around the same age as Susannah, so it's possible. Her name was Erica, and I remember it was her first murder case."

Alex made a note of the name. Gus might need DS Mercer to pave the way, but they might get a clearer picture if they spoke to DS Barge directly. She was there on the day; DI Cook and DS Fry weren't. As for DI West, he was retired and might not be available to answer their questions.

"The CSI crew operated on both sides of the hedge, didn't they?" said Gus.

"Terry West ordered a fingertip search of both fields," said John. "There was nothing on or near the body to identify the victim. So the forensic crew concentrated on the victim first to facilitate the removal of the body. Next, DI West called for additional uniforms to assist in the extended search. They arrived around noon after the ambulance had left. Despite their exhaustive efforts, they never found a bag, purse, phone, or anything the victim or killer might have conceivably discarded."

"How did West and Barge approach the next forty-eight to seventy-two hours of the investigation?" asked Gus. "Those can be the most important hours when evidence is collated, witness statements taken, and the initial results of the autopsy become available."

"They drove out to the morgue at Flax Bourton the next morning to watch the pathologist at work," said John. "West remained in the viewing room throughout, but his DS disappeared after the first ten minutes. It was her first autopsy. The results of the post-mortem confirmed what West had been told to expect. Their victim had been struck with a heavy metal object, and Danute Zukas was likely dead before reaching the field. The killer had set the body alight after dumping it in the ditch. When Barge recovered, West drove them back to the office, and they started checking reports for missing persons."

"They had little else to go on," said Gus. "The fire didn't achieve what the killer planned, but based on the crime scene photos, there was little chance of producing an artist's impression of what the victim looked like."

"Nobody came forward to say their wife or daughter hadn't returned home on Sunday night," said John Cook. "So Terry West asked the media for help. They were clamouring for news of the murder soon after the forensic crew's orange tent got erected in the field around lunchtime on Monday. At last, the cordon did its job, keeping the press and public at a distance. Nevertheless, murders attract interest. Terry West appealed to people using the A36 Warminster Road between ten o'clock on Sunday night and seven the following morning to report anything odd. They had so little evidence it was hard to frame a meaningful press release. The response was sporadic. Although people wanted to help in any way they could, it was soon clear to West and Barge that a vehicle in a field by the side of the A36 for thirty minutes in the early hours hadn't registered with a single person."

"What were the chances of driving past the gateway to

the field at the exact time the vehicle entered or left the field anyway," said Gus. "The killer wouldn't have advertised what they were doing, and the killer didn't need headlights once he'd left the main road. The fire most likely showed something odd was going on, and the accelerant would have caused a brief burst of flame. The body was smoking by the time the dog walker arrived. Understandably, West didn't receive hundreds of potential sightings. When did they adopt a different approach to the search?"

"DS Barge queried after several weeks whether there had been anything distinctive about the victim's body," said John. "At that stage, they didn't know Danute had a tattoo. The pathologist mentioned that it surprised him not to find any tattoos, rings, or piercings on someone of the victim's age. He wished Terry luck identifying her, considering what little they had to work with. Any clothing Danute wore that hadn't suffered fire damage was mass-produced, and she was barefoot."

"Did DI West wonder whether the killer had dressed Danute in those clothes to confuse the investigation?" asked Gus.

"I don't think so," said John Cook. "His sergeant wondered whether the young woman had had dental work done or had an accident resulting in her having a metal plate inserted. Erica Barge thought outside the box and developed a novel way to identify the archetypal Jane Doe. Terry West called the pathologist and was told Danute Zukas had never had an operation of any kind as far as he could determine. However, he agreed to recheck the body the next time he visited the morgue."

"A further delay to the investigation making progress," said Alex.

"According to this report," said John, "the pathologist's

next visit to Flax Bourton took place two days later. The examination of the deceased incorporated dental X-rays, models of the maxillary and mandibular teeth, and a written and taped description of the dental structures. That gave West and Barge something positive to circulate to neighbouring police forces. Bath is a cosmopolitan place, with thousands of overseas students and tourists on its streets all year round. So DS Barge suggested they spread their net wider."

"It was still a long shot," said Gus.

"DS Barge wasn't suggesting they circulate details to every police force in Europe. The autopsy had shown they were dealing with a female between twenty and twenty-five, white and of northern European descent. So they targeted dentists across Europe, asking for their cooperation. They confirmed identification nine weeks after the murder when a dentist compared the post-mortem records with ante-mortem records held at a practice in Kaunas, Lithuania."

"The fire damage didn't distort the results then?" asked Alex.

"Teeth are incredibly durable," said John. "They can withstand heat to twelve-hundred degrees. Consequently, they are often the only identifiable feature left if a victim perishes in a car crash or remains exposed to the elements for a long time. After meticulous checks, Terry West received a letter from a Dr Kazavinicius, who said the dental records matched her patient, Danute Zukas. She had last treated Danute in November 2010, when she was nineteen-and-a-half years old."

"Who informed her family?" asked Alex.

"The local police," said John, "someone from a charity in Lithuania, helping the victim's mother, then contacted Terry West. Karolina Zukas couldn't afford to fly to the

UK, and the charity staff helped get Danute's body back to Lithuania for the funeral. They also shared details with Terry West that Karolina and her daughter Natasha had provided, which they hoped would help the police find her killer."

"Hang on," said Alex. "You said you got handed the murder file at the end of September. That was only days after Terry West received a confirmed identity for the victim."

"Exactly," said John Cook. "Manvers Street couldn't wait to get rid of the case. But, don't forget the pathologist said right from the beginning Danute was killed elsewhere and brought to the field in Claverton. So, they had a name and place where Danute worked between the early summer of 2011 and April 2012. Natasha Zukas knew her sister worked in a late-night bar, and Terry West didn't take long to determine it was Nyx. He and Erica Barge interviewed the manager, David Hodges, who told them Danute lived in a flat in Trowbridge."

"West realised the murder site had to have been in Wiltshire and saw an opportunity to wash his hands of the affair," said Alex. "He realised with over two months hanging around before they started the search for her killer, they were odds-on to come up empty. West was less than two years from retirement. He didn't want a botched murder case to blight his career."

"So, did you re-interview Hodges and the others at Nyx?" asked Gus.

"We saw Hodges. Besides confirming Danute worked for him, DI West hadn't progressed matters once he learned the girl had lived in Trowbridge."

John Cook looked at his watch. Gus sensed he was itching to get rid of them.

"Is there somewhere you need to be, John?" he asked.

"I have several meetings scheduled for this afternoon. I didn't expect you would want to go into this level of detail. Can we call it quits for now?"

"I think we might benefit from speaking to DS Barge," said Alex. "She was directly involved in the case during those first two months. That's a lot of time for subtle changes in the facts of the case. The files you inherited from Manvers Street should precisely reflect what occurred, but you told us you only received a sparse information folder. You liaised with your opposite number, DI West, to add flesh to the bones. We know how telephone conversations can result in someone receiving a different message to the one intended."

"Send three and fourpence; we're going to a dance," said Gus.

John Cook looked flummoxed. He hadn't heard that one.

"Send reinforcements; we're going to advance, sir," said Alex. "Army recruits learned that one after a series of radio operators misheard an order and passed on what they thought they'd heard. Clarity of communication was vital in WWII, and it's just as important today."

"I will get DS Sherman to arrange a second meeting, John," said Gus. "After we're positive everything West and Barge contributed to the investigation aligns with your starting point. Then we'll need to hear what happened when you started searching for Danute in Trowbridge."

"It would help if you spoke to Susannah Lamb before you get back to me," said John. "I'm swamped, and it would be a nightmare if you dragged me away from my duties for a whole afternoon."

"We'll accommodate you as best we can, John," said

Gus, "but we're not discussing anti-social behaviour statistics here. We're investigating a brutal murder. Danute's family have waited far too long for her killer to be unmasked and brought to justice."

Gus and Alex left DI Cook at his desk and headed back through reception to the front door.

"I hope I never get like that, guv," said Alex.

"I pray you'd never get like Terry West either, Alex," said Gus. "He was just as guilty. West was last to arrive at the crime scene. He dithered for several weeks before his Sergeant suggested checking dental records and then played 'Pass the Parcel' with the murder file; in case what might have been his final major investigation didn't put a stain on his CV."

"Back to the office, guv?" asked Alex.

"Yes, please. We'd better ask Geoff Mercer to get Avon & Somerset Police to grant us access to Erica Barge. I reckon you're right. We can't move forward with this case until we speak with someone there. For a while, I wondered whether the dog walker might be our best bet."

"Did you notice that even when DI Cook had the file in front of him, he couldn't name any of the people who attended the crime scene? Except for DI West and DS Barge. It made me wonder whether anyone bothered to take names, addresses, and contact numbers to include them in the murder file."

"It wouldn't surprise me if there were two files," said Gus as Alex drove away from Polebarn Road and headed to the A361. "One for the botched enquiry overseen by DI West and a sparse excuse of a murder file cobbled together by DS Barge to get Manvers Street off the hook."

"Do you think DS Mercer will have a few words to say, guv?" asked Alex.

"We'll leave that to him, Alex. I intend to approach this case as if we're the first to tackle it. All I can trust, at present, are the reports supplied by the pathologist and the chief fire officer. Everything else is subject to interpretation."

Chapter Six

GUS AND ALEX emerged from the lift twenty minutes later, just as Lydia returned from the restroom with a tray of coffees.

"Perfect timing," said Gus. "We didn't get offered a cuppa in Trowbridge. They were far too busy."

"Two coffees, one black and one white, with one sugar coming up," said Lydia.

"Any progress, guv?" asked Neil.

"Yes and no," said Gus, picking up the phone to call Geoff Mercer.

"What Gus means," said Alex, "is we now realise what a shambles the Bath detectives made of the first investigation. No wonder Cook and Fry couldn't make progress when they inherited it. Mind you. DI Cook doesn't strike me as having the right credentials."

"We measure everyone we meet against the best," said Luke.

Lydia returned with the coffees just as Gus ended his call.

"Right, Luke. Can you find a number for a DS Erica Barge from Bath? We need at least two hours of her time as soon as possible. If she can't see us tomorrow morning, you and Alex can visit her in the afternoon. He knows what we need."

"Got it, guv," said Luke.

"Listen up, everyone," said Gus. "Forget everything you've read in the file I brought back from London Road. We can't rely on anything except for reports on the autopsy and attempted burning of the body."

"Gus agrees we should start from scratch," said Alex. "That's why we're leaving the Trowbridge element to one side for a spell. DS Barge was present at the crime scene, parts of the post-mortem and eight or nine weeks before the victim was identified. So we need to verify everything that happened and the order in which it happened in that phase of the original investigation."

"I've traced DS Barge, guv," said Luke five minutes later. "Manvers Street tell me she's finishing a college course today and is due back in the office at two o'clock tomorrow afternoon. A colleague rang her, and she's agreed to see you at ten in the morning. DS Barge lives in Falconer Road, off Lansdown Lane."

"That's perfect, Luke," said Gus. "Alex and I will be happy to oblige."

"Do we need to rearrange the wall, guv?" asked Blessing.

"The map and the crime scene photos won't change, Blessing," said Gus. "Apart from that, everything else can go back into the file folder until we verify its authenticity."

Gus cast his eye around the three walls of the office. He'd known they couldn't expect to close the Jones and Burnside cases this week, but he hadn't expected to go back to square one with the Zukas case. Had the Chief Constable known this lay behind the file he'd handed him?

It could make for an exciting week. At five o'clock, Gus headed for the lift. The others wouldn't be far behind him. They had had little to get their teeth into this week yet. There was always tomorrow.

Wednesday, 12 September 2018

AS GUS DROVE past the London Road entrance, his dashboard clock read twenty-past eight. He had left Suzie getting ready at the bungalow in Urchfont. Gus knew how notorious Bath traffic could be. He and Alex needed to leave the office as soon as possible if they weren't to keep Erica Barge waiting.

Gus hadn't been surprised to find the house empty when he got home yesterday evening. Suzie hadn't left a message with any of the team, but he'd known that if a chance arose to call in on Vicky Bennison, his partner would grab it with both hands. Suzie still felt responsible to a degree for the attack Vicky had suffered.

Gus had used the two hours before Suzie reached home to plan today's interview and review the few scraps of information they'd gleaned from John Cook. Then, while Gus prepared a meal, he wondered whether Susannah Fry or Lamb, as she now was, had been cast from the same mould as her ex-boss.

Admin had always been a necessary evil as far as Gus was concerned, but he'd never let it run his life. His bosses chased him for reports, and he always promised to produce them. While he worked at Bourne Hill in Salisbury, his Chief Superintendent would shake his head and say:

"I know, Freeman, you'll do it just as soon as you get back from arresting the guilty party. The trouble is the report I'm chasing is for someone you nicked *last* week."

Suzie had breezed through the front door at twenty to eight, full of apologies for not letting Gus know what was happening. Vicky had needed a lift home from the hospital, and Suzie had driven straight there from London Road.

"Is Vicky feeling well enough to cope on her own?" Gus asked.

"I think she'll be back on her feet in a day or two," said Suzie. "Maddy, one of her colleagues, arrived before I left and stayed until Vicky was ready for bed. So I don't think it will be a late night. I asked Maddy to keep me in the loop if they needed someone to cover an evening shift. It's not the physical wounds that need healing now."

"Vicky isn't ready yet to be alone in the house. Too many memories."

"It will take time," said Suzie. "I'm going to shower and change. Whatever you're cooking for us smells terrific."

"It will be ready when you are, darling," said Gus.

After they had eaten, Gus updated Suzie on his unproductive day.

"That's life," said Suzie. "There's always tomorrow."

With that thought, it hadn't been a late night for them either.

Alex Hardy was standing beside Lydia's Mini when Gus pulled into the car park behind the Old Police Station at a few minutes to nine.

"Do you trust my old Focus to cope with the hills on Lansdown?" he asked.

"I hadn't a clue where we were going, guv," admitted

Alex. "Luke gave me directions before he and Blessing went upstairs."

"We'll get going then," said Gus. "While we're heading to Falconer Road, can you remind Luke to fix a meeting with DS Lamb in Warminster? If she's available this afternoon, it might make sense to take Lydia with you. She might open up more with another woman present."

"What about the others he might arrange, guv? I thought you wanted Luke and me to meet the leading lights while you were out of the office."

"Stick to that, Alex," said Gus. "Especially for that chap Hodges. We'll use Neil and Luke as a pairing after I get back. It should only be for this afternoon, anyway. If everything goes to plan, I'll be in the office at nine tomorrow."

Gus slowed to a crawl on the A4 as they approached the turn-off to pass Alice Park and creep along London Road. It took ages to negotiate the traffic lights onto Cleveland Bridge. Five minutes later, Alex told Gus to turn right up Lansdown Road.

"Crikey, that's steep, Alex," said Gus. "Are you sure there's not another way?"

"We can carry straight on via Queen's Square, guv," said Alex.

Gus saw he was grinning.

"Luke gave you both routes, didn't he?"

"Yes, guv. The road through Lower Weston and past the Royal United Hospital is still a gradual climb but not scary for your ancient Focus. That's the trouble with Bath; you can't avoid the hills."

Traffic was much lighter the further they got from the centre. Most vehicles ahead of them were heading for the RUH and soon hunting parking spaces. When they reached the top end of Lansdown Lane, everything had calmed down. Gus followed Alex's instructions and turned onto Falconer Road with five minutes to spare.

"Let's hope Erica Barge isn't a late riser, Alex," said Gus.

"How long ago were these houses built, guv? The late 90s, do you reckon?"

"At a guess, Alex," said Gus. "With a view like the one below us, I doubt you'd get much change out of four hundred thousand. I can't see a DS coping with the mortgage on this place alone. We've waited long enough. Let's see what Erica Barge has to say."

The two detectives left the Focus at the side of the road and walked up the short pathway to the front door. Alex stretched out an arm to ring the bell, but the door swung open, and a short, fair-haired woman greeted them with a beaming smile.

"I don't need to ask if you're the detectives I'm expecting," said Erica Barge. "I saw you park the car, complete a rapid assessment of the housing estate, and wondered how a bog-standard DS could afford a property up here with the Gods. Come inside."

Erica led them through the hallway to the kitchen at the rear. Alex was envious. He and Lydia never had time to use their kitchen, and the fact it was basic and a tad dated didn't bother them. Things must be different for officers working in the city of Bath.

"Take a seat," said Erica. "How do you take your coffee?"

Gus and Alex stated their preference and watched as Erica expertly tackled the Gaggia.

"We have one of those in our restroom," said Gus.

"Lucky you," said Erica. "When I'm at home, I use the best blends. You know what muck most station offices dish up. In the old Manvers Street squad room, the table with the kettle and stock of mugs was dubbed the Culture Club."

Erica returned with three coffees and sat opposite Gus and beside Alex.

"I know what you're thinking, Mr Freeman," she said. "How can I afford this place? We're not married yet, but my partner works as a chef for a well-known establishment on Royal Crescent. Gareth moved here from London three years ago, and he could contribute heftily to us getting our foot on the property ladder."

"It strikes me you got on the ladder a few rungs further up than most," said Alex. "What a splendid view you have over the city."

"I'm a lucky girl in more ways than one," said Erica. "Now, how can I help you?"

"We've started a cold case review, Erica," said Gus. "The murder of Danute Zukas, four years ago. Yesterday, we spoke to DI Cook at Polebarn Road, Trowbridge. But, frankly, we were disappointed with the information he received from your old boss, DI West."

"I knew this was likely to happen," said Erica, leaning back in her chair. "We didn't cover ourselves in glory on that one."

"We have questions about what happened the morning the body was discovered," said Alex. "But most of the problems that followed could have been avoided if the uniformed officers and yourselves had arrived sooner. Why did it take so long for you and Terry West to reach Claverton, anyway?"

"If I tell you the truth now, it can't hurt him anymore," said Erica.

"He retired soon after this case, didn't he?" asked Gus.

"You need to hear the entire story," said Erica. "Terry

was a drunk. When I joined the police as a PC in 2004, I was eighteen, keen as mustard, and Terry was soon someone I admired. He was a good copper, married, with two children, and he encouraged me to become a detective. I took my time deciding it was the right move for me, but I joined the team in 2007 as a DC, and three years later, I got teamed with Terry soon after being promoted to sergeant. However, Terry's world fell apart over the next four years. His youngest child got knocked off her bike on the way to school. She died before the ambulance reached the Royal United."

"That must have been terrible," said Alex.

"Terry threw himself into the job, even more than he already did," said Erica. "Then, a year later, the team had been out in Bath celebrating a successful court case, and Terry staggered home to find a letter from his wife. She had taken their son and run off with a builder working on the house. She'd found someone who finished work at regular times and paid her attention. After the divorce, Terry went from bad to worse. I lost count of the number of times I covered for him. He'd had to sell the family home and move into a bedsit on Newbridge Hill. If he wasn't working, he was drinking. To be fair, he was drinking in the office, too. The bottle of spirits in the bottom drawer of a copper's desk was a regular sight in every TV drama in the old days. Things have changed, especially with more female and ethnic minority officers around. That hard-drinking culture is becoming a thing of the past, but Terry was a stickler for tradition. So every time he had a mug of coffee in his hand, I knew he'd topped it up with whisky."

"Didn't his superiors notice a change in his performance, let alone his appearance?" asked Alex.

"Terry had me to cover for him, didn't he?" said Erica.

"I always carried a packet of extra-strong mints for when we visited witnesses or paid a visit to a superior's office. I bought a pasty or hot sausage roll on the way to work in the morning to ensure he had something to line his stomach. I made his coffees as often as possible and sat with him, hoping he wouldn't dive for the bottom drawer while I was still in the room."

"What happened that morning?" asked Gus.

"I got to the office on time, but Terry hadn't arrived. The emergency call came through, and I rang his mobile. It went to voicemail, so I drove the two miles to Newbridge Hill to pick him up. Terry's car was badly parked outside, so I knew he had gotten home the night before. I hammered on the door but got no reply. The woman in the next room came out into the corridor. She told me Terry kept a spare key under the spider plant on the window sill at the top of the stairs. I thought that was risky. She shrugged and said nobody had used a duster in the communal areas since she moved in, so it was safe as houses. I heard her door close as I pushed open Terry's door. He must have collapsed as soon as he got inside. Somehow, I woke him up and forced down several black coffees. He kept apologising about the state of the place. I told him we needed to get to Claverton. Finally, Terry shook himself and grabbed a jacket. He thought he was ready to leave. I told him we weren't going anywhere until he'd had a shower and changed his clothes. I waited for him outside in the car, and he thanked me for being a mate all the way out to Claverton."

"That explains why you took so long to get there," said Gus.

"I lost my rag once I saw what was happening," said Erica. "Ian Joseph ought to have known better."

"Who was that?" asked Alex.

"PC Joseph was the more senior of the two uniformed officers that attended the scene. I can't recall the other guy's name now. He quit the force a year later. They were both kids in their early twenties, but even so, it wasn't rocket science. Terry told me he was glad I hadn't brought him any grub that morning. If I had, he wouldn't have held on to it when he viewed the body."

"Can you run through what happened at Claverton once you arrived, Erica?" asked Gus.

Erica's version of events matched Gus and Alex's story from John Cook the previous afternoon. So the details in the murder file were relevant as far as that investigation phase went.

"What did you do when you returned to the office?" asked Gus.

"I warned Terry not to start drinking once I turned my back. Then I popped out to buy us both a pasty."

Erica laughed.

"Sorry," she said. "I hadn't met Gareth then. I enjoy my food and the occasional glass of wine, but I wouldn't dream of existing on takeaways, baked goods, and cheap bottles of plonk now. I prefer fine dining these days, and I've become a wine snob, too, I'm afraid."

"What happened after lunch?" asked Alex.

"The weekend was catching up with Terry," said Erica. "He couldn't concentrate on anything as the afternoon wore on. He kept telling me not to worry. Someone would ring in saying so-and-so hadn't come home last night. So we couldn't do much until after we had been to Flax Bourton in the morning, and then we had several days waiting for the forensic test results."

"We heard about the post-mortem," said Alex.

"I've improved over the years," said Erica. "They're still not my favourite experience."

"Nothing from the post-mortem or the forensics provided a lead on the killer," said Gus. "What else did you try?"

"We used an artist's impression of the victim in the Bath Evening Chronicle on Thursday. That's a weekly paper these days, and although plenty of people still read it, the image wasn't anything like the girl we saw in the photo that arrived eight weeks later."

"How was Terry behaving in the weeks after the murder?" asked Gus.

"He wasn't drinking any less," said Erica. "I wanted to try a different approach, but he kept knocking back my suggestions."

"Such as?" asked Alex.

"We were well aware drug use was common among people of our victim's age. So we should have tested for it. Terry said if Snowy had thought it relevant, he would have ordered the tests."

"Who's Snowy?" asked Alex.

"Daniel Hill, the pathologist," said Erica. "Dan was in his sixties, white-haired, and lived in Bath. He's retired now and lives in France."

Erica could see Gus and Alex were none the wiser.

"Snow Hill is a very steep road off London Road. The council estate on the hillside built in the mid-60s is one of the city's more deprived areas today. Before his hair turned white, he was Mr Hill or Daniel. Ever since I'd dealt with him as a DS, we knew him as Snowy."

"Why did Terry think Daniel Hill discounted drugs being involved?" asked Gus.

"They didn't play any part in her death," said Erica.

"Snowy said the victim died from blunt-force trauma, and the killer started the fire to destroy any hopes of gathering evidence."

"Did you ever consider someone had trafficked the victim to this country? The post-mortem suggested she came from Northern Europe. She may have arrived here illegally. The people exploiting her could have controlled her using drugs, depending on why they brought her to the UK. It might have been slave labour or prostitution."

"Terry didn't see any signs of that being connected to the girl we found in Claverton. It wasn't certain she died in the city, was it? Snowy said she died somewhere else between midnight and four. Terry said that could have been anywhere between an hour and six hours' drive from Claverton."

"Until he knew where the murder took place, he wasn't concerned with progressing the case," said Alex.

"We'd tried the photo-fit," said Erica, "then Terry appealed for witnesses who had been on the A36 at the relevant times. But, of course, he didn't expect to hear from anyone. If the murder occurred in South Wales at midnight, that stretch of the A36 wouldn't have been involved until ten minutes before they set the body alight."

"What did he say when you asked whether there was anything unusual about the victim's body?" asked Alex.

"He told me if I hadn't run outside to throw up, I would have known the answer," said Erica. "I knew it wasn't my finest moment. But I reminded him I'd had to drag him off the floor of his flat to get him to the crime scene. I could have easily reported him to his superiors and had him sacked. So he listened, at last. Snowy checked the body and confirmed no signs of past operations, tattoos, or piercings on the unburnt skin. He photographed the teeth and sent the details through to Terry. After we got those circulated, we made progress."

"A dentist from Kaunas, in Lithuania, contacted you," said Gus. "At last, you had a name."

"I went to Bournemouth that weekend," said Erica. "I needed to get away. Terry was drinking more heavily and getting on my nerves. Terry had been getting earache from his boss for the previous two weeks. After we'd spent weeks on the case without getting a break, they were on the verge of re-assigning us. Then, when I returned to work on Monday morning, we had a call from a charity in Lithuania. They told us Danute had a younger sister. She had spoken to our victim on the phone and learned Danute worked in a Bath bar. The woman from the charity told Terry it might be somewhere he wouldn't want a daughter of his to work."

"They couldn't have known," said Gus.

"No, but it narrowed the field we needed to search and made Terry hell to work with for the next few days. We checked the likely rough dives without luck. Then I thought of Nyx, which was a more upmarket place. They didn't cause us many headaches, and I thought they were worth trying. Terry and I visited the premises, and the manager confirmed Danute had worked for him for around ten months. She left in April 2012. David Hodges told us she'd been a good worker; they hadn't wanted to lose her. Terry asked where she went after leaving them, but Hodges didn't know. He assumed Danute had found a job in Trowbridge because that was where she lived, and the travelling back and forth to Nyx six nights a week must have taken its toll."

"Who did you interview next?" asked Alex.

"Nobody," said Erica. "Terry handed me the murder file the morning after we'd spoken to Hodges and told me to hand the case over to Wiltshire Police in Trowbridge. I flicked through the contents and realised it was thinner than it should have been. Terry told me it wasn't our problem; the murder site was somewhere in Trowbridge, end of story."

"You couldn't have been happy about that," said Alex.

"I was livid," said Erica. "I spoke to DI Cook, sent the file through, and gave him Terry's name as his point of contact. I wanted to wash my hands of the case. So I asked to be assigned to a different DI, and when they asked why, I told them Terry was an alcoholic."

"How long did West last after that?" asked Gus.

"Only a couple of months. They did not make the real reason public. Instead, they dressed it up as early retirement and brushed it under the carpet."

"Could we speak to Terry?" asked Gus.

"Only through a medium," said Erica. "He was dead within a year."

"Cirrhosis of the liver?" asked Alex.

Erica shook her head.

"He died in a car crash. The brakes failed as he drove towards Bath. Terry didn't look after that car any better than he did himself. He was on the B3110, but nobody knew why he was out near Hinton Charterhouse that night. The road drops en route to Bath as you drive along Midford Road, and there are a series of bends before reaching Southstoke. Terry missed a right-hand bend and ploughed into a dry-stone wall at seventy miles per hour."

"Had he been drinking?" asked Gus.

"What do you think?" asked Erica. "Terry was twice the legal limit. The inquest was a formality. The coroner described it as an accidental death where the driver lost control of a poorly maintained vehicle while impaired by alcohol."

"A sad end," said Gus. "Did you ever speak to Terry after he retired?"

"I saw him, just once, shuffling along the Upper Bristol Road, drunk as a skunk. That was a week or two before I met Gareth, so we're talking about the Spring of 2015. Around three months after Terry had retired. I'd heard whispers he couldn't let our last case rest. Officers on patrol in the early hours had spotted him on his hands and knees outside Nyx the previous weekend. A barmaid was helping him regain his feet. They recognised her; she had worked there since it opened. Phoebe was her name, but I can't tell you her surname. It was clear to the patrolling officers Phoebe knew Terry West well. She gave them a wave, suggesting she would see he got home safe. When I saw him on his way home in late March, he was rambling. I couldn't make sense of what he was saying. I asked him where he'd been; had he been drinking in Nyx, you know? I wondered what was bothering him. Terry muttered Phoebe's name and something about the Olympics."

"What did it sound like?" asked Gus.

"Why was she carrying the flowers?"

"Who, Phoebe?" asked Gus.

"Heaven only knows," said Erica. "That was the last time I saw Terry. After that, the whispers surfaced from time to time over the next few months, and then he was gone."

"If Terry was fretting over your last case, he could have meant Danute," said Alex.

"We need to speak to Phoebe," said Gus. "If she's still working at Nyx."

"I've just received a text from Luke, guv," said Alex. "DS Lamb isn't available until the morning. So if you're in the office at nine tomorrow, we can drive to Station Road, Warminster, together for a ten o'clock appointment."

"OK, Alex," said Gus. "It might help to speak with Susannah before we switch our attention to the people from Nyx. I want to learn where Dante Zukas lived while she worked in Bath and trace where she went next."

"Refills, gents?" asked Erica, waving her empty coffee cup.

"I think we're finished here," said Gus. "Many thanks for the offer, though. I want to confirm one more thing with you before we leave. After you moved to work with a different DI, did you see or hear of anyone working on the Zukas case?"

"DI Cook should have advised Manvers Street he was visiting their patch," said Erica. "Just a courtesy call before he interviewed David Hodges and his staff. I don't recall hearing any gossip in the squad room about those interviews. I was busy with the cases my new team got involved in. Then six months later, I met Gareth, and my career didn't have the same appeal."

"You're still taking courses," said Alex. "That suggests you want to progress further up the ladder."

"Or maybe, they get me out of the office and provide me with skills that would help me in the future."

"Gareth plans to strike out on his own," said Gus, "and while he concentrates on his fine dining menus, you could handle the business side."

"Can you blame us?" asked Erica. She collected their three cups and put them in the dishwasher. Gus and Alex made their way from the kitchen to the front door.

"You've been most helpful, Erica," said Gus. "If you think of anything relating to the Zukas case that might help, don't hesitate to get in touch. What happened to Terry's car, by the way?"

"It was a write-off," said Erica. "They took it straight to the breaker's yard."

"Didn't anyone check the brakes?" asked Alex.

"Of course," said Erica, "but the mechanic said they were so badly worn they could have failed at any time. There was no suspicion of foul play. Why would there be? Terry was a washed-up ex-copper. He might have put plenty of criminals behind bars while he was still on his game, but there wasn't a queue of ex-cons waiting to murder him, DS Hardy. Everyone could see he would self-destruct sooner rather than later. Why risk getting caught when you could have a front-row seat if you wandered around the city centre streets."

Gus reached the car and looked back. Erica Barge had closed the door. If Gareth were as great a chef as she thought, it wouldn't be long before she closed the door on her police career.

"What did you make of that, guv?" asked Alex.

"Erica removed doubts about the contents of our murder file and confirmed my fears. But, unfortunately, Terry West short-changed John Cook with the information he sent him. I'm not convinced Cook would have made significant progress even if he'd had a full deck to work with, but Susannah Lamb might help us understand what went wrong there. So back to base, Alex, and we'll try again in the morning."

Chapter Seven

GUS DELIVERED Alex to the car park behind the Old Police Station. As he drove home to Urchfont, he wondered what Terry West had been up to on the night he died.

Was it relevant? Erica Barge said he was a wreck, physically and mentally, and it might have been something as simple as hearing about a half-price Happy Hour in a pub in Hinton Charterhouse.

As Gus swung the Focus through the gateway of the bungalow, he forgot the case for the rest of the day. After all, four years ago, Terry West hadn't had a problem forgetting it. A few weeks later, neither had John Cook.

Gus parked the car under Tess's trailing roses and let himself indoors. He glanced at the kitchen clock and realised Suzie would leave London Road in ten minutes. What could they have for lunch? One of those pasties Erica Barge mentioned would have gone down well now.

Gus consulted the contents of the fridge and elected for a mock pizza. They had fresh ingredients for the topping on hand, plus wholemeal bread. In ten minutes, he could have a tasty snack ready. He imagined Suzie would be too excited or nervous to be hungry before she had been for her scan. All things being equal, they could celebrate over a proper meal this evening.

Suzie came through the front door twenty minutes later.

"How did your trip to Bath go this morning, darling?" she asked.

"Very well," said Gus. "My old jalopy sprang up the hills like a gazelle. DS Barge served up a superb cup of coffee, and we learned why it took so long for her to arrive at Claverton that day. Of course, we still have several unanswered questions, but we'll make a start on those in the morning with a trip to Warminster. Will a mock pizza keep you going until tonight?"

"Mmm, that sounds delicious," said Suzie, "leave the spring onions until you've taken the pizzas from under the grill and scatter the raw chopped pieces on top."

"Really?" asked Gus. "We have spring onions, but I hadn't planned on using them."

"The more, the merrier," said Suzie. "They're good for us, as well as tasting great."

They sat in the kitchen and savoured their mock pizzas with a glass of lemonade.

"It's good, but not the same without a cold beer or glass of white wine," groaned Suzie.

"What time do we have to leave?" asked Gus.

"We've got time to shower and change," said Suzie. "I'll go first, and then I'll sit and read through the bumf they gave me when I arranged this scan,"

Gus found Suzie sitting in the lounge after he had finished getting ready.

"A sonographer who has been specially trained carries most scans out," read Suzie.

"I would have hoped they wouldn't let anyone near complicated equipment without the necessary training," said Gus. "How long does it take?"

"Twenty to thirty minutes. They'll take me into a private room with a bed, and I'll need to uncover my stomach by lowering these trousers to my hips and raising my top over my belly."

"You had better let me read that booklet," said Gus. "I doubt they'll let me sit and hold your hand."

"They had better, buster," said Suzie. "You're my nominated partner."

"I'll read it anyway," said Gus, "in case I have to close my eyes."

"You're incorrigible, Gus Freeman. Come on, let's get it over with."

Suzie grabbed her handbag and car keys.

"Where do you think you're going?" asked Gus. "I'll drive."

Suzie threw Gus her keys.

"Very well, oh sensible one. Why not think positive thoughts?"

"I was," said Gus. "I didn't want to get stopped on the way home by an over-zealous traffic cop who mistook your whooping and hollering for drunken behaviour."

Suzie was unusually quiet in the car as they drove into town along Nursteed Road. They passed the Fox & Hounds within minutes and turned onto Marshall Road. They arrived at the modern clinic on the right-hand side, and Gus parked the Golf a mere seven minutes after leaving home.

"It didn't take long to get here, did it?" he said.

"You could experience this every day if you drove something other than that old Focus of yours," said Suzie.

Not for the first time, Gus wondered whether he needed to let go of the past. Tess had always loved the Focus, and they shared many happy times in it on holiday. But, moving forward, the Family Freeman might warrant a reliable and spacious vehicle. Anything except one of those dreadful people carriers.

"Stop daydreaming," said Suzie. "We'll be late."

Gus followed Suzie into the light, airy reception and waiting area.

Even when Gus was a youngster, a doctor's receptionist had always been a formidable barricade for patients to overcome. His mother hadn't needed to take him to the doctor's more often than his school friends, but it was never easy to get beyond the front desk.

Screens protected the modern version of the battle-axe, both toughened glass and computer. The patient wasn't leaving the waiting area until the computer said 'Yes'. After Suzie successfully negotiated the Spanish Inquisition, they were instructed to take a seat until called.

They didn't have long to wait. Suzie grabbed Gus's hand and followed the young nurse to the consultation room. He wondered whether Suzie's move was for reassurance or to stop him from trying to escape.

Twenty minutes later, it was finished. Gus could tell the ultrasound gel must have been cold, judging by Suzie's reaction. The sonographer merely smiled and didn't pass a comment. Gus supposed the gentle torture made coming to work worthwhile if you carried out the same procedure day in, day out. So he sat and watched as the probe slid across

Suzie's stomach and black and white images appeared on the screen opposite.

Gus tore his eyes away from the moving images on the screen to study the sonographer. She concentrated on the screen, as did Suzie, but nobody said a word.

You could cut the tension with a knife.

Then the middle-aged woman leaned forward and adjusted the volume control.

Wow, thought Gus.

"Everything looks and sounds fine, Ms Ferris," she said. "Baby has a good, strong heartbeat."

"Wow," said Suzie.

"Just the one?" asked Gus.

"Were you expecting to find more?" asked the sonographer. "I can keep looking if you wish."

"No, one healthy baby is perfect," said Gus.

"I can't detect any anomalies," said the sonographer. "We'll see you again in around eight weeks. I can give you a rough due date today, but I won't confirm the sex of the baby until your next scan. You're a healthy woman, Ms Ferris. I fully expect your pregnancy to progress normally over the coming months."

The atmosphere in the room had changed. It was as if someone had flicked a switch. And now, everyone in the room was smiling. The young nurse escorted Gus and Suzie back to the waiting area. The nurse collected the next expectant mother and disappeared along the corridor. Suzie booked in for her next appointment, and Gus led them outside.

"Well, that's a weight off your mind, darling," said Gus as they walked across the car park to the Golf.

"Did you stop breathing when she started moving that probe across my tummy?"

Gus had to admit that he had.

"Who do you want to tell first?"

"Mum and Dad know already," said Suzie, "but we should let them know today went well. So let's drive to the farm, and we can call the gang in the village after we get home. Maybe they'll join us in the Lamb for a meal. As for our work colleagues, they can hear first thing in the morning."

Suzie stood by the driver's door and raised an eyebrow.

"Drive safely," said Gus, handing over the keys.

Suzie had little choice but to reduce her speed. Traffic in town and on the A360 through Potterne was heavy as the aftermath of the school run swelled the number of vehicles.

As Suzie turned off the main road onto the long track leading to the family farmhouse, she spotted her father's Land Rover two hundred yards ahead.

"That's good. Dad's home," said Suzie.

Suzie parked the Golf close to the kitchen door and sounded her horn. John and Jackie Ferris appeared in the doorway seconds later.

Suzie had hardly stepped from the car before getting wrapped in her mother's arms. John was soon pumping Gus's hand and offering congratulations.

"We'd better get these two inside, Gus," said John. "There's bound to be tears, and I don't want the animals upset."

"I sense you farmers don't get too emotional about the circle of life," said Gus.

"True, but it's great news, Gus. Jackie's been fretting ever since she got out of bed this morning. I might get a good night's sleep tonight now."

"You're all heart, John Ferris," said Jackie, wiping tears from her eyes.

John wanted to open a bottle of champagne to mark the occasion, but Suzie tutted.

"There will be plenty of time for that when the baby's here," said Jackie. "How would coffee and cake do instead?"

Nobody objected, and soon they were seated around the large table with a mug of coffee and a large slice of fruit cake.

"What were you thinking just then, Gus?" asked Jackie. "You suddenly started grinning."

"Ever since we saw the baby and heard its heartbeat, everyone has been smiling, Jackie. I saw the joy on your faces the minute we pulled up outside. Even when you and Suzie had a few tears outside, you were still grinning from ear to ear. It's infectious."

"We're going to be grandparents," said Jackie. "That's the best news we've had this year."

John looked at the clock on the wall.

"I suppose you need to do the rounds, John?" asked Gus. "To make sure the horses are okay."

"They can wait a while longer yet, Gus. I thought I heard a car. Would Blessing finish work early today?"

"We haven't been able to make the progress I would have liked on our latest case," said Gus. "I put a freeze on material we received from Kenneth Truelove on Monday. It wouldn't surprise me if Alex Hardy made an executive decision and sent the team home early. We'll be back all guns blazing tomorrow. Alex and I had a fruitful meeting this morning."

Blessing Umeh stepped into the kitchen. Gus detected a trace of concern in his Detective Constable's voice.

"Ah, you're here, guv," she said. "I saw Suzie's car. Is everything OK? Will you be back at work in the morning?"

"You'd better sit, Blessing," said Gus.

"Oh dear," said Blessing.

"One coffee and cake, please, Jackie," said Gus.

"Don't tease her, Gus," said Suzie. "I went to the clinic for a twelve-week scan this afternoon, Blessing. We haven't told many people yet, but I'm expecting. My due date will be around the thirty-first of March."

"Oh dear," said Blessing. "I mean, that's wonderful news. It's just that when my mother rings me later, I will have to tell her. You'll hear her tutting, even here in the kitchen, because you and Mr Freeman aren't married."

"We have no plans to change that situation, Blessing," said Suzie. "So, Maryam will just have to get used to it."

"Are you excited, guv?" asked Blessing.

"He can't stop smiling," said Jackie.

"I await the future with cautious optimism, Blessing," said Gus. "I can't afford to let the excitement show on my face too often. It could prove most disconcerting for any witnesses I interview."

"Alex told us you learned a few fresh facts this morning, guv," said Blessing.

"That can wait until the morning, DC Umeh," said Gus. "Suzie and I have places to go, people to see. My best wishes to your mother and father. Say hi to Jamie, too, if he drops by this evening. We'll make tracks now, and I'll see you in the office at nine."

Suzie said her goodbyes to her parents and joined Gus in the farmyard.

"Everything okay, darling?" she asked.

"Will everyone ask the same inane question?"

"It's only natural," said Suzie. "They notice the thirty-year difference in age. We ignore it because it isn't relevant to how we feel about one another. Some people will just assume you might have reservations over starting a family late in life."

"They couldn't be more wrong," said Gus.

"Good," said Suzie. "Now, let's get home, change, and see who's available."

"I'll leave you to make the calls," said Gus. "I'll double-check with the landlord at the Lamb that he pencilled us in for tonight. I thought it best to warn him he might have half-a-dozen hungry souls descending on him."

They needn't have worried. The landlord hadn't forgotten, and Clemency Bentham and Brett Penman expected the call. They had cleared their social calendar soon after Suzie broke the news several weeks ago. Brett rang his grandfather, and at half-past eight, Brett and the Reverend, together with Bert Penman and Irene North, joined the happy couple in the Lamb.

"Everything's still okay then?" asked Brett.

"Nothing to worry about at this stage," said Suzie.

"We're both happy for you," said the Reverend.

"Did I miss something, Mr Freeman?" asked Bert.

"No, Bert. We wanted to be sure before we told everyone."

"There will be another mouth to feed at the bungalow by April next year," said Suzie. "I'm pregnant."

"Well, bless my soul," said Bert. "Congratulations, Miss Ferris. Isn't that wonderful news, Irene?"

"It is that Bertie," said Irene. "I shall start knitting this weekend. It will keep my hands warm and flexible through the winter months."

Gus had visions of their little mite getting swamped with brightly coloured woollen goods if Irene's wardrobe was anything to go by.

"We won't know whether we're having a boy or a girl for

another couple of months, Irene," said Gus. "Best hold off for now."

"I can do neutral colours before switching to blue or pink," said Irene. "You can never have too many booties and hats to keep their heads warm."

Gus groaned. At least Irene hadn't asked if he was excited about becoming a father.

"Will we ever persuade you to call us Gus and Suzie, Bert?" asked Suzie.

"Hard to change the habits of a lifetime, Miss…. Suzie."

"That's a start. I hope everyone's hungry," said Suzie. "I know I am. Don't hold back. Gus is paying."

Gus looked around the table at a sea of smiling faces. Everyone placed their orders, enjoyed a hearty meal, and agreed it was the best night ever. As Gus left the Lamb to wander along the lane to the bungalow, he thought times spent with loved ones and friends were special. Why couldn't the world always be like that?

Thursday, 13 September 2018

GUS WAS first out of bed in the morning. He felt good.

Although Brett had shared a bottle of red wine with him last night, Bert had stayed true to his pints of cider. Clemency and Irene had stuck to soft drinks so that Suzie didn't feel left out.

Gus made another mental note while waiting for the waffle maker. He would cancel replacing that bottle of McCallan's. Firstly, the two hundred quid it would cost would come in handy for things in the nursery; and Erica

Barge's tale of how the hard stuff wrecked Terry West's life was a wake-up call.

Suzie soon joined him, and they ate breakfast together, mulling over the highlights of yesterday afternoon and evening. When they left the bungalow and set off for work, Gus hoped the positive mood would last.

Neil Davis was upstairs in the office when he exited the lift.

"Morning, guv," said Neil. "Good to see you back."

"It was a half-day, Neil. I haven't been off sick for a month."

"Sorry, guv," said Neil.

"What do you want the rest of us to do this morning, guv?" asked Neil. "While you and Alex are in Warminster."

"Hold your horses, Neil," said Gus. "The others are on their way. We'll sort out who does what when everyone's present and correct."

Alex and Lydia arrived together as always. Gus expected the third-degree from Lydia, so he got in first.

"Good to see your more sober suit is back from the cleaners, Lydia. We can safely send you out to meet the public again. Make yourselves comfortable, you two, while we await Luke and Blessing."

"Got it, guv," said Lydia.

Luke Sherman was alone when he entered the office.

"Any sign of Blessing yet, Luke?" asked Gus.

"She was just parking her car, guv," said Luke. "It's busy down there this morning. Blessing's on her third attempt at reversing into the one remaining space. She seems excitable today. I don't know whether that's Jamie-BT's influence or something else."

"When Blessing solves the parking dilemma, we'll make a start," said Gus. "Is everyone on the same page with where we reached on the Zukas case after our conversation with DS Barge yesterday?"

Neil, Luke, and Lydia confirmed they were. Seconds later, Blessing Umeh trotted out of the lift.

"Sorry, guv," she said. "I made a fuss of parking to ensure I was the last to arrive."

Gus knew Blessing would have found it impossible not to tell the others what she'd learned last night if they'd been alone in the office for over thirty seconds. Bless her.

"What's going on, guv?" asked Neil.

"Blessing got home earlier than usual yesterday evening. She walked in on Suzie and me, updating her parents on our appointment in Devizes. Suzie's expecting and her twelve-week scan went well. The baby's due at the end of March. So no further bulletins will be given at this time."

Gus waited for the clamour of congratulations to cease.

"Right, Alex, are you ready? We need to get to Warminster to meet with DS Lamb."

"Ready, guv," said Alex.

"Can you fix up a meeting with David Hodges at Nyx, Luke? Also, he had a barmaid called Phoebe for several years. No idea whether she still works there. Find out her surname and arrange an interview. I'm hoping they can identify regular customers who might have been responsible for Danute leaving Nyx. Also, they should know who Danute travelled to work with."

"Got it, guv," said Luke. "Shall Neil and I pair up with one of the girls to handle those?"

"Good thinking, Luke," said Gus. "Alex and I might uncover several people in Trowbridge who knew Danute we can split between the four of you. Alex and I will talk to Hodges. We should have enough to keep us occupied into the middle of next week."

Gus and Alex walked towards the lift.

"Are you excited about the news, guv," asked Alex.

"The times they are a'changing, Alex," said Gus. "Neil and Melody's child will be born first. Have you asked whether he's excited?"

"Sorry, guv," said Alex. "That was crass. You aren't the first guy in his sixties to become a father for the first time."

"When you're in a hole, it's best to stop digging, Alex," said Gus as they left the lift and walked to Alex's car.

"Got it, guv."

"Suzie and I have six months to work out how we'll cope with being new parents plus working full time," said Gus once they were inside the car. "There will be bumps in the road, but we'll get there."

Alex drove out of the Old Police Station car park, took the A350 through Westbury, and turned into Station Road, Warminster, twenty-five minutes later.

Gus stood back while Alex dealt with the formalities inside the police station. They were soon shown into a small side office. Within two minutes, a young woman joined them. Gus remembered what John Cook had said. Erica Barge and Susannah Fry had been around the same age. However, while Erica Barge was short, fair-haired, and of stocky build, the person sitting opposite him and Alex was six-foot-tall, slender, and with her long, dark hair secured in a ponytail.

"I'm Susannah Lamb," she said. "How can I help?"

"Good morning, Susannah," said Alex. "I'm Alex Hardy. My boss here is Gus Freeman. Our Crime Review Team is taking a fresh look into the murder of Danute Zukas in July 2014. You worked on that case with your former boss, DI John Cook, while stationed at Polebarn Road, Trowbridge."

"I remember," said Susannah. "What prompted the review?"

"The Chief Constable persuaded me to come out of retirement," said Gus, "because he believed I could assist a small team of excellent junior detectives in putting right past wrongs. Danute Zukas didn't deserve to die, and so far, we haven't done enough to find the person responsible."

"I imagine you've spoken to John recently?" asked Alex.

DS Lamb gave a wry smile.

"He called within minutes of you leaving his office. John was shocked at the level of detail you wanted. He will have told you what a mess the Bath detectives made of things."

"Well, there were gaps in John's memory," said Gus. "On more than one occasion, he suggested we ask you for confirmation he had things in the correct sequence or hadn't forgotten something altogether."

"Shall I take you through how DI West ran his investigation?" asked Susannah Lamb.

"Please," said Alex. "But stick to the facts. We spoke to DS Barge yesterday."

"I see," said DS Lamb.

Gus relaxed in his chair as he listened to Susannah Lamb tell them what she remembered of the case. Her understanding of events in the Claverton field matched those of Erica Barge, who was there in person. DS Lamb didn't appear to know the explanation for Terry West's late arrival. Gus sensed the two sergeants had never met or spoken to one another.

"John will have told you we didn't even get involved until the end of September," said Susannah. "I got into the office that morning, and John called me. He showed me a file he'd received from Manvers Street. I asked why the case had been transferred. He said DI West, who had dealt with the case since the discovery of the body, now had evidence the murder took place in, or close to Trowbridge."

"What did you do then?" asked Gus.

"We went through the murder file, but it was sketchy. John said he would phone DI West and clarify several issues. That conversation is where everything I just told you came from. John spoke to Terry West, and then John told me. We didn't drive into Bath to see him. John wasn't keen on questioning anyone. Terry West had already got to provide statements. He was happy to take them at face value."

"John Cook didn't want to make it appear he thought DI West hadn't done a good job," said Alex.

"Especially since they were across the county border," said Susannah. "City of Bath Police always thought they were better than the country coppers from Wiltshire. Even after they disappeared under the Avon & Somerset banner."

"From what we've learned, DI West didn't take statements from that many people," said Gus. "Other than the pathologist and emergency services personnel at the crime scene."

"DI West had received a communication from the city in Lithuania where the victim came from. Her dentist finally gave the victim a name."

"How soon were you able to interview David Hodges, the bar manager?" asked Alex.

"Several days after that first contact with West. He called John to say a Lithuanian charity was helping Danute's mother get the body home for a funeral. The charity had told him there was a younger sister. She had spoken to her sister regularly during the first nine months Danute spent in this country. West told John the sister said Danute worked at a bar called Nyx. He told John where it was, and that was it. After that, we never heard from him again."

"You recognised Erica Barge's name earlier," said Gus.

"I knew West worked with a DS Barge, but we never met. I only saw Erica's name when quoted following DI West's death in a newspaper report. That was months after we got handed the file and after we'd both moved on to other cases."

"OK," said Alex, "so when John Cook learned where Danute worked, what did you do?"

"John and I went into Bath to speak to the manager within twenty-four hours of receiving the call from Terry West. David Hodges said Danute was a beautiful young woman, popular with colleagues and customers. Her English was initially limited, but she had improved by the time she left. She would never lose her accent, of course. Hodges told us he was sorry to see her leave."

"Danute started working at Nyx in the summer of 2011," said Gus. "Did Hodges confirm she left at the end of April 2012?"

"He did, yes," said Susannah Lamb. "John asked the standard questions. Did they have any trouble that might have led to Danute leaving? Were there any regular customers she got close to? Did any of those regulars over-step the mark? You know the sort of thing. Did she attract a stalker? She was a beautiful young woman."

"Hodges told you there was nothing like that," said Alex.

"It seemed a dead-end," said Susannah.

"In what way?" asked Gus.

"Well, John asked where Danute went after leaving Nyx. Hodges said he didn't have a clue. Danute didn't give a reason for leaving. She just called in one afternoon and said she wouldn't be in that night."

"Did you or John Cook wonder whether David Hodges was telling the truth?" asked Gus. "He could have been the person who stalked her or grew close to her, and she tired of him."

"Hodges didn't seem the type," said Susannah.

"Is there a type?" asked Alex.

"I can usually tell," she replied. "Look, Hodges was married with children. I saw the framed photograph on his desk. He was a genuine bloke in my book. The way he spoke about Danute wasn't false emotion; he genuinely cared that she was dead."

"Was there anything else to make John Cook think Nyx was a dead end?" asked Gus.

"He thought DI West had been rushing to get the case off-loaded to us. John accepted someone had killed her elsewhere and then took Danute to that field out at Claverton. But what was to say the murder didn't take place in Bath? It made just as much sense."

"Did you visit the field where they found the body?" asked Gus.

"I thought it a good idea, but John took persuading. You've met him. He's decent, but he prefers to spend his days in the office hidden behind a barricade of paperwork. The trend to ask burglary victims to collect evidence to enable the police to pursue a case suits them fine. He doesn't have to get off his backside. So, under sufferance, John drove us out to Claverton, and we spent thirty minutes checking the crime scene images against the field as it was after three months of activity. The only way we could be certain we were even in the right spot was where the farmer planted young saplings to replace the fire-damaged parts of the hedge. It was raining heavily that day, and we both struggled to get through the muddy ground by the gateway. John thought the trip was a waste of time."

"David Hodges told you Danute lived in Trowbridge, though, didn't he?" asked Alex. "Surely, that must have opened up the possibility the murder happened there?"

Susannah Lamb kicked back her chair, burst into tears, and left the room.

Chapter Eight

"SORRY, GUV," said Alex. "Was I being too hard on her? Terry West had spoken to David Hodges, and Erica Barge confirmed Hodges told them Danute lived in a flat in Trowbridge. So what was that about Cook thinking West foisted the case onto Wiltshire Police for no good reason? The victim lived in Trowbridge, didn't she?"

"I can't see where else she could have been living, Alex," said Gus. "However, we mustn't forget the murder took place in July 2014, not a few days after Danute stopped working at Nyx. That's a long time. Perhaps Cook got it right. If Danute's circumstances changed, she might have been able to afford a place in Bath or somewhere other than Trowbridge. I still think it was a good starting point for Cook to pinpoint exactly where she lived while working at Nyx. It would have given them something to build on. Not least, finding out who drove her daily to and from Bath. Did the driver live at the same address, or did they collect Danute and drop her off in the mornings?"

"Where do you think Susannah has gone, guv?" asked Alex.

"Call yourself a detective, DS Hardy? Find another female officer and ask her to fetch DS Lamb from the ladies' loo."

Alex left the room and returned with a red-eyed Susannah Lamb two minutes later.

"Are you ready to carry on, DS Lamb?" asked Gus.

"I'm sorry," said Susannah. "I always knew someone would ask questions about this case, eventually. So when John told me how deep you were digging, I knew we were in trouble."

"We don't carry out a hatchet job on the detectives who ran the initial investigation, DS Lamb," said Gus. "But as I stressed to John Cook when we met, we won't stick to the same steps he took; we won't ask the same questions. There's no point since you didn't have success following that path."

"Once you had familiarised yourselves with the only crime scene available, you must have searched for an address in Trowbridge where Danute lived between April 2011 and May 2012," said Alex. "It was the only logical step."

"Even if John Cook thought Hodges might have been mistaken," added Gus. "Our approach hasn't changed in over a century. Conan Doyle coined a phrase we forever associate with Sherlock Holmes, When you have eliminated all that is impossible, whatever remains, however improbable, must be the truth. It's what we do. Check the pieces are from the jigsaw we're trying to solve, discard the rest, and then put the remaining pieces together."

"If you proved, beyond doubt, Danute never lived in a property in Trowbridge, then you would have re-interviewed Hodges to ask why he misled you," said Alex. "Hodges maintained Danute travelled to work each day; she didn't live in the city. However, he didn't appear to know who her companion or companions might have been. Furthermore, there's no sign in the file that you or John ever went back to interview him. So, what did you do to resolve the rental issue?"

"DI Cook assigned our duties, and we followed them," said Susannah. "Ours not to reason why. We just did as we were told."

"You said we, so was there another detective on the team?" asked Alex.

"DC George Collins," said Susannah. "He's still at Pole-barn Road and hasn't risen in the ranks yet. George was wet behind the ears back then. He didn't look old enough to drink, let alone work on a murder case. None of us had ever handled a case that big."

"Tell us how DI Cook got you to spend your time," asked Gus.

"I got tasked with visiting the letting agencies covering Trowbridge and the surrounding villages," said Susannah. "John asked George to check the local press, newsagent's windows, and social media for random private adverts from people with a room to let."

"That must have thrown up plenty of possibilities," said Alex.

"The first letting agent I talked to was Andrea Beavan," said Susannah. "She explained what records landlords had to keep. They needed to record rental and deposit payments, and they had to record any other income, for example, if they charged a tenant for maintenance or gardening services. She said they should be able to show me details of each tenancy, with a start and finish date. I had rented nowhere myself. I lived at home with my parents until I married Brad, and he had a house here in Warminster. Brad is fifteen years older than me and had moved south from Leeds. Anyway, what Andrea said seemed complicated, but I felt sure if that much had to be recorded, we'd find Danute in no time."

"Landlords are advised to keep records for six years," Gus said to Alex. "In theory, we might find a tenancy record, other than in Trowbridge, even now."

"We might be pushing it, guv," said Alex. "If a landlord kept records for the absolute minimum term, we would only get back as far as September 2012."

"Good luck with that," said Susannah. "Andrea Beavan told me not every registered landlord was renowned for keeping meticulous records. And what about the ones George Collins checked? Chances are if the only evidence someone was renting out a room was a handwritten card in a newsagent's window for a week or two, they're not declaring the income to the taxman."

"Are you saying you couldn't find Danute Zukas's name on any tenancy agreement in Trowbridge during the months concerned?" asked Gus.

"She didn't appear among the ones I checked," said Susannah. "Do you know how many records I had to search through?"

"Not really," said Alex. "I don't suppose it's computerised?"

"Each landlord records the detail differently, if they record it at all," said Susannah. "Thirty-three thousand people were living in Trowbridge in 2011. If only Danute Zukas had arrived before the end of March that year. We could have found her through the census details published in July 2012. A lot has changed in how the population is made up, but one thing stays the same: the two-point four average number of people per household. Eleven percent of people in Trowbridge rented their properties through a private landlord or letting agency in 2011. I know that for a fact. So it took ages to collect the data, and then George and I ploughed through it."

"Did DC Collins turn up anything from the other avenues he followed?" asked Alex.

"Only a handful. You'd be surprised how many people only want a short-term let. George found a young couple who completed the sale of their home and moved out in case they broke the chain. They couldn't move into their next home for a month, and they didn't have family in the area who could house them. Then there were people working on a building site who needed somewhere for three months, six months even. George had one property with a registered landlord who kept accurate records showing six residents during the period in question. The shortest stay was four weeks, and the longest was fifteen. Danute wasn't among that list either."

"How long were you ploughing through these lists?" asked Gus.

"We went from letting agency to letting agency, private landlord to private landlord, collecting the data as we went. John couldn't get additional resources. Then we picked each batch apart, searching for our victim. That took three weeks."

"Is it possible you missed her?" asked Gus.

"Of course," said Susannah. "I was never confident George was concentrating on the job. He wasn't keen on mundane, boring jobs. He signed up to be in the thick of the action. Something on social media or local papers could have slipped through the net. I was more confident I'd collected as much as possible from the agencies and checked it thoroughly, but even so.….."

"Go on," said Gus.

"John kept getting pressure from his superiors. Finally, they demanded a result."

"Did he suggest a different approach?" asked Gus.

"No, John caved in when they wanted George for a case with a more likely positive outcome. I had to work on the searches alone."

"What was DI Cook doing?" asked Alex.

"He checked on my progress every morning," said Susannah. "You know how it is in a station like Polebarn Road, and it's worse here. We have to keep half a dozen plates spinning in the air; we don't have the luxury of only one case to occupy our minds. John was swamped with paperwork, as usual. All he committed to was dropping everything to interview the landlord or Danute's driver when I found them. If that was the same person, even better. It meant he spent less time away from his desk. In the end, I took things into my own hands."

"In what way?" asked Gus.

"We're talking October now, four years ago. I hadn't met Brad then, and I went to Bath on a Saturday afternoon with a girlfriend. Saskia works for Wiltshire County Council at County Hall. We went by train from Trowbridge and planned to catch the last train from Bath Spa at around half-past eleven. We started drinking in All Bar One by four o'clock, and although we had a meal early in the evening, I was well away by ten. So I suggested to Saskia we make Nyx our last stop."

"Did David Hodges recognise you?" asked Gus.

"He wasn't anywhere to be seen that night," said Susannah. "Phoebe said he was in the office, upstairs."

"You spoke to Phoebe, the barmaid?" asked Gus.

"Do you know her?" asked Susannah.

"No, but Erica Barge said Phoebe has worked at Nyx since it opened. So what was the plan?"

"I didn't plan to visit Nyx," said Susannah. "I was drunk, and I knew it could get me into trouble with John, but I thought it was better than doing what we'd done so far. When I asked Phoebe if Terry West had ever spoken to her, she said he had. That wasn't in the murder file they sent us. Even though I'd drunk too many vodka and tonics, I knew she was watching every word she said. She straightened a beer cloth on the bar and moved returned glasses onto the shelf behind her. She bought a few seconds while deciding how much to tell me."

"What did you sense she was hiding?" asked Gus.

"I reckon something was going on between them," said Susannah.

Gus remembered what Erica Barge had told them. Police patrolling the city centre had seen Terry West outside of Nyx on more than one occasion. Erica Barge thought it was because Terry couldn't forget the Zukas case. Perhaps something else drew Terry West to the bar.

"That might explain why West removed items from the murder file John Cook received," said Gus. "If he and Phoebe became involved after interviewing people at Nyx, it wouldn't look good."

"Did Phoebe open up?" asked Alex. "Or did she continue to be evasive?"

"Saskia realised the time was ticking by, and she was desperate not to miss that last train. We needed to leave the bar and get to the station. I told Phoebe Terry West wasn't who I was interested in. It was Danute Zukas. Phoebe told me to meet her at a coffee shop near the Abbey on Monday afternoon. Saskia and I caught the train home, and I called in sick on Monday morning. I told John I'd had a dodgy burger on Saturday night and hoped to be back at work in the morning. He never found out I drove into Bath that day to catch up with Phoebe Sawyer."

Alex made a note of the barmaid's name. Luke could arrange for them to interview her when they talked to David Hodges.

"I found Phoebe already sitting in the café when I reached the Abbey courtyard," said Susannah. "She was keen to tell me about her and Terry West before she answered my questions. Phoebe had seen how drink changed people and ruined lives. Her ex-husband had been an abusive drunk. Phoebe saw men and women on the same downward spiral when she worked at Nyx. When Terry West interviewed her at the beginning of October 2014, Phoebe knew he'd had several drinks before visiting David Hodges upstairs. West spoke to her and the other staff members. Later that day, she'd asked her friends if they knew Terry's history and soon learned of the tragedy that started the decline. She felt sorry for him. Terry turned up at Nyx late the following Friday night, asking if he could speak to any regulars about Danute. He relied on Phoebe to point him in the right direction, and they talked until closing after he'd spoken to a couple of guys."

"Did Phoebe mention any names?" asked Alex.

"Phoebe said their names were Jerry and Graham, but she didn't give me their surnames. Both men were in their mid-forties, wore wedding rings, and enjoyed a few drinks every weekend. They would arrive at around nine o'clock and leave between twelve and one. Now and then, they mingled with other customers, but mostly, they were content to sit together and chat. Phoebe remembered they chatted to Danute more often than the other bar staff they had working there at the time. They were regulars, never any trouble, and Phoebe said she chatted to them too if she served them drinks. It was normal to have a few words with people you recognised. So why would people return to the bar if they never saw a friendly smile or a kind word?"

"That's why they call it the hospitality sector," said Alex.

"That's what Phoebe meant," said Susannah. "After they closed that night, Phoebe continued chatting with Terry West. They agreed to meet up for a drink somewhere else in Bath. She was at pains to tell me there was never anything physical between them. Phoebe didn't fear Terry being abusive towards her, but she had hoped to save him from himself by being a good friend. Terry would turn up at Nyx, and Phoebe knew he was drunk, but he'd learned to disguise it well. Nobody at Manvers Street had worked out Terry was an alcoholic, and they were coppers. If he could fool them, he could persuade a youngster working behind a bar to let him have one more drink. Phoebe made sure Terry got home safely. When he was too drunk to walk, she virtually carried him home to her flat, and he slept on her sofa. Phoebe said she cried for days after she heard how he died."

"Had Terry told Phoebe where he went that night?" asked Gus. "Did he elaborate on what he was investigating? His ex-colleague, Erica Barge, believed something about Danute Zukas's murder was eating at him. Any idea what that was?"

"Phoebe said Terry was drinking more heavily and didn't visit the city centre as often in the weeks before he died. Phoebe heard he bought his spirits at an off-licence up at Bear Flat and drank at home. The last time they spoke proved to be his last visit to Nyx. Terry kept mumbling something Phoebe had mentioned. It had happened not long after Danute stopped working at Nyx. The Olympics dominated the summer of 2012, and although the actual Games were weeks away, the build-up touched most major towns and cities in the weeks leading up to the Opening Ceremony."

"That would have been the Torch Relay," said Gus.

"That's right," said Susannah. "We had officers working overtime while the runners came through the county's western side and made their way to Bath via Bradford-on-Avon. Phoebe reckoned it was the first week of June. She awoke late after a busy night in the bar because of the higher visitor levels in the city. They were there to join in celebrations for the twenty-fifth anniversary of Bath gaining World Heritage Site status. Phoebe walked into the city centre after lunch and went shopping. Traffic was horrendous, and the streets were packed with people. She decided to have a coffee, walk home, and sit tight before returning to Nyx for another busy night. She needed to walk from the Abbey Courtyard and negotiate Milsom Street to reach her flat. Both sides of the street were full of people. People hung out of office windows on the upper floors, and everyone had a smile. Phoebe watched the procession as it came past. Phoebe stopped by the HSBC Bank to watch. She spotted Danute Zukas on the other side of the road. Phoebe called out, but Danute couldn't hear her because of the noise. Phoebe told me it was the only time she saw Danute after quitting her job. Phoebe watched Danute make her way up the slope to the top of Milsom Street and followed suit. She lost sight of her for a while as the sheer number of people made it impossible to see which way she went on George Street. Finally, Phoebe pushed through the crowds to reach the junction and glimpsed Danute further up Gay Street, heading towards The Circus. They were still heading in the general direction of Phoebe's flat on Burlington Street, so she continued to follow. Danute wasn't alone; there were three, maybe four young women, dressed similarly, in a light grey shift dress and sandals."

"Did that seem odd to Phoebe?" asked Alex.

"It wasn't how they were used to seeing Danute at Nyx," said Susannah. "Phoebe said Danute was a natural beauty and only needed a light touch of make-up, but she always dressed smartly. David Hodges didn't appreciate his staff looking cheap. Skirts couldn't be ultra-short, and tops had to cover their assets. The closest Phoebe got to Danute and her companions was on Brock Street, where they appeared to be en route to the Royal Crescent. The girls were stopped talking to a group of students and handing out flowers. Danute and her companions looked happy and relaxed. Then another crowd emerged from Victoria Park and surged across Brock Street. The excitement of the Torch Relay was dying down. When Phoebe looked back to where Danute was standing, everyone disappeared. Phoebe walked home, cooked a meal, and got ready to return to the city centre to start work at eight o'clock."

"There doesn't seem to be any confusion over the date," said Alex.

"No," said Gus, "and Erica Barge mentioned Danute and the flowers when we spoke with her."

"What do you think it meant?" asked Susannah.

"We can only speculate," said Gus, "but Phoebe Sawyer told Terry West about that sighting because Erica Barge saw Terry stumbling home to Newbridge Hill one night, eight months later, and he was still searching for an answer. Erica told us he wanted to know why Danute was carrying the flowers. It made no sense to DS Barge, but something Phoebe told you might shed some light. Phoebe said the modestly dressed girls were handing flowers to that group of students during a light-hearted discussion. We should be able to trace the organisation they represented."

"They couldn't operate on the streets here in Warminster without a licence," said Susannah. "Although, the rules aren't the same everywhere."

Alex was scrolling through his phone.

"Bath and North-East Somerset Council's Trading Standards and Licensing teams were receiving reports of emotive causes being used by street cash collectors during the summer of 2012, guv. Several teams of young people who didn't represent a registered charity were reported as persuading unsuspecting residents and visitors to part with their money. The Olympics gave them an ideal umbrella to shelter under, especially with the Paralympics scheduled shortly afterwards. Some individuals they received complaints about had the materials you would associate with legitimate charity collectors, such as branded outfits or buckets. However, the causes they were collecting for were rather ambiguous, which raised doubts whether any of the monies donated ever reached good causes."

"Did Phoebe have any other gems to offer that afternoon, Susannah?" asked Gus.

"We finished our coffees, and I asked Phoebe to call me if she remembered anything else that might help us with our enquiries. She was going to find out the surnames of those two regulars, but I never heard from her."

"What did you do with the information when you returned to work on Tuesday?" asked Gus.

"There wasn't much I could do, was there, without admitting to John I'd gone off-piste. So, I kept my head down, slogged through another batch of tenancy checks and waited for Phoebe to call."

"How long before John's superiors pulled the plug on the investigation?" asked Alex.

"John asked me for a report on everything he'd asked George and me to do. I handed that over in the second week of November. John told me they would take no further action until fresh evidence surfaced. Evidence that offered a reasonable chance of a successful outcome. I transferred to another case concerning travellers on a site near the West Wilts Crematorium. John attended a coaching and mentoring skills workshop which occupied him part-time for eighteen months. We didn't work together much during that period. When we teamed up again at the end of 2016, I was engaged to Brad, and the cases were domestic abuse-related or helping to round up workers in local restaurants that had overstayed their visas. Nothing as exciting as a brutal murder."

"Do you ever wonder?" asked Gus.

"What would have happened if I'd told John I'd met Phoebe, do you mean?" asked Susannah.

Alex thought he might have to fetch her from the Ladies again.

"It's water under the bridge," said Gus. "I can't explain why you couldn't find an address for Danute somewhere in Trowbridge. Even the CCTV sighting just before she died two years later suggests it was where she lived. So what did you make of that sighting?"

"The image was grainy and unstable," said Susannah. "I had to agree with George and John; it was Danute in the end."

"Why was George Collins involved?" asked Alex.

"George was on another case, and like everyone else at

Polebarn Road, he'd seen the photo sent to us from Danute's mother. George thought the girl on his CCTV search in the town centre reminded him of Danute. John finally agreed, although she looked little like the nineteen-year-old in the original photo. That was what got George added to our team. We took the original photo when we visited letting agencies and private landlords. Nobody ever recognised her from it, though."

"Did you have any doubts about the image?" asked Gus.

"You worked as a detective for many years, Mr Free-man," said Susannah. "The family photograph is always done professionally. Danute's hair was short and brushed within an inch of its life. She wore no make-up, and her mother insisted her daughter wear her Sunday-best clothes. When we compared that photo with a grainy image of a young woman who was now twenty-three, with a different hairstyle, dressed in casual clothes, and side-on to the camera—it would be natural to have doubts. We had never seen Danute alive. How could we spot any mannerisms she might have had? If the CCTV camera had caught a close-up of her face from the front, it would have removed any doubts. I asked John if Danute's mother should see the CCTV image to confirm it was her daughter. He didn't want to cause her any further distress."

"I've seen a copy of that CCTV image," said Gus. "So have the Chief Constable and my boss, DS Mercer. We accepted it was Danute Zukas, based on the murder file reports. Our initial impression was Danute had transformed in the two years between leaving Nyx and one day before her murder. We thought drink or drugs could have contributed to that change. The evidence pointed to Danute being exploited by a gang. Or an individual who had got their claws into her in the weeks before she left Nyx. What you told us this morning about Phoebe Sawyer's sighting of Danute doesn't tally with that. Six weeks after leaving a job she enjoyed, Phoebe saw Danute in Bath with several young women, looking happy and relaxed. They could have been working for a charity. Nothing Phoebe saw suggested Danute was being exploited. Of course, Danute may have signed on with an agency, and that job was only temporary. After the Olympics, she could have taken more temporary work or found a permanent position. Was that in Trowbridge or Bath? That will be another avenue for our team to follow. What in that CCTV image convinced us Danute had changed?"

"DS Mercer said Danute looked rough, guv," said Alex. "If we didn't have the family photo, would we view the image differently?"

"Maybe we're seeing what we expect to see," said Gus. "Remember Daniel Hill and Terry West in the early days of the investigation. Hill said drugs didn't feature in the cause of death, so he didn't carry out exhaustive tests on the body. West pointed out it wasn't uncommon for people of Danute's age to use drugs. Police officers think along the same lines. Because a significant proportion of eighteen- to twenty-five-year-olds admit to using drugs, when we see a young woman like Danute, we assume the worst until convinced otherwise. With a picture already in your mind of a teenage Danute, it was natural to suspect something had altered her situation since she left Lithuania."

"Phoebe didn't see Danute alive again after June 2012, guv," said Alex. "What if Danute never found a job, and her landlord, or landlady, threw her out? Nine or ten months on the streets would make her look scruffy."

"Danute wasn't begging in that CCTV image," said Susannah.

Gus tried to recall the image from the murder file.

"No, that's true," he said. "Danute was carrying flowers to hand to the pub-goers. However, that doesn't mean Danute still mixed with the girls Phoebe saw her with in Bath. I wonder whether we could still check the CCTV record on either side of the sighting we have of Danute? Phoebe might recognise someone on the nearby streets. Failing that, we might spot three or four young women dressed similarly, handing out leaflets or flowers."

"We've got places to go, people to see, guv," said Alex. "Shouldn't we be heading back to the office?"

"Unless DS Lamb has something to add," said Gus. "We're done here."

"I've got nothing," said Susannah. "Will you need to see me again? Can I do anything to help?"

"Unlikely, to the first question," said Gus. "We'll have a word with George Collins to see where he put that CCTV material. As for checking whether anyone employed Danute, either temporarily or full-time, we'll handle that. But, no, you've done enough, DS Lamb."

Chapter Nine

ALEX DROVE BACK to the Old Police Station while Gus sat in quiet contemplation beside him. Alex knew better than to disturb him.

Gus spoke for the first time as they travelled in the lift to the office.

"Between them, Manvers Street and Polebarn Road made a right dog's dinner of our case, didn't they?"

"That's being kind, guv," said Alex. "We're no closer to finding out who might have killed Danute. But, if either set of detectives knew what we know today, would they have ever been able to get a result?"

"I somehow doubt it," said Gus. "Although, there's no guarantee we can do anything with what we've learned so far. We still have several missing pieces of the jigsaw. Let's debrief this morning's meeting with the team and agree on our action plan."

Luke and the others were eager to hear their news. Apart from a couple of interviews with people on the edges of the case, there wasn't much to get excited about.

Everyone listened as Gus and Alex told them what DS Susannah Lamb, nee Fry, had told them.

"Blimey, guv," said Neil. "They'd never get a job in this office."

"Erica Barge was the pick of the bunch, Neil," said Luke. "At least she tried to be creative for answers, despite her boss's shortcomings."

"I think DS Barge should have reported DI West earlier, guv," said Lydia. "You wouldn't be happy with us if we covered for you that way."

"I wouldn't be happy with myself if I ever needed you to," said Gus. "Anyway, as I told DS Lamb, it's water under the bridge now. We need to use the new information, plus follow the leads we gained, to find what the other detectives didn't."

"Discover where Danute Zukas lived between April 2011 and when she died," said Neil.

"And identify her killer," said Blessing Umeh.

"Where do you wish to start, guv?" asked Luke.

"Alex and I will interview David Hodges and Phoebe Sawyer," said Gus. "If they can't tell us the surnames of the two regulars Phoebe mentioned, we'll need two of you to visit Nyx on Friday night to speak to them."

"It's a tough job, but someone has to do it," said Neil. "Why don't you and I volunteer, Luke?"

"I'll need to rearrange something," said Luke. "I'm sure I can manage."

"How will we tackle finding this person who drove Danute to Bath each night, guv?" asked Alex.

"Let's see what the people from Nyx can offer first, Alex," said Gus. "As DI Cook was obsessed with finding the murder site, he ignored anything relating to where Danute worked after leaving Nyx. DS Lamb caught sight of Danute on Milsom Street and near the Royal Crescent, possibly involved with a charitable organisation, but where did Danute earn a living in the next two years? Luke and Lydia can concentrate on that task within office hours. Blessing, I want you to liaise with a DC George Collins, at Polebarn Road. We need to see as much CCTV coverage for Saturday, the twelfth of July 2014, as possible. George spotted Danute at 10.45 pm on the corner of a side road leading to a late-night bar near the town park. We may gather more information from Nyx to aid you in your search but look for other young women of Danute's age dressed similarly. They could hand out leaflets and flowers or just chat with other youngsters on the streets, hoping to collect money. What they were up to, we'll discover in due course. Last but not least, Neil, see whether Danute's mobile phone number is in the murder file. Her younger sister, Natasha, had that number on her phone for a minimum of nine months after Danute left home. Follow up with Danute's service provider for detailed call logs. DI West and DS Barge went part way down that route, but I want to know more than where Danute was when she made the calls to her sister. I need to know who she called here in the UK when she worked at Nyx and afterwards."

"Got it, guv," echoed around the room.

"The game's afoot, guv," said Neil.

"Any idea what game we're playing, Neil?" asked Gus.

"You lost me, guv," said Neil.

"Do you remember when we were investigating the Grant Burnside case?" asked Gus. "There's a village called Stanton Fitzwarren, off the Cricklade Road. It would be an hour's drive from here. Forty years ago, it was always in the news because of the Unification Church members' arrival. Sun Myung Moon, who died in 2012, was a multi-millionaire

South Korean business executive who claimed to be the second messiah. He devoted his life to establishing The Kingdom of Heaven upon Earth after founding the church in 1954. It has been described as a hybrid of Christianity, Confucianism, Shamanism, and anti-communism. The cult spread, and in the Seventies and early Eighties, it claimed to have over four million members in one hundred and twenty countries. Their numbers have dwindled since then, but the so-called Moonies still maintain a presence in many countries."

"What on earth attracted them to Stanton Fitzwarren, guv?" asked Lydia.

"A cynic would say money, Lydia," replied Gus. "The first local to fall under their spell was the daughter of the Lord of the Manor. Most of the villagers worked on farms owned by the family and lived in properties on the estate. The young girl's parents, upstanding churchgoing community members, were appalled. Who wants their child in the clutches of a weird sect?"

"I'm guessing they got rid of them sharpish, guv," said Neil.

"Quite the contrary, Neil," said Gus. "The daughter soon lost interest, but her father outraged the locals by donating his entire estate to the Moonies. He and his wife visited the sect's training centre in Reading, liked what they saw, and joined. So Stanton Fitzwarren lost a councillor, churchwarden, parish councillor and Women's Institute president overnight. The couple moved to the States, and the national director and several converts moved in."

"The locals didn't sit back and take it, did they, guv?" asked Alex.

"Stories of alleged brainwashing spread like wildfire," said Gus. "Naturally, the Moonies refuted those claims.

Stanton Fitzwarren, on Swindon's doorstep, became the Moonies' most fruitful recruiting ground in Britain. However, it couldn't last, and the sect's activities dramatically downsized. The bulk of their followers headed for the States. Everything went quiet in Stanton Fitzwarren. The estate continued to be run as a farm, and with around twenty properties rented out to the public, the estate generated a healthy revenue for the Moonies."

"What happened to the Lord of the Manor?" asked Luke.

"He maintained joining the Unification Church was the best thing he ever did. He and his wife wanted to deepen their faith in God, and it pleased him to see the farms at Stanton Fitzwarren run by the Church's young people as a Christian cooperative."

"That isn't what happened to Danute Zukas, though, is it, guv?" asked Blessing.

"I don't believe the Unification Church groomed Danute, or whatever name it operates under today, Blessing. However, when Kenneth Truelove handed me the murder file, I must admit I bought into his idea Danute had been groomed by a sexual predator. Hundreds of cults use mind control to recruit and control members operating in the UK. Experts believe that figure to be over a thousand, most of which operate in secret. Most masquerade as health courses and addiction treatment programmes to lure unsuspecting victims. The girls that Phoebe Sawyer saw on the streets of Bath intrigue me. What message were they peddling? Who persuaded Danute to get involved? They appeared to focus their attention on teens and early twenties."

"Where do we start, guv?" asked Neil. "These secret

operations can be tricky to locate. But it goes with the territory."

"They're not keen on members leaving the sect either, guv," said Luke. "If they do, they must sign a non-disclosure agreement."

"When stories appear in the press, it's often because an investigative reporter has gone undercover to learn what really goes on," said Blessing.

"Let's take it a step at a time," said Gus. "We'll split these interviews between the six of us and see whether we can identify the organisation behind these possible street missionaries."

"Could Nyx have been where Danute first came into contact with someone from this organisation?" asked Lydia. "Perhaps we're jumping the gun, guv. We haven't established it's a sect, or cult, yet."

"Phoebe never mentioned seeing the girls in the bar, Lydia," said Alex. "And it's possible they only operated on streets in Trowbridge too. The CCTV coverage Blessing will interrogate can help confirm that."

"I agree with your assessment of the situation, guv," said Luke. "Danute didn't get caught up in a sect like the Moonies. They might not be innocent in how people get persuaded to join them, but they spread the message that Jesus loves you, and God is good, don't they? It would be the sinister variety we need to watch for. When he died, which leader faced incarceration, kidnapping, rape, and incest allegations? That would have been twenty-five years ago now."

"You're talking about David Berg and the Children of God," said Gus. "A group that gained ground quickly in the late 60s and disappeared as fast. Because I was brought up in Wiltshire, I heard the Stanton Fitzwarren story soon after becoming a detective in Salisbury. Various news items in the national and local press kept me aware of the Moonies and what they were doing. Over the years, there have been other groups Wiltshire Police needed to monitor. Extremists, mostly, whether their passion was politics, religion, ecology, animal cruelty, or merely the latest cause célèbre in the spotlight. Did I ever encounter an organisation that murdered one of its members and attempted to destroy the body? No, I didn't, and I would hope if such a group were on our doorstep, Wiltshire Police would be aware of it."

"If a thousand secret sects exist in the UK, guv, we probably don't have the resources to keep track of every single one," said Neil. "They could be out there, hiding in plain sight, and nobody sees what's happening behind closed doors."

"I know only too well how many wide-open spaces there are on Salisbury Plain," said Blessing with a shiver. "If this group was small, they could have set up in a house near Trowbridge. Perhaps they recruited Danute Zukas that way."

"You might have hit on something there, Blessing," said Alex. "It would be easier to operate from a place in the countryside. Stanton Fitzwarren was a village with a population of less than two hundred. That's the setting I would choose. Members could travel to Bath, Trowbridge, or any local town, hunting new members and gathering funds."

"I'll check with London Road," said Gus. "Perhaps Divya can help us by interrogating the Hub's data banks for more information on these secret organisations. Right, for the rest of the day, Alex and I need to update the Freeman Files with the details of our meetings. We'll head into Bath in the morning to meet with David Hodges. I don't know what business hours he keeps, but unless he wishes to attend a local police station for an interview under caution, I suggest he's in his office above Nyx at ten o'clock,"

"Got it, guv," said Luke. "I'll tell him the good news and warn Phoebe Sawyer she won't have time for a quiet coffee in the Abbey Courtyard tomorrow lunchtime. You and Alex can speak with her as soon as you finish with her boss."

"You had better warn him two likely lads will be in Nyx tomorrow evening at nine as well while you're on the phone, Luke," said Neil.

"I hadn't forgotten, Neil," said Luke. But, of course, he hadn't forgotten he needed to text Tom Spencer yet to postpone their next get-together, either.

"Shall I contact DC Collins at Polebarn Road direct, guv?" said Blessing.

"Luke can pave the way with a courtesy call to DI Cook. He knows what to say. Unless I'm mistaken, you'll have clearance to drive to Polebarn Road tomorrow morning at nine o'clock and start working with young George straightaway."

"OK, guv," said Blessing.

"I'll make a start on the job search, guv," said Lydia, "Luke can join me when he's free."

"I think I've found that mobile number we needed, guv," said Neil. "It was scribbled in the margin of a copy of the letter the Lithuanian charity sent Terry West."

"Good," said Gus, "that should keep each of us busy until the close of play tomorrow."

Neil turned to speak to Luke.

"Our close of play will be much later than five o'clock."

"You can't do too much for a good boss, Neil," said Luke.

Neil hoped Melody would agree.

At five o'clock, Gus decided he'd done enough. Time to

get home to Urchfont. He and Alex had finished updating their files and run through the questions they wanted to ask David Hodges.

Luke had been the first to leave the office. He had planned for the meetings in Bath and Trowbridge, plus re-scheduled his date in Swindon. Nicky wouldn't learn about that one.

Blessing and Neil travelled down in the lift together. The young DC wanted Neil to move his car first to give her wiggle room for her Nissan.

Alex and Lydia were the last to leave.

"Do we have any plans for this evening?" asked Alex.

"A quiet night at home," said Lydia. "After we've eaten, I must phone Eleanor. We haven't spoken for a week or two. Unless Chidozie has altered his plans, we should holiday in Dubai towards the end of next month."

"The weeks keep whizzing past," said Alex. "It's Friday tomorrow again already. That holiday will be on us before we know it."

"Don't expect to lounge around doing nothing this weekend," said Lydia. "We need to shop for clothes."

Alex groaned.

"That reminds me. I must dig out my sunglasses."

"Plenty of time for that," said Lydia.

"Not if you're shopping for clothes," said Alex.

His arm still stung when they exited the lift. Blessing was leaving the car park. Luke and Gus had already gone. Neil Davis stood beside his car, watching Blessing inch her way into traffic.

"Problem, Neil?" asked Lydia.

"Not at all," said Neil. "While seeing Blessing out of her parking space, I thought about Natasha Zukas."

"And you a married man," tutted Alex.

"With Melody expecting a baby," said Lydia.

"What prompted that flight of fancy, Neil?" asked Alex.

"I asked Gus if he had ever seen a photo of her. Natasha was two years younger than Danute, but they were supposed to look like twins. They had the same tattoo. I wondered whether it might help if we flew her over here to jog a few memories. A photo of Danute is fine, but a living, breathing look-alike in Nyx, on the streets of Bath, or strolling around Trowbridge town centre at night could have a positive result."

"What did Gus say?" asked Lydia.

"He said he would take it into consideration," said Neil. "I guess it will depend on what we discover in the next few days. He would have to persuade Geoff Mercer to stretch the budget yet again. I remember he turned pale when Alex and Gus flew out to Malaga."

"Didn't we learn Ryanair had regular flights to and from Kaunas?" asked Alex. "That wouldn't break the budget. I think it's a grand idea."

Gus pondered Neil's suggestion as his Focus eased its way through roadworks on London Road. Perfect timing, as always. Get the traffic cones out before rush hour, ready to dig holes in the road on Friday. Then they can ensure they choke the town centre with idling traffic over the weekend, waiting for the lights to change. Meanwhile, the employees were enjoying the weekend at home.

Gus wondered whether Suzie had already escaped the madness and was waiting for him. After last night's mini-celebration, he hoped they would spend a quiet evening at home.

Gus spotted Bert Penman in the gateway to the allotments as he passed the church. Bert waved his walking stick, trying to catch Gus's attention. Gus parked on the left-hand side of the lane and trotted back to chat with his old friend.

"Everything okay, Bert?" said Gus.

"I noticed you spent time on the land last weekend, Mr Freeman," said Bert. "Just a word of warning. I'd get your vulnerable crops, like your carrots, into storage before the middle of next week. This hip is telling me we're due the first frost of winter."

"Well, we wouldn't want to rely on the Meteorological Office for our weather forecasts, would we?" laughed Gus. "I shall put it on the list for the weekend. Anything else I forgot?"

"The leaves on several of your sprout plants were turning yellow. So I snapped them off at the base and threw them on your compost heap. It improves air circulation."

"I remember, Bert," said Gus, "you told me it makes the sprouts easier to pick on cold, wet and frosty days. It's written in the notebook I keep in my shed."

"You'll find less free time in the future to read that book, Mr Freeman," said Bert.

"Don't get much now, Bert," said Gus. "Things will change once the baby arrives, and I'll take advantage of something that wasn't available in your days. I never thought I'd need to apply for paternity leave. I didn't dream I'd have the opportunity."

"You might find you'll wish you were like me when Cora had the bairns," said Bert with a smile. "I had to work to keep food on the table, and I was glad to get out of the house on more than one occasion when the little ones wouldn't settle."

"Are you off to the Lamb?" asked Gus.

"Is grass green, Gus," laughed Bert. "There, I remembered to do what Miss Suzie asked."

"Well done. One out of three isn't bad. I'd better get to the bungalow to help Suzie in the kitchen. I'll see you at the weekend."

Gus trotted back to his car while Bert strolled towards the Lamb.

"I didn't realise you would be late," cried Suzie as Gus pushed open the front door.

"I would have been home five minutes ago if I hadn't stopped for a gardening lesson from Bert," said Gus. "Although, those roadworks on London Road didn't help."

"They'll be a nightmare," said Suzie. "I was fortunate to escape the car park before the cones reached the gateway. But heaven knows what it will be like in the morning."

"Alex and I are driving to Bath first thing. We might spend most of the day there. Why don't I take you in the Focus and drop you off at the traffic lights?"

"That could work, provided you promise to collect me on the way home."

"Right. That's sorted," said Gus. "What are we eating?"

"I thought we'd try a layered aubergine and lentil bake," said Suzie.

"Do you need me to do anything?" asked Gus.

"It's almost ready. You've got time to shower and change if you're quick."

Gus headed for the bathroom, wondering if he could phone for a pizza later.

Friday, 14 September 2018

GUS AND SUZIE left the bungalow at twenty-five past eight. The aubergine and lentil bake proved less terrible than Gus imagined. He hoped Suzie didn't plan on making it a permanent fixture on their menu, but he could live with it reappearing once every six months. As they stopped for the fourth time on their slow way into Devizes, Gus congratulated himself for suggesting they left the Golf at home today.

"The next enforced stop will be as close as we'll get to the car park entrance, darling," said Suzie. "I'll hop out there and await your call later today."

"I don't see any reason we can't finish our work in Bath by early afternoon," said Gus. "I'll call when I leave the office."

"Don't forget," said Suzie. "I know you when you get deeper into a case."

The traffic lights ahead of them changed to red, and Suzie soon kissed Gus on the cheek before getting out of the car. He sat and watched her cross the road and disappear around the side of the main building.

After their meal last night, they discussed the team's daily progress. Suzie agreed with Gus; if there was a secret sect with violent elements operating in the county, it had never raised concerns for the people at London Road.

As Suzie pointed out, a sect's leaders could cover a wide area of Avon and Somerset from a base on the county's western borders. Danute Zukas, being seen in Trowbridge that night, could have been an isolated incident.

Gus eventually escaped from Devizes and descended into the valley. He could see possible nooks and crannies for isolated properties on both sides of the road as far as the eye could see. Perhaps it was the aubergine and lentils playing tricks on his mind.

Gus found that Alex and Lydia had arrived before him

when he pulled into the Old Police Station office car park. He exited the lift, and they were deep in conversation.

"Good morning, you two," said Gus. "Sorry to break it up, but we should get moving, Alex. If the trip through Devizes signifies things to come, we need every minute we can get."

"I brought my car again this morning, guv," said Alex. "We can leave straight away."

They heard the lift descending to the ground floor. Another team member had arrived.

"Can we book a week's holiday, guv," asked Lydia. "I spoke to my mother last night. The three of us have been invited to join my father and his partner in Dubai. They will take a well-earned break after a busy summer at the Lady Eleanor."

"It sounds great," said Gus. "When would it be exactly?"

"The last week in October, guv," said Alex.

"I'll inform DS Mercer," said Gus. "If we're snowed under with another case, I'll ask for a helping hand."

"Rick Chalmers, guv?" asked Alex.

"He would be useful," said Gus.

"Anyone except Amelia Cranston, guv," said Lydia. "Am I right?"

Gus winced.

"DS Mercer was a huge fan of Amelia," said Gus. "Or at least I thought that was why he pestered me to give her a shot. But maybe it was because she'd upset every other department head he had available. But, no, if we need an extra pair of hands, I draw the line at Rick. He's a team player."

Luke Sherman and Neil Davis emerged from the lift together.

Alex nodded to Gus, and they prepared to leave.

"DI Cook will be speaking to Blessing now, guv," said Luke. "He was happy for her to work alongside DC Collins at Polebarn Road this morning."

"Of course, he was, Luke," said Gus as he joined Alex in the lift. "He can get on with his paperwork undisturbed. We'll see you this afternoon."

The trip to the centre of Bath was uneventful. Alex followed Gus's suggestion that they park in the multistorey car park on Manvers Street, then prepared to walk through the busy streets of the Roman city.

"There are so many side streets and alleyways in an old city, aren't there, guv," said Alex as they left the car park. "Unless you know your way around and stick to the wide thoroughfares, it would be easy to miss dozens of shops, pubs and clubs oozing with character. I've never heard of Nyx before. Is it near the Abbey?"

"Everything is near the Abbey in many ways, Alex," said Gus. "Nyx is in a passage off North Parade, a three-minute walk from the car park."

They soon found themselves in a cobbled passageway. The high Georgian buildings on either side meant the route would be semi-dark for most of the day. Nevertheless, the September sun offered a brief glimpse of the layout ahead. Gus saw stone steps leading to a set of double doors. An ornate wrought-iron sign to the left of the entrance showed they were in the right spot.

The passageway rose to join North Parade, the historic terrace John Wood the Elder built in the middle of the eighteenth century.

"I was right," said Alex. "This place has character, alright, but how on earth do people find it?"

"Word of mouth," said Gus. "If they serve a good pint, word soon gets around."

Alex spotted a modern doorbell discreetly masked by a trailing ivy plant. He rang the bell and heard a faint ringing in the distance.

"If Hodges is in his office, he will have heard that," said Gus.

Less than a minute later, David Hodges opened the right-hand door.

"Come inside, please," he said. "Welcome to Nyx."

"Thank you for agreeing to speak to us, Mr Hodges," said Gus. "My name is Freeman, a consultant with Wiltshire Police. DS Hardy and I wish to see the bar area first, if we may?"

"Of course, whatever you need," said the manager. "Anything that will help you solve Danute's murder. I'll get the lights on for you."

Gus and Alex soon realised the stark exterior of the premises bore no relation to what Hodges had achieved on the inside. Instead, the décor was twenty-first century and of top quality. Gus scanned the various seating areas separated by smoked glass partitions. Sixty customers would be its capacity if seated, plus another twenty maximum standing at the bar or perched on high stools on either side of the room. It wasn't a country pub like the Lamb that he loved, but it had more warmth than Gus had imagined. Maybe it was the lower ceilings.

"It's like being wrapped in a warm blanket, isn't it?" said David Hodges. "We have a solid clientele that comes back to us time and time again. We don't drown out conversation with loud music or have wall-to-wall television screens showing sports from around the world. I was told I was mad when I went into partnership with a mate twelve years ago. Yet, we're still here, despite many other businesses failing."

"I can see the attraction," said Alex.

"Do you get many people my age here, Mr Hodges?" he asked. "Or would you say the majority were between eighteen and thirty?"

"Far from it," replied the manager. "The art of conversation isn't a requirement for younger people today. They communicate via their mobile phones, sometimes even in the same room. We always saw our target audience as the over-thirties, with no upper age limit. Customers from those generations enjoy the chance to talk with others, whether or not they know them."

"Phoebe Sawyer has worked for you since you opened," said Gus. "She's a mature woman according to two people we've spoken to, yet you employed Danute Zukas despite her tender years."

David Hodges allowed himself a wry smile.

"If you've seen enough of the bar area, perhaps we can continue this meeting upstairs in my office? I can get us a cup of coffee, tea, or a cold drink."

Chapter Ten

GUS AND ALEX followed David Hodges upstairs. They quaintly identified the main toilet facilities as Ladies and Gents at the top of the stairs. A private door on the far righthand side of the landing kept the customers from the inner sanctum of the Nyx operation. When Gus stepped inside the office area, he realised David Hodges wasn't a one-man-band. Instead, there were two desks, one considerably larger than the other, covered with phones, computers, and the paperwork paraphernalia vital to a thriving mini-concern such as Nyx. Whoever had the role as David Hodges's secretary or personal assistant wasn't at work this early in the day.

Gus's appraisal of the layout hadn't escaped David Hodges's notice.

"My PA works in the afternoons, five days a week," he said. "Ms Emily Griffiths is her name. Emily's been with us since we opened, like Phoebe. She's in her late thirties now, and her son is doing very well at school. Sorry, I'm rambling. You don't need to hear about Emily. It's doubtful she ever came into contact with Danute."

"I'll make a note of the name, sir," said Alex. "If we need to speak to her, we'll get in touch for her contact details."

"Right, now, what did you want to drink? We have our own restroom behind you and a kitchenette."

Gus and Alex told the eager-to-please manager what they wanted and sat by the bigger desk. Gus could hear a kettle boiling in the next room. He hoped the brand of instant coffee was palatable. Then he remembered how much thought and money had gone into the decor downstairs. Hodges soon proved him right; his black coffee was every bit as good as brewed by their Gaggia.

"Now, where were we? Why do we employ attractive young women to serve behind the bar?" asked David Hodges once he'd seated himself in his high-backed leather chair with his cup of tea. "Well, that's a loaded question, Mr Freeman, as you know only too well."

"A valid question though, Mr Hodges," said Alex. "Danute's English was poor when she arrived here, as we understand it."

"There were various factors in play, DS Hardy," said Hodges. "We're a small business, and staff turnover can be high in the hospitality sector. I've been fortunate with my two senior staff members, who have remained loyal throughout, but the competition was high that summer. Several new stores had opened their doors on Southgate Street, and two large hoteliers had upgraded their facilities and were hiring in greater numbers than in previous years. We've employed students from the University here at Nyx in the past, but they don't have the same work ethic as Danute. So, we've also employed young girls from Poland, Spain, and Brazil behind the bar at various times. Their English was often better than the students from the Claverton Down campus. As for a willingness to get stuck in and to stick to our house rules, they were certainly far better."

"You have strict house rules, then?" asked Gus.

"I wouldn't describe them as strict, no," said Hodges. "I know it helps my business if I have pretty girls behind the counter when my customers arrive. But those on both sides of the bar must act with the utmost decorum. Phoebe instructs the girls not to wear clothing with plunging necklines or skirts so short when they fetch a bottle from the bottom shelf one can see next week's laundry. Our bar staff must be polite to the customers, and although a brief conversation is acceptable, they shouldn't give them ideas by spending too long with them. Our customers soon get told when they've overstepped the mark, and we will show anyone with wandering hands the door."

"There was never any incident involving Danute that prompted a customer to receive a warning or get ejected?" asked Gus.

"Certainly not," said Hodges. "And Danute's English came on leaps and bounds within a few months. She was a quick learner, not afraid of work, and the customers loved her. Whereas the Scottish student she replaced would slouch behind the bar and sulk, Danute would greet everyone with a smile and be on the move as soon as a new customer stepped inside the door. By the end of the summer, Danute was an integral part of the team. We were glad she'd opted to come to this part of the country and thanked our lucky stars we'd found her so soon after Moira left."

"Moira was your Scottish lass, I presume," said Gus. "How did Danute know you suddenly had a vacancy?"

"Word of mouth, I believe," said Hodges. "I mentioned

the competition that summer earlier. There had to be more than a dozen employers simultaneously looking for permanent and casual staff. Those businesses had money to advertise in the Chronicle and online. Soon after those adverts appeared, people were leaving their present job and moving to one of the new retail outlets or a hotel. That meant we smaller businesses had to work fast to find replacements. I feared we'd be struggling for weeks. Students were taking exams or disappearing for the holidays, and we might not have found the right person until late September when the next student intake arrived. Moira left us after a busy Friday night, and I was going to ask Emily to contact the employment agencies first thing Monday afternoon. Then, at eight o'clock on Saturday evening, just after we'd opened, Danute walked in and asked Phoebe whether the vacancy had been filled."

"That wasn't luck," said Alex. "She must have heard from someone Moira had left."

"Which begs the question," said Gus. "Who told her?"

"I suppose it does," said Hodges. "I don't know if Phoebe asked how Danute knew; she was just glad not to have to cope with one fewer member of staff."

"Did Danute start straight away?" asked Gus.

"Phoebe asked her to come to see me on Monday afternoon to sort out the details. So, after we'd met, Danute's first shift with us was that evening."

"When did Danute tell you where she lived?" asked Alex.

"Danute told me on Monday afternoon she lived in a flat in Trowbridge she shared with two other girls."

"Why couldn't you give that address to the detectives who visited you after her murder?" asked Gus.

"When Danute tried to explain where the flat was, apart

from the number 22, it got lost in translation. So I asked for her bank details to pay her salary directly into her account. Danute said she didn't have one yet. Her mother had taken control of the family's finances after her husband died. So I agreed to pay Danute cash until she got her affairs in order. Danute gave me her mobile phone number as her main contact point; for the next nine months, our arrangement functioned. I'd tell her from time to time I hadn't got her address or bank details yet, and she'd smile and promise to let me know, but they never materialised."

"I wonder why?" asked Alex.

"Did Danute ever mention her family?" asked Gus.

"We knew her father had died, and her mother struggled to put food on the table for Danute and her sister. That was the sum of our knowledge."

"Was Danute friendly with anyone still working behind the bar here, apart from Phoebe Sawyer?" asked Alex.

"Danute was friendly with everyone, DS Hardy," said Hodges. "However, I'm afraid none of the girls here in 2011 is still with us."

"Time marches on," said Gus. "They could be old enough to be customers now, though. Might any of them drop by tonight?"

"A cynical view of the service we provide, Mr Freeman," said Hodges.

"I didn't intend to offend," said Gus. "but Danute Zukas spent three years in this country. For the first nine months, she worked here, late at night, serving drinks to people, most of whom were old enough to be a parent. Then, something made her leave, and two years later, someone killed her. It's difficult not to imagine the answer lies in something that occurred between the walls downstairs. Although you paint a picture of harmonious socialising, I can't help wondering whether a predator stalked our victim. They may even have been a regular at Nyx in 2011. Does that suggest any names, Mr Hodges? Who were the people who defied your house rules seven years ago? Perhaps we need to speak to them?"

"Phoebe would remember the offenders better than me, Mr Freeman. We don't have lists of members; we're not a club. However, we liaise with many other premises in the same business. They send details to us of people thrown out for drunken behaviour, fighting, and so forth. We reply in kind. Phoebe has a list behind the bar of people currently barred from Bath's licensed premises. Her memory is better than mine; she might recall the trouble-makers from those days. But, as I said before, we could never remember Danute being involved in any unpleasantness while she worked here."

"Was Danute friendly with any customers who still drink here?" asked Alex.

"Graham Davies and Jerry Day are still around," said Hodges. "The odd couple."

"Phoebe told the detective they were both married," said Gus.

"That's true," said Hodges. "They work for Airbus. Graham and Jerry arrive here every Friday evening, rain or shine, at nine o'clock on the dot. They order drinks and sit in the same spot until they're ready to leave. Sometimes other customers engage them in conversation, but mostly they prefer their own company, and while away the three to three-and-a-half hours of their lives they share with us chatting to one another."

"That sounds normal enough to me," said Gus.

"They're cross-dressers," said Hodges. "Friday nights are when they can experiment with the female side of their fundamentally male personalities. That's how they explained their behaviour to Danute. She was the only staff member they had ever spoken with about it. Graham and Jerry talked to Danute more often than with others on our staff.."

"What about your customers?" asked Alex. "How do they react?"

"This is Bath, DS Hardy," said Hodges. "It's like the News of the World used to proclaim, although that might have been before your time. All human life is here. I'm sure you understand the reference, Mr Freeman?"

Gus nodded. Neil and Luke might need a word to the wise before they interview those two this evening. Luke would be sensible enough to tread with care; Neil might need a steadying hand.

"How did Danute get to work each day?" asked Gus.

"One of her flatmates brought her into Bath," said Hodges. "I never met the girl, but she worked in one hotel or restaurant. I do not know what hours she worked, but it appeared to mesh with the hours we offered Danute."

"This girl drove Danute home in the mornings, too?" said Alex.

"I believe so," said Hodges. "I'm sure Phoebe will confirm the details. Danute's flatmate's hours must have been flexible enough to enable her to cope with the extra hour we require staff to work on Fridays and Saturdays. I don't recall any problems arising where Danute couldn't get back to Trowbridge."

"Perhaps this girl was a customer," said Gus. "It could explain how Danute reacted so promptly after Moira quit. How long was Danute in this country before she applied to work here?"

"I believe Danute told me she had arrived ten days ago when we spoke for the first time."

"I wonder why Danute chose Trowbridge?" asked Alex.

"Every town surrounding Bath is cheaper to live in, DS Hardy," said Hodges. "But, as it turned out, Trowbridge chose her. Danute told me she flew into Bristol International, asked a fellow passenger how to get to the beautiful city of Bath, and started looking for work as soon as she arrived. A business that offered staff accommodation would have suited Danute best, but someone offered her a room in Trowbridge. You might be right, Mr Freeman. Perhaps the woman who owned the flat pointed Danute in our direction."

"A business with staff living in," said Gus. "We could be looking at one of the major hotels. Wherever Danute's land-lady worked was one of the first places our victim sought employment. We need to confirm whether that woman was a customer here and how long Danute occupied a spare room at her home."

"I wasn't privy to any information relating to her living arrangements," said David Hodges. "We don't intrude on the private lives of our staff. However, Phoebe might have overheard something. She'll be here shortly. I can occupy myself downstairs while you speak with her in my office. Was there anything else?"

"Not today, Mr Hodges," said Gus. "If you could supply DS Hardy with contact details for Ms Griffiths, that will be sufficient for now."

The manager wrote the details on a card and handed it to Alex.

"I hope you solve the mystery, Mr Freeman," he said. "Danute was only with us for a short period, but she left a lasting impression. Not just with the staff we had working here then, but with our customers. Everyone was sad when they heard she'd left. But, unfortunately, we didn't have the chance to thank her properly and give her a decent send-off."

"Danute called on Friday afternoon and said she wouldn't be in that evening. Is that correct?" asked Gus.

"Exactly," said David Hodges. "A brief call. Phoebe asked if she was homesick. Danute told her it was nothing like that. When Phoebe asked why Danute was leaving and where she would live and work, Danute apologised for the short notice and ended the call. We kept her wages in the office, waiting for her to collect them, but we never saw her again. I rang her mobile number two weeks after she left us, but the number was unobtainable."

"Interesting," said Gus.

"Because she hadn't provided her bank details, you couldn't get the money to her," said Alex. "I wonder if Danute ever set up an account at a bank in Trowbridge?"

"We'll follow up on that later," said Gus.

David Hodges collected the empty cups and returned them to the restroom.

"Can I get you a refill, gentlemen?" he called.

"Yes, please, sir," said Alex. "The same again for both of us."

"I think I can hear Phoebe on the stairs," said Hodges. "I'll make her a cuppa before I get out of your hair."

The office door opened, and Phoebe Sawyer entered.

Gus remembered what Susannah Lamb had told her. Phoebe had taken the damaged Terry West under her wing; Gus was never over-confident saying how old a woman was, but Phoebe couldn't have been more than five years younger than him, if that.

Alex was forming his own opinion. The woman in the

doorway was petite, smartly dressed, with ash-blonde hair that looked natural but probably wasn't. It was likely Phoebe Sawyer had come straight from the hairdresser. The senior staff member at Nyx was in her fifties, didn't wear a wedding ring, and looked anxious.

"One green tea with a slice of lemon coming up," said David Hodges.

"That doesn't happen very often," said Phoebe with a nervous giggle.

"Good afternoon, Ms Sawyer," said Alex. "Thank you for coming in early to speak with us. Mr Freeman and I have a few questions about Danute Zukas and her time here."

David Hodges breezed into the room with three cups on a tray. It surprised Gus to see he'd added a small plate of biscuits.

"Use my chair, Phoebe," said Hodges. "No point in playing musical chairs; these detectives don't bite. I told them they could rely on you to fill in the gaps in my knowledge. I'll make myself useful downstairs."

With that, he left the room and headed to the bar.

"That makes three rare occurrences on the same day," said Phoebe. "The boss making me a cup of tea, handing out free biscuits, and allowing me to sit in his chair. Now, what do I need to explain that David couldn't?"

"Do you recall what happened when Moira, your Scottish barmaid, left Nyx?" asked Alex.

"Gosh, that was a while back," said Phoebe. "A slacker was our Moira. I wasn't heartbroken to see her leave, but her timing couldn't have been worse. We were just approaching the start of a busy tourist season, and she decided that working in a shop selling posh frocks was more her style."

"I believe you didn't need to advertise the position," said Alex.

"No, that was when Danute appeared out of nowhere. I was working behind the bar, hoping we could cope over the weekend without Moira, when I spotted a young woman at the end of the counter by the stairs. She asked if we'd found someone to replace Moira in her broken English. I said no, we had only learned she was leaving us yesterday. I told Danute I couldn't decide to hire her without checking with my manager first, so I told her to come back on Monday afternoon to meet David. She must have thought I was delaying the inevitable, and my boss would say we couldn't take on someone with no references or UK work experience. However, Danute made me think she would soon overcome any communication issues. She was attractive, eager to find work, and frankly, I knew we might struggle to find someone suitable from the employment agencies."

"Do you know any staff from the major hotels in Bath that visit Nyx for a drink?" asked Gus.

"It's possible," said Phoebe. "Although I couldn't give you a name off the top of my head. Staff at many hotels in the city wear a uniform with a name badge that identifies them to the guests. When they socialise elsewhere in Bath, it's impossible to tell where they earn a crust. Some dress casually, while others wear loads of make-up and designer gear. David doesn't have a specific dress code for Nyx's customers. We expect people to behave like grown-ups and dress accordingly."

"Did Danute ever tell you how she learned about the vacancy?" asked Alex.

"Word of mouth," said Phoebe. "A friend told her."

"They must have been a new friend," said Gus. "Danute flew to the UK just over a week before she spoke to you."

"Younger people today make friends far quicker than we used to," said Phoebe, looking at Gus. "Danute told me the girl who suggested trying Nyx was her flatmate."

"Did you ever get a name?" asked Alex, taking a digestive biscuit from the plate. He took a bite and made a face.

"I told you how rare seeing biscuits was," said Phoebe; "they've probably been hanging around in the restroom for ages. No, I'm afraid I didn't get a name."

"Mr Hodges said you had a list behind the bar of people barred from licensed premises in Bath," said Gus. "Can you recall anyone added to that list while Danute worked here?"

"The detective from Trowbridge asked David that question," said Phoebe. "David told him there was never any trouble inside the bar while Danute worked here. We don't attract the sort of person likely to cause trouble. That type gravitates towards the bars and clubs where teenagers drink. That's where most of the fights break out."

"What can you tell us about Terry West?" asked Gus.

"I miss him," said Phoebe. "If you could see past the hard-drinking image he showed to almost everyone he met. Terry was a decent bloke who had suffered more tragedy than he could bear. I don't suppose Terry would ever have given up the drink and found his way back to a normal life, but he didn't deserve for it to end as it did. Terry was desperate to discover who killed Danute. Her murder was almost the last case he handled."

"We understand you saw Danute just once, here in Bath," said Alex. "That was in June, a few weeks after she left Nyx."

"That's right, on Milsom Street it was, although I couldn't get close enough to speak to her. But, despite the clothes she wore that day, she was still as pretty as ever and seemed cheerful. So on Friday night, I told Graham and Jerry I'd seen her. They were pleased to hear she looked well."

"You mentioned those names to DS Fry from Polebarn Road," said Gus, "but you failed to mention the cross-dressing. She visited Nyx with a friend one Saturday night, and two days later, you met for a coffee in the Abbey Courtyard."

"I remember that girl and the conversation we had. We discussed Terry and Danute. As for Graham and Jerry, that's nobody's business but theirs," said Phoebe. "Live and let live, I say, Mr Freeman. I don't see how it would have helped find Danute's killer, anyway."

"Only a couple of questions left, Ms Sawyer," said Gus. "Mr Hodges told us Danute was driven to work each evening by a friend from Trowbridge. Any idea who that was and where they might have worked?"

"I wondered how Danute planned to cover the unsocial hours we ask staff to work when she first came to speak to me. When she told us she lived in a Trowbridge flat with two other girls, I assumed one of them must work somewhere in Bath and forgot about it. We don't worry as long as they turn up on time, do the work as required, and don't develop sticky fingers. Danute never mentioned the woman's name nor where she worked. Although, I overheard her mention a restaurant to Graham and Jerry on one occasion."

"Danute left for home at different times, especially when you stayed open later," said Alex. "Did that ever cause problems?"

"No," said Phoebe. "Danute would ring her friend and give a time when she would leave. Then, I'd let her out the front door, watch her dash up the rise to North Parade and

see she got there safely. Her friend would be waiting. Danute said it took them twenty-five minutes to reach home."

"When was the last time you spoke to Terry West?" asked Gus.

"Several weeks before he died in that dreadful crash," said Phoebe. "If you've spoken to your colleague, she will have told you Terry was drinking more heavily in the weeks leading up to his death. Terry stopped coming here and drank at home, alone. When I spoke to him last, he was propped against the bar downstairs, nursing a double scotch. Terry mumbled something about not being able to make sense of the flowers Danute had been holding when I saw her near the Royal Crescent. When was that, exactly? Maybe at the end of February or early March 2015. Around six months after Manvers Street had made him take early retirement. The car accident happened on the eighteenth of September. He was driving towards Bath, and his brakes failed. His car was a wreck before it hit the wall. I'll be putting flowers on his grave on the anniversary again next Tuesday. Ironic, isn't it? If Terry had stopped fretting over those flowers' significance, he might not have been in the back of beyond that night."

"Did Terry ever share his ideas with you about why he thought the flowers were important?" asked Alex.

Phoebe shook her head.

"He was incoherent most of the time by then."

"Terry told no one where he was going that night?" asked Gus.

"He didn't tell me. Apart from the guy at the off-licence, I don't think he spoke to anyone in the weeks before he died."

"I wondered why you described the area as the back of beyond," said Gus.

"If he took a B road, it meant he was in the countryside, not the city or the suburbs. There are several villages out that way where he could have gone."

"Two colleagues will come here this evening to speak to Graham and Jerry," said Gus. "They'll know who to look out for now."

"I hope they're of the more understanding and sensitive breed of police officers," said Phoebe. "We don't want to upset two of our best customers."

"Oh, they will have been well-trained and briefed on what to expect," said Gus.

"Is that it, then?" asked Phoebe. "Don't you have any more questions?"

"Why?" asked Alex. "Is there something you think we haven't queried?"

"No, I don't think so," said Phoebe. She stood and collected their cups, and placed them on the tray. Then she tipped the mouldy contents on the plate into a waste bin beside Emily's desk.

Gus and Alex prepared to leave.

"I'll walk out with you," said Phoebe. "I don't start work until eight this evening. I might take a nap this afternoon; these late nights are catching up with me. You must know how that feels, Mr Freeman."

Gus could only remember a couple of occasions in the past six months when he'd not been in bed by midnight.

"Early to bed, early to rise, Ms Sawyer," said Gus.

They found David Hodges sitting at the bar reading a newspaper.

"Finished?" he asked.

"For now, Mr Hodges," said Alex. "Two of our team

will pay a brief visit this evening. We hoped there were other staff members from Danute's time still working here, but we'll content ourselves with a chat with Mr Davies and Mr Day."

"I'll see you later, David," said Phoebe. Hodges was already heading upstairs to the safety of his office.

As they stood in the passageway outside, Gus looked to his left towards North Parade.

"Did you watch Danute make her way to the street up there every night, Ms Sawyer?"

"The girls call me Mother Hen," said Phoebe. "I see everyone off the premises every night, Mr Freeman. The streets in any city are dangerous places in the early hours. Young girls are more at risk than most. I feel responsible for them. I need to know I've done everything possible to ensure they get home safe to their loved ones."

"Who makes sure you get home safe, Ms Sawyer?" asked Alex.

"Are you offering DS Hardy?" said Phoebe with a smile. "There's usually a staff member heading in my direction, and we keep one another company."

"Did Mr Hodges never offer to ferry a staff member home?" asked Gus.

"Never," said Phoebe. "Not because David doesn't care about their safety. His wife would kill him if she got in the car and smelt even a whiff of perfume. Where are you heading?"

"Manvers Street," said Alex.

"I'll say goodbye then," said Phoebe. "I'm off to North Parade. Goodbye."

Gus and Alex turned to head back the way they had come and soon emerged out of the dark passageway and into the sunlight.

"Make a note of that B road, Alex," said Gus. "We need a map of the area on the office wall at once."

"Got it, guv," said Alex. "It might narrow the search for Blessing's country hideaway."

"If that's what it was, Alex," said Gus. "I must admit, I'm leaning towards the notion Danute fell under the spell of a cult. However, I'll wager the charity malarkey was a smokescreen. Call Luke, and put him in the picture regarding tonight. I don't want Neil putting his foot in it."

Alex made the call as they made their way along Pierre-point Street. He drove them back to the Old Police Station office five minutes later.

Chapter Eleven

EARLIER THAT MORNING, at Polebarn Road in Trowbridge, Blessing Umeh had met DC George Collins. Blessing had panicked when she saw the parking bays outside the modern building. She was so like her father. If only Gus had given her time for a practice run.

Of course, there weren't many spare spaces when she got there just before nine. So she waited for the people who'd arrived several minutes ahead of her to disperse. Blessing hoped to park her little Nissan without mishap when the coast was clear.

As Blessing prepared to reverse for a second attempt, she heard a tap on the window.

"Are you having trouble, darling?"

Blessing stalled the car and glared at the tall man looming over her.

"Just leave me alone," said Blessing. "And I'm NOT your darling."

"Suit yourself," said the man.

Blessing watched him stroll across to the glass doors and disappear inside.

Once she'd started the car and calmed her nerves, Blessing parked successfully. Then, with a massive sigh of relief, she walked inside, got through reception, and received directions to a room at the rear of the building where DC Collins was waiting for her.

Blessing's heart sank when she looked through the glass panel on the door. Only one person sat inside, with his feet on a desk, staring out of the window—her tormentor from the car park.

"You must be George Collins," said Blessing as she entered the room. "I'm DC Blessing Umeh."

"You're not local, are you?" asked George.

"I was born near Warwick," said Blessing, "and I started as a police constable in Royal Leamington Spa. When my father moved to Bath University to work, I asked for a transfer to be near my parents."

George Collins slid his feet off the desk and sat up straight.

"How did you get a cushy gig with this Crime Review Team?" he asked.

"I had impressed my superiors in Leamington, and I was starting as a raw detective constable when one of Mr Freeman's team met me on a kidnapping case. Lydia Logan Barre recommended me to her boss. I moved south and loved every minute of my time with them."

"I wish I could get a transfer like that," said George, "I'm wasted here."

"Perhaps," said Blessing. "Have you got the relevant CCTV camera footage for us to view?"

"Do you need me to sit with you while you run through it?" asked George. "It's so boring."

"Are you always this negative?" said Blessing. "Do you ever wonder why you're still a DC four years after you worked on the Danute Zukas murder case?"

"Susannah and I slogged through reams of paperwork searching for that girl. We never found a thing. If you ask me, I don't think she was ever here in Trowbridge. I reckon she lived in Bath."

"Why would she tell her boss she lived here?" asked Blessing.

"These foreigners, you can't trust them. That Danute was probably working a benefits fiddle. She flew here, pleaded poverty, and got a council flat. Then she got a job, working nights, where she told everyone she lived in Trowbridge to cover her tracks. It wouldn't be the first time. If the council sent someone round her place to check on her, she'd be there during the day, acting as if she didn't have two pennies to rub together. Double bubble, she was on, I bet. We're a soft touch."

"How do you explain finding Danute on CCTV in Trowbridge just before she died?" asked Blessing.

"She was still working nights, wasn't she? A quarter to eleven at night, handing out stuff to everyone passing. Whoever she was working for when the camera caught her that night, you can guarantee it was her second income."

Blessing shook her head. George Collins was nothing like her ex-boyfriend, Dave Smith. She wished she could get up and walk out, but her parents had raised her to be better than that. It was essential to Gus that she checked this CCTV footage to answer his questions.

"Right," said Blessing. "Let's get started. Show me the images that made you suspect the girl on screen was the same girl on the photograph DI Cook received."

George swung into action like the turtle preparing to race the hare. Blessing sighed.

"The image is grainy, and the street lights aren't great on that corner," said George.

Blessing studied the image and nodded.

"That's the girl in the photo her mother supplied," said Blessing. "A little older, with a different hairstyle, but that's her. Can we use the original footage now to see if anyone else appears on that corner?"

"Loads of kids walked by her," said George. "It's a busy bar; people come and go all night."

"I mean, someone dressed the same as Danute. Someone carrying flowers or leaflets."

George searched for the footage where the image had been captured.

"How far back do you want to look?"

"Run it back slowly for fifteen minutes. Then return to the start point, and we'll check the fifteen minutes after you spotted Danute. Did you already do that?"

"Are you kidding? Cooky wanted to know if we had identified the murder victim. He didn't ask for anything else. We wasted enough time trying to find this flat where she was supposed to have lived."

Blessing studied the footage closely as George tapped his pencil on the tabletop and looked thoroughly bored. It was no use; nobody matched the description of the young girls she had hoped to see.

"Did you set up the relevant footage from the other cameras in the town centre?" asked Blessing.

"Yes, ma'am," said George. Blessing bit her tongue.

"Let's start at ten o'clock," said Blessing.

Blessing spotted George glancing at the clock on the wall in front of them.

"I'll work my way through the first few minutes," she said. "Why don't you get us a coffee? White, with one sugar for me, please."

"I need a fag," said George. "So, I'll be ten minutes, okay?"

Blessing was concentrating on the screen.

Fifteen minutes later, George was back with two coffees.

"Find anything?" he asked.

Blessing turned the screen towards him.

"Which camera covers the streets just beyond the top left corner of the screen? Can you see that girl there, crossing the road?"

"You're joking," said George. "We can only see her from the waist down."

"Yes, but the girls we're interested in will dress the same as Danute, and that girl is wearing a plain dress with sandals on her feet. The same sandals as Danute."

George found the right camera footage and cued it up to start from around ten o'clock.

"Well, I'm blowed," he said.

As soon as the images moved, four young women appeared. They stood in a group, chatted for a few seconds, and then split up.

"There's Danute," said Blessing, "making her way to her designated spot on the corner. The others will have occupied positions with the greatest footfall. They have flowers, and the leaflets are probably in those bags they carry around their necks."

"We couldn't see that bag," said George. "Danute had one on her left-hand side, hidden from the camera. I didn't realise the mark's significance or shadow on her right shoulder. It was the thin leather strap securing the bag."

"Can you get me the best close-up images of the other three girls, please, George?" asked Blessing.

"Will that be it?" asked George.

"No. I want to send a message to DS Sherman back at the office. He might have an update for me, but the sooner he knows we're on the right track, the better."

"How does this CCTV stuff help, anyway?" asked George.

"Danute may have been vulnerable," said Blessing. "A young woman, a thousand miles from home. Her family were devout Roman Catholics. Maybe Danute rebelled and started searching for a different way."

"Drugs, you mean?" asked George.

"The body didn't show any signs, George. Don't you remember anything? We can't rule out someone controlling Danute with drugs, which might explain how she looked in that image. But there are other ways to get people working in unison like those four girls on the footage we both watched."

"God botherers," said George, clicking his fingers.

"I wouldn't have put it that way, George," said Blessing. "Why? Are you aware of such an organisation in Trowbridge? Please don't tell me you've had the answer to this mystery all along."

"Look, I'm not stupid," said George. "I know what's going on in my town. We've got the usual denominations, and until fifty years ago, that was enough for anyone who wanted to follow a religion. But, since we opened our doors to people from four corners of the world, they brought in different ideas, and they established different types of churches because the traditional sort doesn't cut it."

Blessing knew her parents would be horrified.

"The Quakers and the Latter-Day Saints were here

years ago," said George, "but two of the newer churches focus on the communities in which they are housed. I don't suppose they have many in the congregation, but they still worship the same God."

"Are you a believer, George?" asked Blessing. "Do you go to church?"

"Not me. I don't always get a Sunday off, but there are a hundred places I would rather be if I do. None of it fits in with what you're looking for, does it?"

"Not really," said Blessing. "Are you sure you missed no one out?"

"I can't think of any other religious buildings," said George. "Although, something could be happening in one of the halls or meeting rooms dotted around town. We've got loads of those. A few years back, there was a storm in a teacup over an old church hall used for yoga classes. A local vicar didn't think it appropriate."

"If you could give me a list of those, that would be useful," said Blessing.

"You don't want much, do you?" moaned George.

"I want to help find out who murdered Danute Zukas," said Blessing. "Are you sure you didn't miss a clue when checking those rental addresses?"

"Look, if her name was Smith, Jones, or Patel, it might have slipped past us. How many people called Zukas do you know? And Danute isn't a name I can recall hearing in the school playground. No, an unfamiliar name should have sprung off the page, and it didn't."

"I wonder why?" said Blessing. "Perhaps the person who owned the flat didn't want people to know they were renting out rooms."

"If they were, we had no chance," said George. "We could only check records from registered addresses and anything I had traced through legwork and social media. Traipsing around newsagents and community noticeboards, taking details of private individuals advertising a spare room was a right pain. Like everything else, it didn't answer where Danute lived for the first year after getting here."

"I'd better get back to the office," said Blessing. "Can you email me the information I've asked for, please?"

"Whatever," said George.

Blessing left him staring out the window and went outside to her car. As she drove out of Trowbridge, Blessing wondered whether anything she had learned would help Gus find Danute's killer.

ALEX TURNED into the car park behind the Old Police Station as Blessing Umeh reversed her Nissan into one of the two empty reserved spaces.

"That's better," said Gus. "Blessing's getting the hang of it at last."

"Mmm," said Alex, "assuming that was her first attempt."

Blessing spotted Alex's car and gave them a wave. She waited for her colleagues before taking the lift to the first floor.

"Any good news, Blessing?" asked Gus.

"George Collins is sending through CCTV images we found of Danute Zukas and three colleagues, guv," said Blessing. "Whether they were the same girls spotted in Bath, I don't know, but they were dressed similarly to Danute, and each had leaflets in a shoulder bag and carried flowers. They arrived together on foot. Someone could have dropped them off in the town centre, and they went their separate ways to cover as wide an area as possible. DC

Collins went through the various religious denominations that populate the town. I didn't get the impression any of them were behind the girls in question. But he's sending a list of several halls and places rented out for meetings. If Trowbridge had a quasi-religious organisation between 2012 and 2014, we might track it that way."

"How did you two youngsters get on?" asked Alex.

"We didn't," said Blessing.

"Never mind," said Gus. "You've moved things forward a tad. Those meeting rooms could be useful, and if we can identify either of the girls with Danute, we'll soon be on the right road. I'm sure of it."

They travelled up in the lift and were greeted by a glum-looking trio.

"Can you give me a progress report, please, Luke?" asked Gus.

"Lydia and I have searched high and low for employment records for Danute Zukas, guv," he replied. "She didn't register with any local employment agencies for temporary work. Although we haven't spoken to employers in the surrounding towns, we drew a blank as far as Trowbridge itself."

"Right, while I think of it," said Gus, "Lydia, can you dig out a map covering the B3110 from Bath to wherever it runs, please? DI Terry West had a reason to be on the Hinton Charterhouse road the night he died. It had something to do with Danute Zukas and those blessed flowers."

"On it, guv," said Lydia. "It will be good to feel I'm doing something useful."

"DI West was searching for the sect's secret hideaway," said Blessing.

"I'm more convinced than ever you were on the right track, Blessing," said Gus. "The girls George Collins helped you find on CCTV are the key. Those images should give us every chance of finally pinning down where Danute disappeared after she left Nyx and why."

"We're assuming whoever's behind this group was responsible for Danute's death," said Neil. "That doesn't have to be the case, guv, does it? When those girls were spotted in Bath, they looked happy and relaxed. Although Danute didn't look as lively by July the twelfth, two years later, there was no sign of anyone forcing her to stand on that street corner. We need more."

"What did the mobile phone checks throw up, Neil?" asked Gus.

"Zilch," said Neil. "We knew Natasha hadn't heard from Danute since March in 2012, and when they tried to contact her, the phone was out of service. I've analysed the call logs, and one number here in the UK cropped up frequently. The name on the contact list was Laura. I've tried the number, but it's no longer available. People change phones so often these days, guv, with the advent of smartphones. They aren't as attached to a number as our parents were to their landlines."

"David Hodges told us they tried to call Danute after she quit," said Alex. "She didn't collect the wages owed to her. Her phone was out of service as soon as she left Nyx, if not before. Laura could be Danute's landlady. We know this girl worked in Bath and took Danute to and from work. Danute called her every night to say she was ready to leave. That's why her number showed up so often."

"Were there any other regular calls, Neil?" asked Gus.

"No, guv," said Neil.

"Where do we go from here, guv?" asked Lydia.

"Luke and Neil will chat to Graham Davies and Jerry Day in Nyx at nine this evening," said Gus. "There's something you need to be aware of, and Alex will fill you in before we leave here today. In the meantime, we'll update the Freeman Files with the results of our labours this morning. Once Lydia has found our map, we'll identify likely locations Danute was between May 2012 and July 2014. We might have a long list, but we have to start somewhere.

For the next two hours, everyone was busy. Lydia removed the existing map showing Trowbridge and the surrounding district. She had little to contribute to the digital files; Luke had covered most of the items they'd worked on earlier. At three o'clock, Lydia took a break and returned from the restroom with a tray of coffees.

"I was ready for this," said Gus. "It's hours since we had a cuppa at Nyx. Thanks, Lydia."

"The map's ready when you are, guv," she replied.

The team gathered at the far end of the room at twenty-past three under the clock.

"Right," said Gus, "let's get our bearings. Terry West lived next to the off-licence on Bear Flat. We know that. If we look at the route he took to return home, it suggests he went as far as Hinton Charterhouse. The B3110 runs from the city and wends its way towards Shepton Mallet. The Romans didn't build that road. Look at how it zig-zags across the countryside."

"How do we know Terry West wasn't searching on the other side of the B3110, guv?" asked Luke.

"Terry West passed the case over to Polebarn Road because he believed the murder took place in Wiltshire," said Gus. "In two years, they hadn't found a murder site, and Terry couldn't let it rest. No, I believe he chose the B3110 for two reasons. First, it was the nearest road out of the city to get him near the Wiltshire border; and second, he'd been drinking. The A36 Warminster road is a major route, so Terry stuck to the quieter back roads."

"The county border isn't a straight line either, guv," said Blessing.

"That it isn't, Blessing," said Gus. "Look at these small villages here. Freshford is just over the border in Somerset, while places like Westwood, Lower Westwood, and Avoncliff are in West Wiltshire, only two miles away. That gives us an idea of our Bermuda Triangle. Danute Zukas disappeared in that locality in late Spring of 2012."

"A simple task to drive from there to join the A36," said Luke, "a road which runs through Limpley Stoke to Bath.

"Danute's body was found five miles away in a field on the same road," said Neil.

"Terry West was close," said Lydia.

"Maybe too close," said Gus. "We're not there yet. We need another search carried out, I'm afraid. Look for properties sold since 2010 and discover what purpose they're being put to today. Don't bother with small houses or bungalows. We want large, detached properties with land attached. Whoever we're dealing with will want isolation and maximum privacy."

The team spent the rest of the afternoon checking estate agency details online. One by one, possible suspects appeared on a list beside the map on the wall.

Alex spoke with Luke and Neil just before five o'clock. Gus listened in, and as expected, Luke took the news in his stride. However, he thought Neil looked nervous.

Gus asked Alex if everything was set for tonight as the office emptied.

"Yes, guv," said Alex. "Neil worried about the other customers' reaction."

"What did you say?" asked Gus.

"I told him to concentrate on finding where this Laura worked. If she's still there, they should leave Nyx and interview her without delay. If not, ask the hotel or restaurant for her contact details. Laura's our best hope for a lead, and as Neil discovered her phone went out of service at roughly the same time as Danute's, Laura could have disappeared too."

"You could be right, Alex," said Gus, "but we haven't found another body, so let's pray she's safe and well."

"What did you think of Neil's comment, guv?" asked Lydia, who was waiting for her partner.

"That there might be another player in the game? No, once we discover who was behind Danute leaving Nyx to hand out flowers and leaflets, I believe we'll have found our killer."

"A lot hangs on what happens tonight, guv," said Alex.

"Then there are the follow-ups on the list of properties we've identified so far," said Lydia.

Gus picked up the phone and rang London Road.

"Vera Butler's phone," came the reply.

"Who's that?" asked Gus.

"DI Packenham," replied Amazing Grace. Just what he needed.

"Has DS Mercer left yet?" asked Gus.

"I saw his car leave the car park at a quarter to five," said Grace.

Oh dear, a black mark for Geoff, thought Gus.

"I don't suppose Kenneth Truelove is there? I need permission for my team to work overtime. We're on the verge of closing a case."

Gus could hear the tutting as Grace Packenham looked across the administration office to the Chief Constable's door.

"He's just leaving," said Grace.

Gus waited as Grace covered the phone's mouthpiece and called out to the Chief Constable. Seconds later, Kenneth Truelove got handed the phone.

"What's up, Freeman?"

"Sorry to bother you, sir. We're close to solving the Zukas case, but it would help our cause if we could tie up more loose ends tomorrow. Is overtime allowed?"

"Go ahead, Freeman. I have every faith in you and the team. We'll talk first thing on Monday in my office. Mrs Yadav gave me details of two more murders late this afternoon with a potential link to our man Jones. I hope to hear good news from you on Monday, and then we must decide how to bring this other matter to a swift conclusion."

"I'll be there, sir," said Gus. "Many thanks, and have a good weekend."

"Good hunting, Freeman," said the Chief Constable.

Kenneth ended the call without giving Gus the opportunity for a friendly chat with Amazing Grace.

Gus sat in the office alone for a few minutes, wondering about those poor victims of Stan Jones's warped mind. No doubt Divya had filled the two missing gaps in the November killings and confirmed their suspicion someone would die in two months if they couldn't locate the long-distance lorry driver.

Gus closed his computer, tidied the files on his desk, and made his way to the lift with a sigh. He sent Geoff Mercer a quick text message at the lift door. He notified him of the need for overtime this weekend and asked Geoff for a huge favour.

Sometimes you have to go with your gut.

As he descended to the ground floor, Gus remembered what he had promised to do this morning. Before leaving the car park, he called Suzie and told her he'd collect her from the London Road HQ in thirty minutes.

"You were later returning from Bath than you thought, I suppose?" she said when she slipped into the passenger seat beside him.

"Not at all," said Gus. "After Alex and I had spoken to David Hodges and Phoebe Sawyer, we had several new pieces of the jigsaw. When we got back to the office, Blessing's news from Polebarn Road allowed us to see where to fit those pieces. We're closer to the truth now. Sadly, we need to continue following our new leads tomorrow."

"Not to worry," said Suzie. "I can't ride my horse for a while, but he still demands care and attention. So I'll spend the morning at the farm and wait for a call to say you've finished for the day."

Gus turned into the gateway at the bungalow fifteen minutes later.

"That wasn't as bad as we feared," said Suzie. "I might risk driving to work on Monday morning."

"Up to you," said Gus as they walked into the hallway, "but I'm meeting Kenneth first thing. Divya unearthed two more murders. I haven't learned whether they were on the continent or here in the UK, but I'd be surprised if they didn't occur in November 2014 and 2017."

"How horrible," said Suzie. "That guy Jones has to be stopped."

"I think Gablecross should step up the surveillance on Richard Chaloner's widow and friends," said Gus. "Even if Jones never strikes outside November, he could still visit Swindon to plan his next attack."

"I'm going to shower and change," said Suzie. "That will give you time to decide where you're taking me for a meal tonight. If I can't see you for much of tomorrow, I need to be spoiled."

"I'll give it thought," said Gus, "but first, I need to phone the others to break the bad news. Alex and I only decided to keep the pressure on after the others had left."

Suzie dropped her keys and handbag on the hall table and went to the bathroom. Gus went to their bedroom, and after hanging his jacket in the wardrobe, he sat on the end of the bed and made his phone calls.

Gus wandered through to the lounge and sat, waiting for Suzie to emerge from the bathroom. Then, the team's replies buzzed on his phone one by one. Everyone would be in the office at nine in the morning—one more call to make.

The Fox & Hounds landlord was happy to hear from him, and Gus agreed that eight-fifteen was a perfect time to eat.

Suzie left the bathroom and disappeared into the bedroom. Gus popped his head around the door to give her the news.

"Eight-fifteen at the Fox & Hounds," he said. "Will that please, milady?"

"Terrific," said Suzie.

After Gus had taken his turn in the shower and dressed, he found Suzie sitting in the lounge. They spent the next hour going over the events of the day and flicking through TV channels, hoping to find something other than a repeat.

"I hope the schedules change before I'm sat at home with our little one," said Suzie.

"You couldn't take your eyes off the screen on Wednesday," said Gus. "I don't think you'll need to worry over something to watch."

Saturday, 15 September 2018

SUZIE WAS STILL SLEEPING at half-past seven when Gus padded towards the bathroom. The meal at the Fox & Hounds never disappointed, and it had been good to spend the evening alone. If he could tear himself away from the case by late afternoon, Gus promised Suzie they would catch up with their friends at the Lamb tonight.

Gus left the bungalow at a quarter past eight and prepared to battle the roadworks on London Road. The traffic lights sequencing appeared to favour oncoming traffic, and Gus tapped the steering wheel in frustration as he inched his way past the Wiltshire Police HQ. Once he had turned right, after passing the brewery, it was plain sailing. Gus parked the Focus behind the Old Police Station at five minutes to nine.

Luke and Neil had beaten him here. He rode up in the lift to find them with an early morning coffee.

"Late night, lads?" he asked.

"We can take it, guv," said Neil.

"Would you care to guess what we found out, guv?" said Luke.

"Let's wait for the others," said Gus. "We could do with hearing good news. I'm hoping it *is* good news?"

"I think so, guv," said Luke. "We found most of the missing pieces of our jigsaw."

Chapter Twelve

ALEX, Lydia and Blessing soon joined them, and Gus urged Luke and Neil to start their story from nine o'clock last night.

"We took your advice, Alex," said Luke, "and parked in Manvers Street car park. Then we found the alley leading to Nyx without mishap."

"Not the brightest lighting I've ever seen," said Neil. "I was glad Luke came with me."

"Once we got inside, it was obvious Friday nights are one of their busiest nights of the week," said Luke. "We went to the bar. A young girl called Sophie served us, and an older woman smiled and nodded in my direction."

"Phoebe Sawyer," said Alex. "Even in plain clothes, you two look like detectives when we have a night out at the Waggon & Horses."

"I looked for a spare table," said Neil, "but apart from one on the far side, there was nothing, so we stood at the side and waited."

"Graham and Jerry arrived at nine o'clock," said Luke.

"Sophie was preparing their drinks before they reached the bar."

"You recognised them?" asked Blessing.

"Only because of the wigs," said Luke. "It wasn't their first rodeo, Blessing, so looking good in a dress and heels is something they've perfected. Unfortunately, their budget doesn't stretch to the finest hairpieces. Anyway, they weren't why we were at Nyx. We wanted to learn what they remembered of Danute and whether they knew Laura."

"As Jerry paid Sophie for the drinks, Phoebe had a quiet word with Graham and pointed us out," said Neil. "Graham came over and introduced himself as Gloria and invited us to join him and Jane at their table."

"The only spare table in the seating area," said Luke. "Everyone knows to stay clear on Friday's because that's their spot."

"Jane joined us, and we started chatting," said Neil. "I told them we were on the trail of Danute's killer. Gloria and Jane were in tune with everyone else you've spoken to. They adored Danute, thought she was a lovely girl and were heartbroken when Phoebe broke the news four years ago. They hadn't seen or heard from her after she left Nyx."

"When I asked about Laura," said Luke. "They knew who I meant straight away. Laura Boyd works in a hotel in Queen Square, a ten-minute walk away. Laura often dropped into Nyx, out of uniform, in the months before Danute started there. So it was more than likely Laura had been there the night Moira had her meltdown and quit. We said we wanted to speak to Laura to learn whether she had been Danute's landlady."

"Gloria said Laura changed shifts once Danute started working at the bar," said Neil. "Laura was working later, which meant the two of them could go home together.

Danute had confirmed to them that Laura had offered her, and another girl, a room at her place."

"They said Laura lived in Trowbridge, guv," said Luke. "Although, they didn't know the address. The third girl was from Poland. Danute told Jane her name was Natalia."

"I didn't think we could learn much more, guv," said Neil. "So I suggested to Luke that we try the hotel in Queen Square."

"You could always go back to Nyx next Friday, Neil, " said Alex.

"I thought it would be one of the stranger interviews I've done," said Neil, "but once the conversation flowed, it felt normal."

"That can't be all the good news, Luke," said Gus. "Were you in luck when you reached the hotel?"

"We spoke to one of the assistant managers, and she fetched Laura Boyd," said Luke. "they showed us into a side room where we could speak with Laura away from the guests. Laura's twenty-nine still lives in Trowbridge but only has one flatmate these days. That's her partner, Natalia Wozniak. Natalia is twenty-seven and works at the checkout at Tesco."

"The first thing we noticed was Laura always referred to her flatmates as Danni and Nat," said Neil. "Laura met Nat in the supermarket, and a casual conversation led to the Polish girl asking if Laura knew anyone renting a room. The landlord where she lived with other girls who'd flown into Bristol from Warsaw had wandering hands."

"How long was Natalia living with Laura before Danute came on the scene?" asked Gus.

"They weren't together in that way at the beginning, guv," said Neil. "Natalia was there for the best part of a year before Danute joined them."

"When did the relationship start?" asked Alex.

"Soon after Danute died," said Luke. "We'll get to that later."

"Danute didn't tell David Hodges her address when she met him," said Neil, "and she didn't appear to have a bank account. Well, that was due to Laura. She admitted to us she persuaded Danni and Nat to pay her in cash and keep their financial arrangements quiet."

"There were never any adverts," said Lydia, "and no links to a letting agency or any of the registered landlords. Laura hid the income from the tax man. That explains why Trowbridge Police couldn't find a trace of Danute."

"Neighbour's wouldn't have heard Danute and Natalia's names mentioned either," said Blessing, "if Laura called them Danni and Nat."

"Carry on, Luke," said Gus, "I sense there's more."

"Yes, guv," said Luke. "Laura said the first nine months went fine. She drove the two of them backwards and forwards to Bath. Danute told Laura she was in touch with her sister. There were things Danute wasn't comfortable with here in the UK. Although she was happy at work and had made friends with the staff and several customers, something was missing."

"Danute spent a lot of time in church while living in Kaunas," said Gus.

"The unsocial hours didn't help in that regard, guv," said Luke. "Then, at the end of February, or early March in 2012, they met a guy called Simeon Lane in Trowbridge. The three girls were walking into town from Gloucester Road one Saturday lunchtime. Simeon stood on the street corner opposite Holy Trinity Church, handing out leaflets to younger people passing. Natalia paused as Laura and Danute tried to get by him, and Simeon grabbed Natalia's arm. He thrust a leaflet into her hand and asked her how she could bear living in a world so obsessed with possessions and empty promises. Laura and Danute went back to rescue their friend, and Simeon invited Natalia to join him tomorrow at a meeting hall just around the corner on Stallard Street. He promised her many other young people would be there, eager to find a better way. Let me lead you out of the darkness, into the sunlight. That was what Laura told us this Simeon character kept saying to them."

"So, the grooming began in Trowbridge, not at Nyx," said Gus.

"The girls eventually got away from Simeon," said Neil. "Another group of younger teenagers were coming out of town, heading home, and he engaged them in conversation. The following day, Natalia suggested they attend the meeting. Just once, she said, what's the harm? We'll learn more about what's involved, and there could be young people we'd want to know better."

"The hall was only a ten-minute walk from Laura's flat," said Luke. "They walked up a narrow lane between two buildings. Another young couple was just behind them. The doors to the building were open, and they could hear chanting. Inside they found two dozen people between fifteen and around thirty years old."

"What were they chanting?" asked Blessing.

"Out of the darkness, into the sunlight," said Luke.

"Then Simeon appeared on the stage at the end of the hall," said Neil. "He wore a white robe, and Laura thought how handsome he looked. Simeon had charisma, she told us and was always smiling. She looked around the room, and everyone's eyes were fixed on him."

"Simeon told them the modern world was darkness," said Luke. "The only way to bring sunlight into their lives was to join with his brothers and sisters. Behind him, three boys and three girls appeared from the back of the stage, also dressed in white robes. They carried flowers and handed a single red rose to each congregation member."

"What happened next?" asked Blessing. "It sounds spooky. I would have run outside."

"That's because you still have your faith, Blessing," said Gus. "Many young people feel lost and are drifting. Nobody ever offered them something to believe in, to belong to; that's what a creep like Simeon Lane relies on to lure them in."

"Laura told us the six members they met called one another brother and sister," said Neil. "They took great care in their appearance. The brothers were clean-shaven with short, tidy hair, no piercings or tattoos. As for the sisters, their hair was straight and shoulder length. They wore little make-up."

"The girls stayed a while longer, but Laura wanted to get into town," said Luke. "They had shopping to do and a meal to cook."

"When did they return to the hall?" asked Lydia.

"The following Sunday," said Neil, "and this time, after hearing the same chanting and receiving another red rose, they were invited to join the group."

"What was the group called?" asked Alex.

"The Haven," said Luke and Neil.

"Simeon stood at the front of the stage," said Luke. "His brothers and sisters mingled with the small group of people happy to join."

"Brother Simeon said he believed mobile phones were responsible for the world's evils," said Neil. "They were banned for those who wanted to become members of The Haven. He told anyone at the front of the hall truly ready to join them to take their phones and place them on the wooden floor. Then they chanted his favourite phrase and stamped on their phones and smashed them. Their new brothers and sisters surrounded them, smiling from ear to ear, and handed them a white robe."

"That explains why Natasha couldn't contact her sister," said Blessing.

"It also explains why David Hodges couldn't get hold of Danute to arrange payment of the money they owed her," said Lydia.

"Hang on," said Gus. "Did the three girls smash their phones and join the group that day?"

"No, just Danute," said Luke. "Natalia didn't want to lose her new smartphone, and Laura was starting to doubt the group was as innocent as it appeared."

"Laura sounded a switched-on young woman, guv," said Neil. "The penny dropped that it was a dodgy outfit during that second visit. When they first met Simeon, he dressed like a normal bloke. I made a note of what she said. 'How could anyone distinguish a member of The Haven from a normal person? They wore the same clothes as you and I and acted normal, but their sole purpose was to brainwash young people like Danute. I watched them in that meeting hall engaging their target in casual conversation, and before you knew it, another victim had abandoned their family and friends. They wouldn't listen to reason.' We reread the murder file notes before we went to Nyx last night. Danute's mother had raised her daughters to be careful in crowds and not to talk to strangers, especially those who seemed over-friendly. Yet that silver-tongued devil had convinced Danute to join him at The Haven in no time flat."

"I thought you said Danute joined The Haven," said Lydia.

"The meeting hall was just that, Lydia," said Gus. "The Haven is the secret hideaway where the brothers and sisters spend their time recruiting new members when they're not on the streets."

"Laura told us she could trust none of them, not completely," said Luke. "Who has a smile on their face all the time? It's not natural."

"The only family those brothers and sisters ever mentioned during those meetings was the one they lived with at The Haven," said Neil. "Nobody had any contact with parents, relatives, or friends from their life before meeting Brother Simeon."

"So, after that Sunday meeting, when did they see Danute again?" asked Gus.

"Not until Sunday the thirteenth of July in 2014, guv," said Luke.

"Hold that thought for a while," said Gus. "Let's start the property search I mentioned yesterday afternoon. We know roughly where we'll find this hideaway. I want to check it out, have a word with DS Mercer, and then a raid is in order."

"We don't have any evidence of a crime yet, guv," said Lydia.

Gus thumped the desk with a fist.

"If Danute's murder isn't connected to The Haven, I'll rip up my consultant's card and retire to my allotment."

"You haven't heard everything Laura told us yet, Lydia," said Luke.

"Neil, can you hunt potential sites for The Haven?" asked Gus. "Blessing, can you help him, please?"

Blessing joined Neil at the far end of the room while the others gathered around Gus's desk.

"Please continue, Luke," said Gus.

"When Laura said Sunday, that was because she was in Trowbridge town centre late on Saturday night with Natalia. Laura's shift patterns had altered since 2012, and the pair had been enjoying a night out. As they left a bar at around half-past midnight, they spotted Danute walking alone. They shouted out and ran to speak to her. Laura could tell at once Danute was nervous. She constantly looked over Laura's shoulder and told them someone was waiting for her. She would get punished for being late."

"Danute was supposed to meet the other three girls at a pickup point," said Alex, "to be driven back to The Haven."

"Exactly," said Luke. "Brother Ralph was the one Danute feared. Natalia asked Danute whether she regretted joining the group or were she and Laura silly not to trust Simeon Lane and his promise of a better way. Danute explained that Brother James or Brother Ralph took them out on Friday and Saturday evenings at the start. They showed them how to raise funds for the cause. Young couples walking on the street or seated together in pubs were easy prey. The girls carried single red roses they'd made during the week. They had to persuade the man his wife or girlfriend needed this artificial flower. A pound coin was a small price for flirting with him and hinting at what his partner would do to him later."

"Gross," said Lydia.

"It gets worse," said Luke. "Danute told them after she'd been at The Haven for a month, Brother Simeon called for her. It was time for Sister Danute to take a further step closer to the sunlight. He told her what they did in love was good and encouraged her to have sex with others in the group after sleeping with him. Simeon was happy for single girls to sleep together until they found male partners. He said it wasn't fair they should feel lonely and unloved.

Simeon encouraged any married couples that had joined the group to share their partners with housemates of the opposite sex."

"Was Danute a willing partner in this, Luke?" asked Alex.

"Laura believed in the first few months, Danute got swept along with the feeling of belonging. Her companions at The Haven provided something missing in her life since she'd left home. Danute was a virgin when entering The Haven. Remember how charismatic Laura said Simeon was? It's easy to imagine Danute believing he thought she was special and went with him willingly. In the months that followed, she realised the truth. Suddenly, Natalia spotted a tall, clean-shaven man in a dark suit standing twenty yards away under a street light. Danute thrust leaflets in their hands and rushed towards him. As she passed Laura, she whispered, 'Tomorrow. The meeting hall' and she and Brother Ralph disappeared towards Fore Street."

"Where is that on the map?" asked Gus.

Lydia retrieved the street map she'd taken off the wall yesterday.

"If we're right about The Haven being in the area you described as the Bermuda Triangle, then they could have been heading in that direction," said Lydia. "The first time the girls saw Simeon Lane was by Holy Trinity Church. Fore Street would lead you straight to the church, and then it's first right onto the A363 Bradford Road. So it's a quick hop to the villages we're interested in."

"What happened the next day?" asked Gus.

"Laura and Natalia went to the meeting hall," said Luke. "The set-up was the same. The room was filled with youngsters persuaded to attend by the girls the night before. Danute joined her friends, and they had to endure the chanting and accept a red rose while listening to more of Danute's story. She told them the group hadn't returned to Trowbridge for months because the bars and restaurants got wise as soon as they saw girls with flowers on the premises. Many places sent them packing. Brother Simeon tried to get around that with fake accreditation on lanyards they wore around their necks for a while, but it was easier to move to another town. Danute wanted to leave The Haven, but her sisters warned her nobody had ever left. Those that had tried got punished. Brother Simeon expected everyone to share their love with him, and Danute learned from her sisters that their first night together had been filmed. It was Simeon's insurance against anybody leaving and revealing what went on behind the walls of The Haven. After Danute had lived at The Haven for a year, Simeon suggested she could attract more new members with her body than with flowers. That shattered any dreams of a special relationship. So when Brother Ralph or Brother James next drove her into town, her mission was to pick up men for sex. Her companions, Sister Monica, Helen, and Mary, had been told the same. When Danute complained that what they were asked to do was wrong, Sister Monica said it was not that big a deal as she already had more sex than in a regular relationship. If they couldn't persuade the men to return to The Haven with them, they had to get them to contribute financially. Danute went along with it initially but soon realised the danger she faced. She wanted to escape. Could Laura and Natalia help her?"

The room fell quiet.

"Something went wrong," said Alex. "Danute was on the verge of escaping the dreadful life they forced her to live. Then, within hours, she was dead."

"Brother Simeon made The Haven sound safe for

young people to find themselves," said Lydia. "To find something to believe in, but he just wanted to sleep with dozens of young women and get them to use their bodies to finance his lifestyle. What a creep."

"What happened, Luke?" asked Gus.

"Brother James realised Danute was spending far too long with two girls whose faces he recognised. He insisted they left the meeting hall and led Danute away."

"Did they see Danute again?" asked Lydia.

"Briefly," said Luke. "Laura and Natalia walked home, discussing whether they should call the police. Minutes later, they heard a knock at the door. It was Danute, with two men, Brother James and Brother Ralph. Brother James said their sister wanted to apologise for lying to them; she was happy at The Haven. Laura could tell Danute was frightened, but Brother Ralph squeezed her arm hard, and Danute said she didn't want to leave the group. They were mistaken and must have misheard her. Brother James led Danute to the car. Brother Ralph took a step forward and leaned over the girls. He's well over six feet tall, according to Laura. He reminded them what a dark world they lived in; it would be so easy to get lost. I know it's corny, but he said, 'We know where you live' as he walked to the car."

"So, Brother James and Ralph returned Danute to The Haven in the early afternoon of Sunday," said Gus. "I wonder what form the punishment usually took. The injuries to her head and torso were severe. Someone lost control. Danute died, and whoever was involved in her murder had to get rid of the body. They left The Haven, drove to Claverton, and dumped the body in a ditch. We have three suspects, the two henchmen, and the cult leader himself."

"If only Laura and Natalia had called the police straight away," said Lydia.

"Danute could have been dead before they found where she'd gone," said Alex. "The girls didn't get a hint of its whereabouts from Danute."

"Why didn't Laura and Natalia come forward after learning about Danute's death?" asked Lydia.

"Laura was in no doubt Brother Ralph would follow through on his threat," said Luke. "She and Natalia agreed to stay together to protect one another. They grew closer from that day forward and have been lovers for the past eighteen months."

"Anything else?" asked Gus.

"Laura asked whether we'd report her, and Neil said we'd leave it to our boss."

Gus made a mental note to file that query alongside the one relating to Eve Chaloner and then called out to Neil.

"Any progress, Neil?"

"Two possible properties, guv," said Neil. "The first is near Lye Green, Upper Westwood. That's a manor house with outbuildings and seven acres of land. It sold for three-quarters of a million in 2010 to a company called Fraser Holdings."

"The manor house is four miles from the field where Danute's body was found, guv," said Blessing.

"The second is near Avoncliff, guv, maybe half a mile further from the field but more secluded," said Neil. "It's a square horseshoe-shaped building facing north towards the river and situated at the western end of Avoncliff. It's a three-storey property built as a group of weavers' cottages during the late eighteenth century. There have been various occupants over the centuries; for a while, it was a hotel, and during WWII, the British Museum stored valuable artefacts in the basement. Several private owners have made improvements to the interior since those days, and when it sold in the Summer of 2011, it fetched upwards of three million."

"How many people could live in a place like that, Neil?" asked Gus.

"Well, I don't know about today. Health & Safety would have a few words to say, but in the mid-nineteenth century, when it was a Poor House, the building held over two hundred wretched souls."

"That's our hideaway," said Gus. "Did you discover who bought the property in 2011, Neil?"

"Lane, Gibbons & Gee, guv," said Neil.

"Are you sure they weren't the solicitors?" asked Lydia.

"Simeon Lane," said Gus, "take your pick between Brother Ralph and Brother James for the other surnames."

"What do we do now, guv?" asked Blessing.

Gus looked at the clock on the wall behind her.

"We take two cars, carry out a brief recce of the approaches to the property, and four of us return to the office while Alex and Lydia keep watch. Before we leave, I'll give DS Mercer a call to arrange a dawn wake-up call in Avoncliff."

"Will someone relieve us later, guv?" asked Alex.

"Don't worry. You don't need to stay out there all night. If we're happy the group still operates out of The Haven, you can leave after you've watched the brothers and sisters leave for whichever town's on their schedule tonight. We don't want to risk getting spotted and spooking them. I can rely on you two to convince them you're a courting couple enjoying the benefits of the countryside. Then, once clear of the property, report in and head home."

"Got it, guv," said Alex.

"Right," said Gus. "I'd better get hold of DS Mercer and make another big dent in his budget."

Geoff Mercer had just returned from Marlborough; he and Christine had been looking at carpets for their new home. So, for once, he was happy to hear from Gus.

"I assume you have news, Gus?"

"We're leaving to carry out surveillance on a property near Avoncliff, Geoff," said Gus. "I'll let you know the lay of the land later today. I expect the people we're after to be inside the building overnight."

"You want me to send a team with a big red key and an early wake-up call, I presume?"

"As many bodies as you can spare," said Gus. "We don't know yet how many will be inside. We hope to discover that later. Over half of the people inside the house will be young women, and three men might not want to come quietly."

"I have no trouble getting volunteers for that raid," said Geoff. "Leave it with me."

"Any luck with the other matter?" asked Gus, crossing his fingers.

"Everything's on track, Gus," said Geoff. "What are you and the team doing tomorrow morning?"

"We'll drive over to interview the three prime suspects as soon as we hear the building is secure. I want to do that before your guys ferry them to the custody suite on the edge of town. If my guess is right, it could save time later."

"I'll warn the Armed Response Team Leader you'll be on your way as soon as he gives the all-clear."

"Many thanks, Geoff. Enjoy the rest of the afternoon."

Gus ended the call.

"Are we ready to leave?" he asked.

"I'll drive the second car," said Luke. "Neil and Blessing can ride with me."

"That sounds like you're stuck with me, Alex," said Gus. "Don't worry. I'll sit in the back and keep quiet."

Gus paused at the entrance to the lift.

"Okay, guv?" asked Neil.

"I've never looked at that brass plate on the wall before," said Gus. "Suitable for eight persons; we've never had cause to use the lift together before. So now's our chance to see whether the manufacturers' claims are justified."

The team travelled to the ground floor together without mishap.

Twenty-five minutes later, they parked in the car park of the only pub in Avoncliff.

"The Crossed Guns, guv," said Neil. "It can't get much passing trade here, can it?"

"Reputation for a well-kept pint and decent food goes a long way in the countryside, Neil," said Gus. "Show me that Ordnance Survey map again, Lydia. How best can we get a three-hundred and sixty-degree view of the property?"

"The lane winding down into the valley could give plenty of warning of approaching vehicles, guv," said Luke. "We can't drive there this afternoon without being spotted."

"We'll split into three groups to cover most of the estate's perimeter," said Gus. "Blessing, you walk with me. We'll take this pathway to get as close to the western side of the building as possible. Luke and Neil, you go down the steps beside the bridge and take the path past the Tea Rooms. That deals with the eastern side."

"We'll drive to this point here," said Alex, pointing to the map. "It looks like the most sheltered corner between here and the property. That will be where we'll stay throughout. Lydia and I will stroll as close to the front of the property as we can."

"Keep your eyes peeled for the brothers and sisters," said Gus. "They could be indoors during the day making those blessed artificial flowers. We don't want to spook them. If they parked their transport in the open, it could tell us how many recruiting teams they send out each Friday and Saturday night. I'm concerned we don't know how many people are involved. Remember where Laura and the others first met Brother Simeon? A van could return from a leaflet run this morning from a nearby town. With luck, they're already inside The Haven, but you never know."

"Got it, guv. How long before we return for a debrief, guv?" asked Alex.

"Sixty minutes," said Gus. "Stay alert, make notes of everything, and if there's an opportunity to use your camera, you know what we're after. DS Mercer and the Armed Response Team Leader will be grateful."

"You can rely on us, guv," said Luke.

Alex and Lydia returned to the car and drove towards the lane to The Haven.

Luke and Neil disappeared down the steps to the right, leaving Gus and Blessing to make their way down the pathway on their left. One hour later, they were back.

"Alex, you go first," said Gus.

"As you can see, we walked back, guv. We passed the gateway to The Haven without incident. Perhaps someone saw us from an upstairs window, but nobody came outside into the courtyard to ask why we were there. The car park is at the rear, and we saw three minivans and three cars. One was a Lexus, and the other two were BMWs. All three cars were carrying this year's registration."

"Brother Simeon and his bodyguards don't consider austerity as a means of reaching the sunlight they're so keen on," said Blessing.

"Did you see anyone at all?" asked Gus.

"No guv," said Lydia, "but I counted the number of windows on the upper storeys that struck me as bedrooms. We know married couples have joined the group, and we can assume they sleep in separate quarters from the single members. You can guarantee Brother Simeon and the senior brothers have their own rooms. It's just a rough estimate, but the transport available suggests The Haven holds a maximum of fifty people."

"That's a fair guess," said Neil. "I expect they leave ten to fifteen members at home when recruiting. Enough of a presence to deter visitors."

"We only spotted people moving across windows," said Luke. "There's a large garden to that side of the property, but nobody was outside working today. Tomorrow morning, a glass-panelled door would be a useful access point at the far end. I've taken shots of the area, and I'm forwarding them to your phone now.."

"All we could see was a large white wall," said Blessing. "There were no windows to the side. The pathway was overgrown and had loads of stinging nettles and brambles. Thank goodness I wore my trousers."

"Despite the state of the pathway, it would be a better approach to the property than from the front or the rear," said Gus. "Far less chance of getting spotted, especially early in the day. What was visibility like on your route, Neil?"

"Limited, guv. The pathway is lined with a high stone wall and outbuildings. As Luke suggested, the door at the rear offers the best chance of a surprise attack."

"There's only one exit road, guv," said Alex, "so, apart from preventing anyone from escaping over the fields behind the property, once our people have secured the lane, the occupants can be restricted to The Haven and its grounds."

"I'll warn DS Mercer to bring half a dozen Denver Boots," said Gus. "Two units can approach the car park from the rear. One can secure the vehicles and stand guard for anyone attempting to escape on foot. The other can enter the house from the side door as the main force bursts through the front doors. We need enough bodies to cope with up to fifty people."

"Do they have enough vans at London Road, guv?" asked Neil.

"DS Mercer might have to make a few phone calls, Neil," said Gus. "We've hired coaches in the past for dawn trips to Stonehenge and the Summer Solstice."

"We'll wander back to the car, guv," said Alex. "Lydia suggested a quick visit to the Tea Rooms to use the loo and fortify ourselves for the vigil."

"No problem," said Gus. "I look forward to hearing from you this evening."

Alex and Lydia said their goodbyes to the others and walked to the steps beside the bridge.

"Shall I drive the four of us back to the office now, guv?" asked Luke.

"Yes, please," said Gus. "I'm sure Blessing has other things to do once she gets home. I know I have. Sorry to interfere with your plans today."

"Nothing that couldn't be rearranged, guv," said Luke.

"We've only just begun, guv," said Blessing. "Who's coming here tomorrow morning for a start?"

"And then there's Rick Chalmers, guv," said Neil. "The video tour of that manor house courtesy of the Avon & Somerset Police raid. What time is that due to start?"

"That slipped my mind," said Gus. "It's only fair I allow

everyone to be in at the death, Blessing. I hope we get the all-clear by eight o'clock tomorrow morning. We can meet in the office before then and drive to interview our suspects. If anyone can't make it, so be it. He's not here, but I'll expect Alex to go with me for the chief interview."

Blessing and Gus joined Neil in Luke's car, and he drove them back to the Old Police Station. The others were leaving the car park as Gus sent a message to Geoff Mercer. He attached the photos from Luke's phone and the few he'd snapped.

Gus went upstairs, sat, and looked at the three walls of the office.

He must wait until Monday to hear about Stan Jones's latest victims. Something had to give in that case soon. The Major Crimes people were looking for Jones and his tractor unit in the wrong place. Stan Jones shouldn't be that hard to find. He had to climb down from his cab sometime.

As for the manor house, the raid was scheduled for dusk tomorrow evening. They should have wrapped up matters at Avoncliff before then. He'd rather have a pint in the Waggon & Horses to celebrate another win for the Crime Review Team, but perhaps he could invite a few people to join them here to watch the conclusion to another case.

Gus called Suzie and said he was about to drive home. He would break it to her later that he'd be leaving home at half past seven in the morning. Perhaps she could come with him tomorrow evening to follow Rick and his bodycam.

With one last glance at the map of the area surrounding The Haven, Gus decided it was time to head for Urchfont. There was nothing to do now but wait for Alex's phone call.

Epilogue

Saturday, 15 September 2018

AT FIVE PAST eight in the evening, Gus received a message from Alex.

'Two vans left The Haven at eight o'clock. One male driver and six female passengers in each. Clothing similar to those described earlier. No sign of Lexus or either BMW. All quiet inside The Haven.'

Gus thanked Alex for the information and told him to get home. He would see him in the office at eight. Lydia could go with him to Avoncliff if she wished.

Thirty minutes later, Gus received a reply.

'We spotted one van ahead of us as we approached Chippenham. No idea where the other van went. We'll both be there in the morning.'

Gus and Suzie left the bungalow minutes later. They had a table booked for nine o'clock in the Lamb. Brett Penman and the Reverend were joining them.

No sooner than Gus had sat at the table with their

drinks, his phone buzzed again.

"No rest for the wicked," said Clemency.

"Is that the text for tomorrow's sermon, Reverend?" asked Gus.

The message was from Geoff Mercer.

'Package arrived. I will arrange transfer in the morning. Please advise timing.'

Gus smiled and switched off his phone.

"Right," he said. "What's the special this evening?

Sunday, 16 September 2018

THE ARMED RESPONSE TEAM vehicles left the London Road car park, in convoy, at five twenty. Their attack was due to begin at six o'clock precisely–ten minutes before dawn. The team comprised male and female uniformed officers. Geoff Mercer had somehow gathered enough volunteers to match the largest number of Haven members they might find inside the property.

The six ART vehicles blocked the exit road by ten minutes to six. By two minutes to six, the crew sent to immobilise vehicles in the car park had completed their task and spread across the property's rear.

At six o'clock, the team leader blew his whistle. They breached the front door with the big red key, and the side door flew off its hinges. Officers rushed inside, shouting at the top of their voices. Those inside were soon aware they were getting raided by armed police, Tasers would be deployed if required, and two police dogs were straining at the leash by each exit door.

The brothers in the bedrooms on the top floor decided

resistance was futile. Most of them were in no position to fight, anyway. Half-asleep, naked, and with no weapons, they followed the example of their sisters and meekly did as they were told. They dressed and made their way downstairs to the main hall on the first floor. Uniformed officers started taking statements.

Officers moved from room to room on the first floor, where bedrooms were larger and occupied by married couples and the senior Brethren. After the briefing from DS Mercer, it did not surprise them to find two young women in Brother Simeon's bed. After a brief check of the basement, the ART team leader breathed a sigh of relief. The Haven might promote moving from the darkness into the sunlight, but they hadn't filled the basement with explosives that would bring them closer to their God via a mass suicide.

He called Geoff Mercer and Gus Freeman and gave the all-clear.

Colleagues prepared to receive their final visitors to the main hall on the ground floor. When Gus Freeman and his colleagues arrived, The Haven's inhabitants would be waiting.

Gus had arrived in the Old Police Station car park at five to eight. The others were ahead of him. They were eager to hear the latest news when he reached the first-floor office.

"Everything went to plan," he said. "We overestimated the total number of cult members. The ART guys found twenty-six people inside the property. We can make our way over to Avoncliff if everyone's ready?"

"What's the latest on tonight's caper, guv?" asked Neil.

"DS Mercer confirmed the raid will go ahead at five to eight this evening. Once we've finished with matters at The

Haven, we can take a break, then return here for a celebration party. If you want to bring a plus one, that's fine with me."

"What a week, guv," said Lydia.

"It's not over yet," said Gus.

Everyone left the office and returned to the car park.

"Take your cars today," said Gus. "Then you can drive straight home."

There was very little traffic on the road through Bradford-on-Avon, and this time they parked near the spot where Alex and Lydia had been yesterday. They walked around the ART vehicles and made their way to The Haven.

"They didn't need the dogs, guv," said Luke as four dogs and their handlers appeared around a bend one hundred yards ahead.

"All quiet?" asked Gus as they met on the lane.

"Seen nothing like it," said one handler. "It's as if everyone's taken a vow of silence."

"Either that or they're on something," said another. "I've never seen such a docile bunch."

Gus and the team continued towards the open front door. Alex stepped inside and explained who they were to the two armed police officers.

"You're expected, sir," came the reply. "The boss is in the hall to your left."

Faces turned towards the double doors as Gus and the others entered the large room. The stage at the far end was empty, apart from two armed police officers. Their team leader walked across the room to meet them.

"We're still searching the rooms upstairs," he told them. "No guns or ammunition inside the building. All sharp knives, etcetera, from the kitchens have been secured. They offered no resistance when we burst through the doors. I've got my second-in-command searching for the pharmacy. Just look at them. They're stoned, or their leaders force them to take something to calm them."

"Docile was how one dog handler described it," said Gus.

"That's it in a nutshell. The majority are uncooperative. No comment appears to be the only phrase these people remember from their life before coming here. If we had the usual documentation and modern paraphernalia at our disposal, we'd have IDs for these people pronto."

"It's not just their mobile phones they leave in the outside world, then?" asked Lydia.

"No, Miss," said the team leader. "I can't see how they can run a group like this without access to computers and phones. But, unfortunately, we have found none here. Although, I've only carried out a cursory check of the basement so far."

"They might not print their leaflets on-site," said Luke, "and the materials they used to make the flowers are available from local craft shops."

"Where are the three people I'm interested in?" asked Gus.

"We've put them in the kitchen at the side of the hall. The door is in the far right-hand corner. There's been zero communication between either of them since we arrived."

"What did you find when you entered their rooms?" asked Gus.

"What DS Mercer suggested we might find. I reckon that Brother Simeon had two girls with him last night, eighteen or nineteen years old. Brother James slept alone, and the tall one, Brother Ralph, preferred the company of a teenage boy."

"I notice the brothers and sisters are wearing the white robes we've heard about," said Neil. "Would that be what they normally wear inside The Haven, I wonder?"

"Perhaps they keep the simple garb for the recruiting drives," said Gus. "I'm more interested in Simeon Lane for now. So follow me, Alex; we'll start from the top."

They found Brother Simeon, flanked by two police officers, sitting on a chair with his hands on his knees. He, too, wore a white robe, but Lane's was decorated with silk and studded with precious stones. Again, the charismatic look that had attracted so many young women was plain to see.

"Ah, someone in authority has arrived, at last," he said, not attempting to get up. "When will this nonsense end? You have no justification for this intrusion. It merely proves how outsiders fear those doing God's work. Persecution is alive and well in this wretched twenty-first century."

"Let's dispense with the quasi-religious patter, Mr Lane," said Gus. "My colleagues and I from Wiltshire Police are looking for someone. We believe she may have joined The Haven six years ago. What can you tell me about Sister Danni, or Danute Zukas, as she was known outside these walls?"

"I don't recall the name," said Lane. "We have met so many young men and women looking for a better way. Some have stayed throughout. Others leave with our blessing to spread the word in other parts of the world. But, of course, a few can't leave the outside world behind, and we have to concede our message will never get them to see the error of their ways."

"You make it sound like members can come and go without punishment," said Alex. "That's not what we've heard."

"Whoever told you that can't have been a member. Jealousy colours many people's opinions of what we've achieved here. It's no surprise to us with the evil in the world that people can't bear to see anyone thriving by not following the herd."

"We have evidence to show you spoke to Danute Zukas in Trowbridge in the first months of 2012," said Gus. "The following day, she and two friends attended a meeting in a hall off Stallard Street. Furthermore, we have evidence you hired that hall regularly throughout 2012 and every year since. Do you deny being present on those occasions?"

"We visit many towns in the county," said Lane. "Our work never ends. Each year, more children became teenagers seeking love and a sense of belonging. But, unfortunately, the world is littered with broken homes...."

"Do those teenage girls realise the love they seek will involve them sleeping with you?" asked Alex.

"You have evidence of us hiring a hall," said Lane. "Of reaching out to young people who feel the outside world isn't listening to them. Do you have evidence of anyone being forced to do something against their will? No, I thought not. That comment could only have come from someone with a vivid imagination and no concept of what The Haven offers."

"I think we should continue this conversation at the custody suite," said Gus. "Maybe you're as innocent as you claim. The sooner we clear things up, the better. Please stay here until we've spoken to James Gee and Ralph Gibbons."

Gus moved to another corner of the kitchen as he mentioned the brothers by name. It was a fifty-fifty guess. Lane's reaction was fleeting, but Gus knew he'd guessed correctly.

Another plus was that it bothered Lane they knew who they were dealing with. What more did they know? Gus hoped that didn't get put to the test just yet. He was following his gut, and Geoff Mercer had the trump card.

Alex could tell Brother James was nervous. They needed to keep the pressure on him.

"James Gee?" asked Gus. "Tell me about Sister Danni? She was close to Brother Simeon, wasn't she?"

"No closer than with others among us," he replied.

"Odd," said Gus. "Mr Lane couldn't remember her, yet you had no trouble casting your mind back six years to the day you first met her. That was in the meeting hall in Trowbridge on a Sunday morning, wasn't it?"

"I don't know. I can't remember. We've had so many meetings in different towns. What's this about, anyway? We've not broken any laws."

"Let's move forward from when you first met Sister Danni," said Gus. "On Sunday, the thirteenth of July, two years later, you were back in Trowbridge. You and Ralph Gibbons dragged Sister Danni to an address in Gloucester Road to let her friends see Danni was safe and happy to return to The Haven. She'd told them the truth about what happened here only twelve hours earlier and was desperate to leave."

"That doesn't sound like something we would do," said Gee. "They must be mistaken."

"We'll be taking you to a police station while we make further enquiries, Mr Gee," said Gus. "You'll have the opportunity to get legal representation before we speak again."

Gus and Alex moved to the far corner of the kitchen, where Brother Ralph perched on a chair. The surly expression didn't jibe with the peace and love the group promoted.

"Well, Mr Gibbons," said Gus, "What can you tell us about Sister Danni?"

"Never heard of her," said Gibbons.

"We understand you threatened Danni's friends after she visited their home in July four years ago. I believe you reminded them you knew where they lived. What happened next?"

"No comment."

"Let's leave our interview until we're more comfortably placed," said Gus. "We can't talk openly in a kitchen. The custody suite is only a few miles away. Perhaps you'll cooperate there."

Gus winked at Alex as he turned to leave.

Alex followed Gus back to the hall. The crafty devil was up to something, but he didn't know what.

After they passed Simeon Lane, Gus called the police officers.

"Escort these three outside and take them away."

"Wait," cried Lane. "I must speak to my flock. They will be worried."

"Very well," said Gus. "Keep it brief."

The armed police officers led the three senior brothers from the kitchen and stood behind them on the stage. Brother Simeon moved to the front, flanked by Brother Ralph and James.

Every face in the hall turned to the stage. Finally, the room fell quiet, and then the chanting began. Blessing Umeh shivered as she realised this was what Danute Zukas had heard in that meeting hall six years ago. Out of the darkness, into the sunlight. Repeatedly, a quiet but hypnotic rhythm filled the room.

Gus Freeman turned away from Brother Simeon as he stood with arms outstretched.

Gus sent a text message and then crossed his fingers and prayed.

Brother Simeon lowered his arms. The chanting ceased, and he addressed his flock.

"The outsiders will not keep us apart for long, brothers and sisters. Love another, and hold on to your faith. This is a test, and we will survive it."

The chanting began once more. Then, from the back of the hall, a young woman strolled to the centre of the room. She was barefoot, clothed in a white robe, and carried a bouquet of black roses.

The Haven members moved aside as the young girl reached the centre. Gus and the team heard gasps coming from the brothers and sisters in front of them.

On stage, Brother James fell to his knees.

The young woman stretched out her right hand and pointed towards Brother Simeon. Then, she turned away, shifted her robe to the side, and exposed the tattoo on her right shoulder.

Simeon Lane looked like he'd seen a ghost.

His eyes darted left and right, but there was no escape.

The young woman turned to face him once more.

Brother James's sobs broke the silence in the hall as he knelt and prayed.

Brother Ralph appeared frozen on the spot. Then, suddenly, he distanced himself from Brother Simeon.

"He made me help him," he shouted, "You were always his favourite."

Brother James lifted his head and pointed towards Brother Simeon.

"He lost his temper after we brought you back here. We couldn't control him. Afterwards, he ordered us to think of The Haven. What damage it would do to our mission."

Natasha Zukas scattered the bouquet on the stage's

apron and walked towards the double doors at the back of the hall where Geoff Mercer was waiting.

"Thank you," said Geoff, "What a performance."

"My wish to become an actress never diminished after Danute's death," she said. "I've pursued my dream ever since leaving school."

Armed officers escorted the three men on stage to waiting vans outside the building. As they passed Gus and his team, Lydia asked:

"When did you come up with that idea, guv?"

"When Neil reminded me the two sisters were so alike in their teens, they could be mistaken for twins. They had a tattoo done on the same day. I wasn't confident we'd get a confession through standard questioning, so I played a hunch. There's always a weak link in any chain, and I believed James Gee was the person to target. Once that link broke, his colleague found the courage to admit they'd helped dispose of the body. Whether we'll ever get Simeon Lane to confess, I have my doubts, but we've got enough to start the ball rolling."

The ART leader crossed the room with more good news.

"Most of these characters hope their Master will return in due course, but several have painted a lurid picture of The Haven. They are giving our officers information on how underage sex and prostitution are part of everyday life. My second-in-command has just uncovered the haul of drugs we suspected the senior Brothers were administering. We'll need to verify what they dished out to these people to keep them in line, but it's one more nail in their coffins."

"A case of out of the sunlight into the dark, guv," said Neil.

"Why did I know it would be you that just had to say that, Neil?" said Gus.

"I thought I could get away with it, as I gave you the idea that broke the case wide-open, guv," said Neil.

"When did Danute's sister arrive, guv?" asked Luke.

"Yesterday evening," said Gus. "It was tight. The timing had to be perfect. Natasha is staying with the Chief Constable and his wife before flying home to prepare for a production with the National Drama Theatre in Vilnius. Enough of this chit-chat. Get off home, enjoy the afternoon, and I'll see you tonight in the office. Don't forget. Curtain up at five to eight, so don't be late."

GUS PARKED the Focus outside the bungalow at two o'clock and walked indoors.

"How did it go?" asked Suzie.

"She was word-perfect," he replied.

Gus didn't want to jinx anything by going over every detail with Suzie. Time enough for that tonight if Geoff Mercer brought good news with him to the Old Police Station office.

"I thought we'd have a light lunch followed by an hour on the allotment," he said, "Then we can come back here and prepare for this evening."

"Do you want us to provide snacks for the gang?" asked Suzie. "I might need to pop into Devizes for supplies."

"Okay," said Gus. "Better add a bottle of bubbly to the shopping list."

"Wonderful," said Suzie. "I'll get soft drinks too."

"Sorry, darling."

Gus loaded the goodies into the VW Golf at twenty past seven, and Suzie drove them to the office. The car park wasn't crowded on a Sunday evening. Geoff and Christine Mercer had beaten them to it. Alex and Lydia arrived as Gus got the hamper out of the boot.

"No sign of the others yet?" asked Alex.

"That car next to DS Mercer looks like Jamie BTs," said Gus.

When they arrived on the first floor, they discovered Jamie and Blessing had collected Neil and Melody in Devizes.

"We're just waiting for Luke and Nicky, guv," said Neil. "Everything's set. We should start receiving the live feed from Rick's bodycam in five minutes."

Gus and Suzie opened the hamper and ensured everyone had a drink and a bite to eat.

"Can you update us on this morning, Geoff?" he asked.

"It was a total success, Gus," said Geoff. "James Gee turned on his brothers as soon as we informed him and his solicitor of the charges we would bring. Ralph Gibbons caved once we gave him the gist of Brother James's revelations. We have keys to an office in Bradford-on-Avon where Gibbons ran the business side of The Haven. There's more damning stuff to come from there, plus the statements given at the scene by members of The Haven."

"Nothing from Simeon Lane?" asked Alex.

"No comment," said Geoff. "Although it won't do him much good. He's bang to rights, and he knows it. He killed Danute Zukas in a fit of rage and forced his minions to get rid of the body."

"Well done, team," said Gus, raising a glass.

The lift descended to the ground floor, and seconds later, Luke appeared.

"Hi, Luke," said Blessing, "couldn't Nicky make it?"

Lydia knew what was coming next.

"We had another row," said Luke. "Nicky didn't appreciate me working yesterday, this morning, and then again tonight, Even though I insisted this was a party, not work."

"Here we go, guv," said Neil.

All eyes switched to the screen Neil had set up next to Gus's desk.

In the gathering gloom, they could make out the shape of Larcombe Manor on the brow of the hill.

"Where are we compared to the road with the cattle grid we used in the summer, Neil?" asked Gus.

"On the opposite side of the main building, guv," said Neil. "Rick said his team was entering through the wood bordering the estate. There's what looks like a pet cemetery as you leave the wood and cross the lawns. On the right are worker's cottages. As we reach the level ground at the top, we might spot the stables and the abandoned ice-house to the right. Over to the left, Rick told me there was a church further into the valley. I don't know whether it's in use these days."

At six minutes to eight, Rick was on the move. They could see armed officers ahead of him now, and the bodycam was bouncing up and down, making it difficult to see what was happening.

"DS Chalmers needs to cut out that fast food," said Geoff. "Even though we don't have sound, I can still hear him panting."

Rick's team entered the main building via the kitchens to the left-hand side. Gus winced when Rick and the others trampled over the plants in the kitchen garden as they rushed to the door. There was a pause, and then they were inside, moving from room to room on the ground floor: a grand dining room, storerooms, and a study. A second team had broken through the front door, and the groups merged.

Ahead of them was a dog-leg staircase leading to the first floor. Rick climbed the stairs behind the others. In the Old Police Station office, everyone prepared for when the families of senior officials in the Olympus charity would have their evening interrupted.

Room by room they went. Everywhere Rick checked was empty. He stood at the open door of an office, wondering where the equipment had gone. The camera only picked up a large basket filled with shredded paper. Whenever Rick caught a colleague exiting a room ahead of him, they bore the same puzzled expression. The manor house was deserted. David Scott and his wife and family weren't here. Nor were any of the other families known to be permanent residents. Intelligence from their bosses at Portishead had given no clue anyone had left the estate.

A third team had checked the orangery, the stables, and the refurbished workers' cottages in the grounds. Not only had the charity officers done a bunk, but every ex-serviceman undergoing treatment for PTSD had also disappeared.

"Blimey, guv," said Neil. "David Copperfield couldn't pull that stunt. So what's going on?"

"It beats me, Neil," said Gus. "I thought we had something extra to celebrate. I need a drink."

Suzie's mobile rang. Gus watched her face as she listened.

"Okay, Clemency," she said, "Thanks for letting us know."

"What's happened?" asked Gus.

"Irene heard Bert coming home from the Lamb. She heard a crack and went outside to find him on the ground. She's worried he's broken his hip or a leg. They've just left in the ambulance heading for Swindon."

"That doesn't sound good, Gus," said Geoff.

"He's over eighty-five," said Gus. "It could finish him."

The euphoria in the room earlier had disappeared.

"This morning, we performed a miracle, bringing in Danute's killer," groaned Gus. "The icing on the cake this evening was supposed to be the arrest of David Scott for the murder of Grant Burnside. Instead, that business has gone pear-shaped, and now my best friend is on his way to the hospital. Trouble comes in threes. What's next, I wonder?"

vinci-books.com/tamethestorm

In the storm of murder, can Gus find the truth?

Gus Freeman and Wiltshire's Crime Review Team face a daunting challenge as they investigate the brutal murder of Clive Palmer, a former history teacher with a shadowy past. With a killer on the loose and a complex web of clues to untangle, Gus and his team are pushed to their limits in this gripping suspense thriller.

Turn the page for a free preview…

Tame The Storm: Chapter One

Monday, 14 December 2015

"Quiet tonight, Dave," said Emily.

Dave Awdry, the landlord of The Volunteer pub, glanced at the clock at the end of the bar.

"Not long before Christmas, Emily," he replied. "They'll be saving their pennies for the holiday period. You'll be glad of an evening like this by the time we reach the New Year."

Emily Chivers looked around the deserted bar, gauging whether anyone was likely to order another drink before Dave called time. She wasn't looking forward to the walk home. Temperatures had dropped over the past week, and the forecast was for another hard frost. Despite being a fit and healthy twenty-year-old, Emily felt the cold. Her mother reckoned it was a cross the Chivers family had to bear.

"Some people swan around in skimpy outfits no matter the weather," her mother would say. "How they don't catch their death beats me. As soon as the nights draw in, I wear a thick jumper inside the house, and I'm never without my winter coat if I venture outside. You should do the same, sweetheart. You can't be too careful."

Emily shivered despite the extra clothing and the space heater behind the bar.

"Any more for any more?" called Dave, hoping to get upstairs to a warm bed alongside Karen, his wife.

Since Emily turned eighteen, she worked for Dave and Karen at The Volunteer and fitted three weekday evenings into her busy social calendar. That allowed Karen to have Monday and Thursday evenings off. Dave took a break on Wednesday night. So far, the pub they took over in 2010 didn't earn enough money to allow them to have a day off together.

The only reply Dave got to his question was silence. His hand hovered under the bell. Nobody would come through the door this late in the day. He groaned when he heard someone pushing back a chair on the hardwood floor.

Emily had spotted movement in the dark corner of the room and was already pouring a pint of bitter for Clive Palmer in a fresh glass.

Dave Awdry watched as Palmer handed the young barmaid the exact money, thanked her politely, and returned to his chair.

Palmer wasn't popular in the village. Dave could remember when he'd arrived in the village just under a year ago. Since then, nobody could accuse Palmer of being a trouble-maker. He wasn't a heavy drinker nor a violent man. In fact, one of the first things Dave had noticed was how well-spoken he was. But the rumours had gathered pace a month or two later.

Purton was a large village just four miles northwest of Swindon. It was only a matter of time before that major town's urban sprawl consigned Purton to history. Ringsbury, at the southwestern end of the village, was a fortified Iron Age camp before the time of Christ. The Romans had settled here, and villagers unearthed many relics in their gardens over the years.

Thirty years ago, they uncovered a Romano-British cemetery when they upgraded the Grade II-listed Northview Hospital. The first written record of the village was in Saxon times at the end of the eighth century AD, about the King of Mercia's dealings with the Benedictine Abbey at Malmesbury. There was confusion over the various ways of spelling 'the Pear Tree' village, but Purton came out tops and stuck.

No, Dave Awdry thought, things *should* stay as they were. There were undoubtedly arguments and disputes over the centuries, notably during the English Civil War. The cannonballs dug up in the pub car park were proof positive a battle had occurred somewhere close by. But, all said and done, it would have been better if Clive Palmer had chosen somewhere other than this quiet spot of Wiltshire to live.

You can't keep a secret for long, though, not today, and the truth came out in time. Clive Palmer had served an eighteen-month sentence in HMP The Verne, near Portland in Dorset. The prison had closed recently, but it hadn't taken a genius to discover the place housed sex offenders. That was good enough for the majority in the village for Clive to be dubbed Palmer the Paedo from that day forward.

Dave and Karen had never been ones to rush to judgement, and they weren't alone. After all, Rob Dolman had given the man a job at his haulage firm. Several of Dolman's drivers used the pub, and it was only natural for Clive Palmer to mix with them.

Nobody had an issue until the rumours started flying. Clive Palmer had always been polite and friendly, but he increasingly drank alone as word spread throughout the village. However, it didn't appear to bother him.

Take tonight, for instance, Dave thought, as he rang the bell for time. Palmer had arrived at half-past eight and had sat quietly in the corner, sipping one pint after another. In five minutes, he'd leave the bar and walk two hundred yards along the High Street to the field where he parked his caravan.

Clive would be fit for work in the morning and back in The Volunteer at eight o'clock for the weekly Quiz Night. Dave and Karen had insisted on teams of four when they first introduced the idea, but with dwindling numbers, they had to allow a little latitude these days. So Clive Palmer entered on his own, and Karen checked his answers as nobody at the other tables was willing.

Karen pointed out anomalies with his answer sheet the first time this happened. But Dave never asked Clive why he crossed out several correct answers or left gaps. Things were hard enough for the bloke. It would have been even worse if Clive had won first prize every Tuesday night.

Clive Palmer never mentioned his life before he'd gone to prison, and nobody asked about the circumstances. Someone in the village had learned Palmer's offence involved a fifteen-year-old girl from Wandsworth. There was an ex-wife somewhere in a nearby London borough and two children. Palmer would have been in his early forties when the attack took place if, indeed, it was an attack. The gossip-mongers weren't interested in the finer points of the case.

Palmer was a paedophile, plain and simple. He was on the Sex Offender's Register, and the police knew where he lived. This was just as well because in the seven months since the truth surfaced, there had been several incidents where uniformed officers had needed to get involved.

After a quiet night in the pub, Palmer had returned home to find someone had smeared excrement over the windows of his caravan. The police blamed youngsters who couldn't spell the word they'd heard their parents mention in conversation.

In October, a thirteen-year-old girl claimed she was followed while walking home from the youth centre. Her parents at once pointed the finger at Clive Palmer and reported the incident to the police. When interviewed, he said he was in The Volunteer that Tuesday night. Twenty people could give him an alibi.

Dave and Karen had told the Police Community Support Officer who came to check that Palmer was in the bar from eight o'clock until closing that night. The officer said nobody else would confirm Palmer wasn't in the pub but merely said they didn't remember seeing him. Karen had fished the scoresheets out of the wastepaper basket in the office and showed the PCSO the quiz sheet she had checked.

"Who else do you think that could be?" Karen had asked. "Nobody talks to him except to make a snide remark. Is there another 'Clive P' in the village? I check his answers every week because no one else will. I'll swear on a stack of bibles he was sitting in the corner on Tuesday night, no matter what the others might like you to believe."

The dust settled within a few days, and things returned to what had become the norm. Most of the villagers shunned Clive and verbally abused him at every opportunity. Yet, Rob Dolman continued to employ him.

"Why not?" Dolman had told Dave Awdry when he

dropped in for a pint after work one evening. "Clive is reliable and hard-working, and I've never received a single complaint from a client. Quite the opposite. Several have called me to say they wished my other drivers were as helpful and polite. Perhaps it helps that most of my business is with customers in neighbouring counties, or on the far side of Wiltshire, towards Salisbury, but I haven't got a reason to sack him. If I did, Clive would have me in court for unfair dismissal, and I couldn't argue."

"Goodnight all,"

Dave heard the comment as he emptied clean pint pots from the glass washer. He glanced over his shoulder to see Clive Palmer making his way towards the door.

Emily waited until the inner door had closed and then went to lock and bolt the main entrance.

"You can get off home now, Emily," said Dave. "I'll put away these last few glasses."

"I'll give Clive a minute to get clear," she replied. "Did you hear the latest?"

"Karen and I don't listen to gossip," said Dave.

"I heard a whisper from one mother on our street last week. She was watching her daughters on the climbing frames in the playground off Church Street that afternoon. Since they learned about Clive Palmer's past, most mums go with their little ones. If they can't get there themselves, they ask a friend to keep an eye out."

"Was Clive Palmer not working that afternoon?" asked Dave. "That seems odd. What happened?"

"One of the younger children, five years old, ran across to her mother. She was chatting with her friends and had lost sight of her daughter. First, she thought the little girl had just tripped and fallen, grazing her knees, but the girl told her she was frightened. A man had picked her up and brushed the dirt from her legs when she slipped and fell."

"That could be innocent enough," said Dave. "The sort of thing any caring father might do, but you risk getting accused of all sorts these days. So it's best to leave any care and attention to the parents. Even if they're not keeping a close eye on what's happening."

"I suppose so," said Emily. "Clive would have been working though, wouldn't he? And the playground is at the opposite end of the village from where he works and lives. So if he *was* there, there could only have been one reason."

"Stop that, Emily," said Dave. "Don't add more fuel to the rumour mill."

"I've heard they're going to force Palmer to leave the village," said Emily. "He's attacked a young girl once. That sort never changes. I'm praying that I'm too old for him. I've got mace in my handbag if anyone tries their luck."

"If circumstances were different, I'd give you a lift home, Emily," said Dave.

"When do you get your licence back?" asked Emily.

"Eight months, three weeks and a day," said Dave. "Karen will kill me if I get done for speeding again."

"I'll be okay," said Emily, adding more layers before venturing outside. "Tell Karen I'll see her on Wednesday night."

Dave followed Emily through the bar and watched as she crossed the road to start her ten-minute walk home. The streets were empty. Anyone with any sense was indoors on a frosty night such as this. Dave locked and bolted the door and switched off the ground-floor lights.

As he climbed the stairs to their accommodation, he wondered whether Karen would still be awake. When he heard her gentle snoring as he closed the flat door behind him, he consoled himself with the thought that their bed would be warmer than the one Clive Palmer was getting into.

Tuesday, 15 December 2015

"Morning, boss," said Ken Webb. "A fresh start, isn't it? So where am I off to today?"

Rob Dolman stood beside the radiator in his office and blew on his hands.

"Peter Wright beat you in this morning, Ken. He got first dibs. I've sent him to collect goods from that injection moulding firm near Chilcompton. Then, after he's dropped off in Swindon, he can fit in a couple of jobs in town. I've marked them on the board."

"You know how much I enjoy making that trip, boss," said Ken. "Ah well, it serves me right. It was tough getting out of a warm bed today. So what's next on the schedule?"

"Cheney Manor, Europa, Callenders, or Clearwater. Take your pick from those industrial estates. The sooner you get on the road, the better."

"Cheney Manor is closest," said Ken, checking the details on the board behind Rob's desk. "I can cover that and Callenders by the end of the day and get the gear where it needs to go. My hours aren't near the limit, but I can't manage any other journeys on this board. So Palmer will have to handle those. No sign of your man yet this morning?"

"No," said Rob Dolman, looking at the office clock. "It's not like him to be late, and he's not taken a sick day since he started working here."

"Maybe he's done a runner, boss," said Ken Webb. "I heard he was seen touching up a five-year-old in the playground last week. Several of the younger fathers are planning a late-night visit to his caravan. Not a baying mob with baseball bats and Molotov cocktails, but scary enough to force Palmer to leave the village."

"I heard the gossip, Ken, but there was no way Clive Palmer was involved. He didn't return to the depot until five to five that afternoon. He left Dorset Autospares in Downton at half-past three. You couldn't make that fifty-mile trip any quicker. So no way was he in that playground off Church Street between three and half-past."

"Did you check on him then, boss?" asked Ken.

"Not a bit of it," said Rob. "That was where he made a delivery, all signed for, no problems reported from Downton. I trust him."

"Why do you stick up for him, boss? He served time for underage sex. Nobody wants him in the village."

"I've run this haulage firm since my late twenties," said Dolman. "After I left school with no qualifications, I flitted from job to job and never settled on anything. There were times when I could have taken the wrong path, like my brother-in-law, Andy Redman."

"Andy's your brother-in-law? I never realised."

"Andy's been in and out of trouble since he was ten. Why my sister, Pat, thought she could persuade him to stay on the straight and narrow beats me. Every time he comes out of prison, he struggles to find someone to give him a break. It's a vicious circle. Andy tries to make a go of it. Either he's on the dole for weeks, and one of his cronies offers him the chance of easy money. Or business drops off at the firm that took him on, and he's first out because of his record."

"Why didn't you offer Andy a job, boss?" asked Ken.

"Pat wouldn't hear of it," said Rob. "She realises Andy's

a hopeless case. She doesn't want this firm's reputation tainted."

"So why was Palmer different?"

"I don't know, Ken," said Rob. "When I interviewed him, he had a clean licence, spoke well, and was keen as mustard. Clive admitted he'd spent time in Portland but swore that nothing similar would ever happen again. So I gave him a break."

"Even when the rest of the village learned the truth?"

"The truth can be a funny thing, Ken," said Rob Dolman. "You get a different version of it with every newspaper you read or TV news channel you watch. Each paints a version of the truth that suits their purpose. Clive Palmer didn't go into details, so I don't know exactly what got him into trouble with the law, but I've had no complaints since he's been here. He's still got a clean licence. He's always polite and cooperative to customers, and his time-keeping has been exemplary until this morning. I was struggling with new paperwork from HMRC last week. Clive stayed behind for thirty minutes to help me make sense of it. He's a clever bloke, you know. I had been thinking of advertising for a logistics manager to take the pressure off me. My wife would appreciate me getting home earlier in the evening. Clive could handle that role; he's developed a good understanding of the haulage business despite only working here for ten months."

"I'd better get moving," said Ken. "How will you cover these other trips if Palmer's done a midnight flit? Peter Wright can't do them."

"Don't worry about that, Ken," said Rob. "You just finish the items on your sheet. I'll walk over to the High Street and see where he's got to."

"Okay, boss. With luck, the heater won't pack up in the van today. See you later."

Rob Dolman took another look at the clock.

No doubt the client at Cheney Manor would be on the phone in a few minutes, wondering when the van would arrive. Ah well. They'd have to wait for Ken to get a move on. There wouldn't be anyone staffing the office for the next twenty minutes.

Rob donned his coat, scarf, and gloves and headed out of the Portakabin. A brisk walk to the High Street lay ahead. Although he'd never visited Clive Palmer's caravan, he knew his employee had persuaded a local farmer to let him park on waste ground behind a long, prefabricated storage building. So the caravan was hidden from view from the street. But, of course, that hadn't stopped those tearaways from finding it and daubing it with muck. But out of sight, out of mind. Clive hadn't mentioned any further cause for a sleepless night since.

There were no signs of life when Rob reached the end of the long barn and spotted the caravan under the trees. He'd already called Clive on his mobile before leaving the office. But, unfortunately, it had gone straight to voicemail. Rob tried once more as he stepped warily across the frozen ground.

The farmer had scattered several hundred cobblestones along the first thirty yards to give his vehicles extra grip when heavy rain turned the grassy stretch into brown sludge. Each stone was slippery enough to bring a man down or twist an ankle in this frosty weather.

Rob finally made it to a safe gravelled surface by the caravan. He could hear Clive's mobile ringing inside. A loud knock on the door didn't get a response. Rob tried the door, but it was locked. He tried to peer inside, but the glass was covered in frost, and the curtains were drawn.

"Something the matter, Mr Dolman?"

"Morning, Mr Oatley," said Rob, recognising the farmer who owned the land. "Clive Palmer hasn't turned up for work. I can hear his mobile phone. It's unlike him to let me down."

"He's not well-liked," said John Oatley. "I'm not sure I made the right decision letting him park his van here, but he pays his rent on the dot every month. I must wait ninety days for my other customers to pay what they owe. Should we call the police, do you think?"

Rob Dolman shivered, and it wasn't the frosty morning that caused it.

"Many people wanted Clive gone from the village," he said.

"Best call them to be on the safe side," said John Oatley.

Rob took one last look towards the caravan and dialled 999.

Tame The Storm: Chapter Two

The emergency call came through to the detective squad room at Gablecross at eight thirty-eight. DS Jake Latimer had just arrived in the office.

A little over six months ago, Jack Sanders had been the Senior Investigating Officer on a case involving the murder of one of Swindon's prolific criminals, Grant Burnside. A sniper shot the gang leader at the Cheney Manor Industrial Estate, and despite their best efforts, they hadn't located the killer.

Jake had worked on the initial phases of the investigation and was still adding titbits to their stack of evidence and witness statements. It was boring, but it paid the bills. Jack Sanders was scheduled for retirement before the murder case and was now on garden leave. Theo Hickerton, Jake's old boss, had blotted his copybook on an earlier case and was licking his wounds in the Traffic Section, which left Jake like a ship without a rudder.

Life would have been dull if it hadn't been for Janina,

the Lithuanian girl he'd met at a massage parlour during his duties. Jake answered the phone.

"DS Latimer. How may I be of assistance?"

"Good morning. My name's Rob Dolman, and I am from Purton. One of my employees didn't turn up for work at eight this morning. I'm stood outside his caravan with his landlord, John Oatley, just off the High Street. We're concerned he may have come to harm."

"What is your employee's name, Mr Dolman?" asked Jake.

"Clive Palmer," replied Rob.

Alarm bells rang in Jake's head.

"I'll get someone to you in thirty minutes, Rob. Don't touch a thing."

Jake ended the call and looked across the squad room.

"Mark. What have you and your gaffer got on today?"

"Nothing that won't wait, Jake," came the reply. "What have you got for us?"

"You won't know until you get to Purton High Street," said Jake. "A guy called Clive Palmer is inside his caravan, condition unknown."

"Palmer? He's on the list, isn't he?" said Mark. "Things have been quiet out there for a while. I hoped they would stay that way. Leave it with us. We'll drive out to Purton and check."

Jake Latimer watched Mark Harvey head for DI Ben Moore's desk, and then he returned to his filing. It was warmer here than in a field in the countryside, ten miles away. Batman and Robin were welcome to it.

"Remind me again, Mark," said Ben Moore when they reached the car park. He jumped into the passenger seat of his sergeant's Ford Kuga. "Why does the name Clive Palmer sound familiar?"

"He's a registered sex offender, guv," said Mark. "Palmer served eighteen months in Portland, and instead of returning to his home in London, he picked Purton's name out of a hat. It's fair to say the locals haven't accepted him as one of their own. There have been a couple of minor incidents where uniforms needed to get involved. But, despite accusations he was up to his old tricks, they proved to be unfounded. Until today, Palmer appears to have been a good boy, holding down a job with Dolman's, the haulage people. You must have seen their vans in town."

"British racing green, with gold lettering?" said Ben Moore. "Yes, they're a familiar sight. Put your foot down, Mark. Have you found the heater on this beast yet? My feet are freezing."

John Oatley had suggested to Rob Dolman they shouldn't stand on the frozen ground for another thirty minutes, waiting for the police to arrive. John was in his late sixties, and although farmers were used to being outside in all winds and weathers, discretion can be the better part of valour.

The pair had moved inside a smaller building opposite the long barn to watch for activity inside the caravan and spot the new arrivals.

"Do you ever take a walk across here late at night, John?" asked Rob.

"I'm in bed by ten," replied John, "and usually awake before the alarm at five. I paid a late-night visit twice after the police got called out, but the kids never returned. We've had security lighting and cameras installed on the sensitive areas of the farm for several years. I've never considered putting anything in this corner of the property. There's nothing worth stealing."

"So someone could have been lying in wait for Palmer when he arrived home from The Volunteer."

"Is that where he drinks?" asked John. "Would he be an enthusiastic drinker? Perhaps he's still unconscious from a heavy night. We should tell the police to check with Dave Awdry."

At a quarter past nine, they heard the crackle of tyres on cobblestones and frozen earth and walked outside. The farmer and the haulage firm owner walked to greet the men getting out of the Ford Kuga.

"You must be the detectives we're expecting," said Rob.

"Yes, sir. DI Ben Moore from Gablecross," said Ben. "My colleague is DS Mark Harvey. Which of you gentlemen called us?"

"That was me, Rob Dolman. John Oatley here owns the farm. Clive Palmer has parked his caravan under the trees for the past ten months. Clive didn't turn up for work at eight, so I walked across from the depot to check he was okay."

"Any reason to assume he wouldn't be okay?" asked Mark Harvey.

"You know the history," said Rob. "Plenty of people in the village wanted him to move on. But, so far, nobody has gone further than name-calling and muck-spreading."

"Wait here, and we'll look," said Ben Moore. "Mark, have you got any kit in your boot?"

"Yes, guv," Mark replied.

"A large screwdriver will be enough to snap the lock on that door," said John Oatley. "I can get one from the barn behind me if you have got nothing."

"Thank you, Mr Oatley," said Mark. "I'll get the kit and gloves on, guv, just in case, and try to get inside without damaging any fingerprints on the door handle."

Mark Harvey delved into the boot of his car, dressed in blue protective clothing, donned his gloves, and accepted a screwdriver and hammer from the farmer. Rob Dolman watched as the two detectives approached the caravan.

"Rather them than me," said John Oatley. "Even if Palmer just fell and hit his head when he got home drunk last night."

Mark Harvey worked the flathead screwdriver under the top left-hand edge of the caravan door. He didn't need the hammer; he could slide the screwdriver between the door and the doorframe towards the handle and apply pressure to the lock. It popped immediately, and Mark swung the door open and stepped inside.

"You'd better call for the full team, guv," he called to Ben Moore. "It's a bloody mess."

Grab your copy...
vinci-books.com/tamethestorm

About the Author

Ted Tayler is the international bestselling indie author of The Freeman Files and The Phoenix series. Ted lives in the English west country, where his stories are based. He was born in 1945 and has been married to Lynne since 1971. They have three children and four grandchildren.

His thought-provoking mysteries appeal to readers of Sally Rigby, Joy Ellis, Pauline Rowson, and Faith Martin. His action-packed thrillers are a must for fans of Mark Dawson and J. C. Ryan.

Gus Freeman's cold case investigations are carried out with reasoned deduction rather than bursts of frantic action. In each of the twenty-four books, unsolved murder is accompanied by romance, humor, and country life. The core message in the twelve Phoenix novels is that criminals should pay for their crimes. Unfortunately, the current system fails to deliver the correct punishment, so Phoenix helps redress the balance.

Acknowledgments

The love and support of my family; without them, this would have been impossible.

www.ingramcontent.com/pod-product-compliance
Lightning Source LLC
Chambersburg PA
CBHW011425010726
47494CB00011B/2514